Through the Tree

The Land of Marqueria, Volume 1

Shana Ren

Published by Shana Ren, 2024.

THROUGH THE TREE

First edition. January 11, 2024.

Copyright © 2024 Shana Ren.

ISBN: 979-8989921010

Written by Shana Ren.

Table of Contents

This is a love letter to my family. JMMSTPH you have all enriched my life. Because of you, I'm a wife, a mother, a mother-in-law, a grandmother. Has it always been roses and sunshine? Bahahahaha, no. But the journey has been beautiful so far.

This is also dedicated to our Lucy, the best dog in the world. We loved you so much and have missed you every day you've been gone.

The Grove

B ehind a red house, twenty-five miles from the nearest small town of Butte, in the foothills of the Rocky Mountains of Montana, stands a large grove of trees. At 6100 feet above sea level, the Grove, set upon a small hill with dips and valleys of its own, appears to be no different from any other copse of trees. A mix of evergreens and deciduous trees, the occasional raspberry and blackberry bush scattered amongst the wild grasses and wildflowers. It's not until you venture into the grove that you realize this is a Grove like no other.

A sense of otherworldliness envelops you in a warm cocoon of silence and nature. As you venture deeper into the trees and the heart of the grove, a huge, majestic, old white birch tree stands before you. Surrounding this beautiful centerpiece, tall evergreens reach toward the sky, their deep green needles forming a lush canopy overhead. Their sturdy trunks contrast with the strong yet delicate beauty of the white birch. A few aspens with their golden, silver dollar leaves and white limbs and the occasional maple displaying dark red leaves dancing in the breeze enhance the perfect sanctuary that only nature can create.

In the pre-dawn, what light there is filters through the foliage, and a gentle glow that seems to come from the Tree itself illuminates the grove, casting enchanting patterns on the early Autumn ground. The air is infused with the crisp, fresh scent of pine and earth, carrying whispers of nature's secrets. The sound of leaves rustling in the breeze creates a soothing symphony, filling the grove with tranquility.

With its smooth, peeling bark, the white birch radiates a timeless elegance and wisdom. Its branches stretch out in graceful arcs, adorned with delicate gold and orange leaves that flutter like confetti in the wind. The tree's age is evident in the gnarled texture of its trunk, a few scars revealing the wisdom and resilience it has acquired over the years. At the foot of the white birch, a few late-blooming wildflowers add bursts of color to the last of the summer grass. The interplay of light and shadow makes the grove an ever-changing masterpiece, a sanctuary of natural harmony.

This Grove is sacred and powerful. Time seems to stand still here, offering solace and inspiration to all who seek its protection. The weary and sorrowful can find peace, and the broken may become whole again. Standing at its center, protected within the Grove, the Tree waits, as it has done for many generations, for the Ones who will heal the world.

Chapter One

J ust before dawn, Kenna left the red house via the back patio door and headed towards the grove of trees behind their house. Lucy, their Bullmastiff, ambled along at her side, her golden coat and black markings just discernible in the predawn light. Eight years ago, at nine months old and having been neglected and ravaged by the two male mastiffs caged with her, Lucy was adopted by Kenna and Jamie. They wanted their girls to have a dog with whom to grow up. After driving five hundred miles to pick her up, Lucy came to them stinking to high heaven and covered in abrasions and bites.

The first thing she and the girls did was give her a bath in the hotel bathtub. After the bath, as Lucy lay on the floor resting, Ember, who was six years old at the time, lay down next to her, giving her gentle pets. Lucy reacted only to wag her tail and give Ember a few dog kisses. Lucy soaked up the attention, her eyes shining with relief and happiness; she had found her forever home.

Eight years later, Lucy was Kenna's constant companion on her walks around the land, sitting on the front deck watching the sunrise or lazing on the back patio, watching the sunsets. Lucy was at her side. Except at night, Lucy slept in the girls' room, on their beds, with her own pillow, or, at times, on the floor in front of their door. She was their companion and protector, chasing off bad dreams and the occasional stray dog or wild animal when they were outside.

A slight breeze blew Kenna's long cinnamon-red hair across her face. She stopped walking, pulled a scrunchy out of her pocket, and then quickly braided the long, wavy mass. When finished, she continued walking after giving Lucy a tickle behind her ear. The smell of Fall was in the air: earthy, crisp, and cold. She carefully climbed the hill in the predawn faint light along the worn path, knowing she needed to pay attention, as a tumble out here would lay her up for several days. "Damn RA," she muttered, rubbing her hands against the small of her back, the pain in her lower back and hips making her grimace. Eleven years ago, Kenna had become very ill while training for a half marathon. It had started with painful finger joints, extreme fatigue, and fevers. A short time later, getting out of bed was a major accomplishment, as she could no longer walk very far, much less run. She spent a year trying different medications, different diets, different everything, to no avail. First, it was monthly injections, then weekly, and it quickly went to daily injections of a medication that burned like fire. Not until they moved to the Red House did her symptoms seem to ease. She was able to walk amongst the trees with little pain, but her running days were definitely over.

Finally reaching the privacy of the Grove, Kenna carefully picked her way to the bench under the huge old birch tree and sat, facing the coming sunrise. Lucy sat at her side, eyes alert and quietly watching. Soon, the sun, peeking over the mountains, began to paint the sky. It began with faint orange, then hints of pink and purple spread across the horizon.

Within ten minutes, the sky was on fire: gloriously vibrant shades of gold, orange, and pink. The few clouds floating above were glowing with that wonderful shade of orange, impossible to replicate outside of nature. "Oh Lucy, my girl, this is one of the best morning shows we've seen, isn't it?" she said to Lucy, who gave her tail a wag and rested her head on Kenna's leg, staring into her eyes. Lucy always knew when she was having a bad pain day and stuck to her side like glue. Kenna laid her hand on Lucy's head, saying, "Yes, today's a bit more painful than yesterday, but I'll be better soon. Just like you will, sweetheart." Lucy had been coming to the grove with her for years now and would always be more energetic afterward.

Kenna closed her eyes and breathed deeply, taking the peace of the grove into herself. Fall was her second favorite season, with the cool crisp air, changing colors, and the promise of the coming Winter, her number one favorite. She leaned back against the white, peeling bark of the large old birch tree, its limbs dressed in its fabulous Fall coat of gold and orange. Leaning her head further back to rest against the tree and looking up, she was amazed at the height of her old friend. Her husband, Jamie, figured it was at least 70 feet tall. Closing her eyes again, hand absently stroking Lucy's head, she listened to the wind gently blowing through the leaves.

As she let the renewing energy from the tree seep into her body and soul, she could feel the pain and fatigue of her disease begin to lessen. Maybe it was a placebo effect of being in nature, but it honestly didn't matter to her if it was placebo or real; she felt markedly better after a visit to the Tree. There were times when Kenna could hear the Tree whispering to her. Faint, soothing sounds. Not quite words, but the impression of words. She had always accepted that nature could communicate if only one would listen. Here, in the Grove, Kenna felt most at home and more connected to the natural world. Even though she felt like she was being watched at times, she never felt unsafe in the Grove.

After sitting for a time, all the pain was gone, and her joints were moving like they had before this insidious disease had stolen her vitality. No stiffness, no pain. Kenna continued to sit on the bench, petting Lucy's soft head and ears, soaking up the peace and quiet energy, looking down at their home. Their house was a dark shade of red with a grey roof and trim. The back of the house had a large patio just off the kitchen doors. In the middle of the patio was a large fire ring surrounded by benches. That is where they would often come to roast marshmallows and hang out with their girls. Off to the right of the patio was a makeshift archery range, with targets set up at 10, 20, 30, and 40 yards. The four of them used the range almost daily, especially before the opening of archery hunting season, which had been three weeks ago.

Facing South, the front of the house, which she couldn't see from here, was covered in raw cedar planks, with a massive covered deck running the length of the home. Large tall windows covered the entire length of the front, letting in the Winter sunshine but keeping out the Summer heat thanks to the prow-shaped roof covering the deck. She had wanted to paint the house a different color after they bought it several years ago, but the girls had loved the color. They asked and received a promise from their parents that they would never paint it another color. It would remain dark red and always be "The Big Red House in the Country," as the girls had named it the day they had moved in. Kenna smiled at the memory.

Feeling immensely better, she stood up, arms over her head, then began stretching her entire body up and to the sides. Lucy stayed where she was, watching. When she had completed her short morning stretches, she began the 108 graceful movements of Tai Chi. Kenna started training in Tai Chi 7 years ago to help with the stiffness and pain of RA. Her trainer, who was a Master, said he'd never had a more naturally inclined student than Kenna. She was a quick study and excelled at it. She had been sparing with the Master for the past three years, and he said he'd never want to meet her in a dark ally. Most don't realize that Tai Chi is an effective self-defense martial art, believing it is just for inner peace, balance, and low-impact movement. She was confident she could defend herself against much larger aggressors than she. After 30 minutes, finished and covered with a light sheen of sweat, she began the walk back down towards the house, Lucy at her side. Her morning coffee was calling to her, plus the chance to visit uninterrupted with her Jamie. Even before the girls were born, the early morning hours were theirs when most of the world was still asleep.

As she walked the faint trail through the grove, Kenna heard her name softly called, startling her. She stopped and turned around but saw no one. Lucy had stopped as well and was on high alert, staring intently back at the Tree. "Did you hear that too, Lucy girl?" she asked Lucy, who continued to stare at the Tree, unmoving. She waited, then quietly called out, "Hello?" and waited again. Nothing. "You're losing it, Kenna." She said to herself, shaking her head. She began to walk back to

7

the Tree, eyeing her surroundings. When she stood in front of the Tree, Lucy crowded in front of her, leaning against her legs, staring intently at the Tree. "Hello?" Kenna called softly. Over the faint breeze and rustle of the leaves, she heard a distinct whisper, "Come home. We're waiting." It was coming from the Tree.

Kenna walked around the large tree, Lucy at her side, looking for the source. When she was back at the bench, she stood with hands on hips, staring up at the Tree. "I'm not crazy. I know I heard someone talking to me," she said to Lucy. Lucy cocked her head at her, then turned to stare at the Tree. Kenna took another glance around and, seeing nothing abnormal, turned to walk back to the house. "Come, Lucy, let's go," she said as Lucy stood still, unmoving. "Lucy, come," Kenna said firmly. Lucy finally looked at her, then back at the tree, gave a sigh, and walked to her side, giving her an almost reproachful look.

They both turned towards the house and continued down the path just a few steps when "We're waiting" was heard whispered on the breeze. Hair standing up on her neck, Kenna again stopped and turned towards the Tree. Lucy stood at her side, again staring at the Tree. But it was the same as it always had been, not one change. Nobody there. "Definitely losing it," she muttered. She glanced around the Grove, seeing nothing different, sensing nothing out of the ordinary. Nothing, that is, but the tingle of magic that emanated from the Grove, which was normal and ordinary for those who knew of and visited the Grove, so Kenna didn't register anything out of the ordinary because she was used to the tingle of magic, even if she wasn't completely aware of what it was or where it came from. Shrugging, she and Lucy turned away from the Tree and continued to the house.

Chapter Two

When she reached the patio door, the scent of fresh coffee was drifting out from the kitchen, greeting her. Jamie had been making her morning coffee for years and would bring it to her in whichever mug was her current favorite, mugs he called 'Kenna's soup bowls.' 'Yep, I am so spoiled,' she thought, smiling. Jamie pulled the door open, asking, "Why the cat who caught the canary smile?" offering her the huge mug filled with steaming rich, dark coffee. After accepting it, she breathed deeply over the mug and took a small sip, then sighed, "Just thinking about how spoiled I am." Giving her a smile, Jamie moved aside a bit to allow Lucy to enter the house, who then headed up towards the girls' room.

Setting the cup down on the counter, Kenna turned to Jamie, who wrapped his sturdy arms around her. She sank into their warmth. "You're all sweaty," Jamie stated, pulling part of her shirt from her back where it was sticking. "Tai Chi," she replied. Jamie nodded, "Aah, got it." They had met in college when they were both eighteen. Kenna hadn't been looking for a relationship of any kind, not after the disaster, which had been her parents' marriage and the trauma she had endured during her childhood. Nope, noway, nohow was she going to get involved with and then trapped by a man. But then along came Jamie, with his golden eyes, mischievous grin, and loud booming laugh. She couldn't deny the chemistry or the connection between them, and the pull had a fateful feeling to it. When she was with him, she felt safe and protected, which was very important to Kenna, as she hadn't had that growing up. Noelle was born one year after they met, and Ember was born one year after that.

Jamie's chin rested on her head, and she breathed in his scent deeply. It was a combination of male musk, laundry detergent, and Jamie's unique smell, woodsy and spice. She always felt so small and dainty in his embrace. She wasn't really small, height of 5'4" and 130 lbs; Kenna considered herself average. Jamie was a bear of a man, 6'5" in his stocking feet, with long muscled arms and legs, and a large brawny chest.

He had begun to lose his dark brown hair in his early 20s, so instead of rocking a George Costanza hairstyle, he had shaved his head. Something he continues to do almost daily. Jamie had a nicely shaped head, and Kenna loved to run her fingers over its smooth skin. With large, shockingly gold eyes, a nicely trimmed chocolate brown mustache, and a beard, Jamie was very attractive and masculine. They stood just inside the door, wrapped in each other's arms for a few more minutes, Jamie gently stroking her sweaty back.

Reluctantly, Kenna moved out of the embrace, and with green eyes twinkling at him, she said, "I love going to the Tree. Seriously, I always feel so renewed." Jamie nodded, smiling, understanding, and glancing up at the Grove, studied it for a few moments. A fleeting expression of longing crossed his face before he turned away. Kenna moved to the counter to sit, calling Jamie to join her. Then, between sips of coffee, they quietly discussed the day ahead. "Will you be taking the girls to the grove today?" Jamie asked, eyeing her as he topped off her coffee. She took a large swallow from her cup, closing her eyes. She sighed, took her hair tie out, unbraided her hair, ran her hands through it at the scalp, nodding her head. "Yes, I think we'll do some schoolwork up there. I don't know, maybe an art session or some botany, or both. The girls have been in front of their laptops too much this week. I need to get them away from the screens and online school for a bit. They don't have Muay Thai lessons today, so it's a good day to go up. Besides, they love the Grove. It's a second home for them.....well, for me too, I guess, " she answered, brow furling a little, playing with the bracelet on her right wrist. Fingering the round gems gently, the Black Tourmaline and Amethyst stones felt warm as she rolled them between her fingers.

"What's wrong? You seem distracted this morning," Jamie asked, looking slightly concerned. Looking up, Kenna gave him a faint smile and shook her head. Nothing, really. I just had a really weird thing happen in the grove earlier. " She looked up at him through her curtain of hair. "You'll think I'm crazy," she said with a smirk. Jamie gave a quiet chuckle and said, "Well, I already know you're crazy."

She gave his shoulder a light swat and laughed. "I married you, didn't I?" she said, then they both chuckled at the old joke. Jamie took her hand and asked, "Now, seriously, what happened in the Grove?" Kenna smiled at his concern, then sighed and replied, "I heard someone call my name when I was in the Grove, alone. I looked around, but there was no one. I'm not crazy; I know I heard my name called. Then, I distinctly heard a voice say, 'We're Waiting' after I started walking back to the house." Jamie stared into her eyes; his expression was odd and unreadable; then he said, "If you want, I'll go have a look around. If you say someone was there, then I believe you."

Smiling slightly, Kenna said, "No, please stay. I looked, and no one was there. I walked back up to the Tree and then walked around with Lucy. Nothing there." She shrugged and said, "After I did that, I heard 'Come Home, We're waiting,' and it sounded like it was coming directly from the Tree. Weird, huh? I don't know. I think it was just the wind through the leaves and my overactive imagination." Jamie rubbed a hand over his head, stared up at the Grove for a few seconds, his expression thoughtful, and said, "Ok, I'll stay. But know this: I'd slay dragons for you." He then leaned over, grabbed the back of her neck, and pulled her in for a soft kiss. "You have time before the girls wake up. Why don't you go shower and wash this sweat away?" he said, then gave her another kiss and pulled her to her feet, gently pushing her toward their bedroom. She nodded in agreement, and the grove was forgotten. Kenna made her way to the master suite.

Chapter Three

An hour later, feeling clean and refreshed, as she walked back into the kitchen, Kenna asked, "Are eggs and toast okay with you?" Jamie grimaced and said, "Hold the eggs, please. Toast will be fine; I'll add some peanut butter for protein." She chuckled and recalled why eggs weren't on his menu anymore. "I promise to hold the shells," she teased playfully. While on a business trip, Jamie had ordered an omelet for breakfast. A few bites in and "crunch." Several egg shells were found alongside the cheese and ham. It has been three years, and he still said no eggs. "Toast it is, then," Kenna said, grabbing the peanut butter out of the pantry next to the refrigerator, smooth for him, crunchy for her.

As they waited for the toast to pop up, Jamie sat down at the counter, grabbed a couple of apples, and began to slice them into quarters on the cutting board. "What's on your calendar today?" she asked, grabbing the finished toast and spreading smooth peanut butter on two pieces for Jamie. "Just finishing up a contract, then a few online meetings," Jamie answered, taking the plates Kenna was sliding across the counter. Dividing the apple slices between the two plates, Jamie asked, "What time are you and the girls going up to the grove?" "I was thinking around eleven. Why?" she replied. Jamie smiled and replied, "Why don't we all head into town for an early dinner? Noelle said she wanted to try the new burger place that opened last week. How about 4:00?" Kenna laughed and replied, "That works. I swear that girl is going to try every burger joint in Montana, then move on to another state. Our burger connoisseur." They were both laughing quietly when a voice from the doorway asked, "What's so funny this early in the morning?"

Standing in the doorway between the kitchen and the hallway was 16-year-old Noelle. She was an extremely beautiful girl with flawless fair skin, dark red arching brows over dark green eyes that had a shining gold circle around each pupil, and a riot of chin-length cinnamon-red curls like her mother's. Amongst the curls at the left temple was a snow-white streak, just like Kenna and Ember had. Noelle was tall for her age, but she always had been. Her goal was to be at least 6 feet tall, and at 5'10", she didn't have far to go.

Walking into the kitchen, she snagged a piece of toast off her dad's plate and sat next to him at the counter. Jamie reached over, giving her a few slices of apples, then gave her a one-armed hug, saying, "Good morning, Bugga." Kissing her head, then taking another bite of his toast, he said, "Tonight is burger night. Be ready to go into town at four. We're going to the new place you wanted to try." A huge grin lit up her face, and she clapped her hands together, making her Black Tourmaline and Amethyst bracelet jangle, excitedly saying, "Yes! Can I drive?" Noelle asked her parents. Exchanging smiling glances, her parents both nodded. Noelle began eating her stolen toast and apple slices, and between bites, she started to tell her parents what she was going to order. Laughingly interrupting her, Kenna said, "We KNOW what you'll be ordering, sweetheart. The same thing you always order: double cheeseburger, fries, and a chocolate milkshake. You're like your father, always sticking to what you like and rarely branching out." Burger, fries, and milkshakes were her favorite foods. She would eat almost anything, but those were her go-to if she had a choice. Noelle smiled and shrugged, "I know what I like, as Father always says."

"Is Ember awake yet?" Kenna asked Noelle. With a loud laugh, Noelle shook her head and then took a bite of the apple slice. Mouth full, Noelle mumbled, "Are you kidding? You know Ember doesn't get up before nine. She's definitely not a morning person." "Chew and swallow before speaking, please," Kenna said, raising an eyebrow. Finishing her toast, she rinsed her plate and loaded it into the dishwasher; turning around, she shrugged and said, "You know, I wasn't a morning person either before your father, and I still prefer the quiet of the night."

Picking up an apple slice, Kenna said, "Noelle, I want us to go up to the grove today for some outside lessons. Maybe some art and botany? Sound good to you?" As Noelle was wiping the crumbs off the counter into her hand, she replied, "Oh, that sounds wonderful. I love going up there, and I can try my new watercolor pencils. What time will we be going up?" "I was thinking around eleven; that way, Ember can sleep in a little more. I know she was up late last night reading", Kenna replied, chuckling. Noelle hugged her mom, breathing in her mother's scented hair, then bent down and kissed her cheek and said, "See you later, shorty. I'm going upstairs to do my online schoolwork. I'll wake Ember up at nine." Before Noelle left the kitchen, she gave her dad a smile, "Thanks for

17

the toast and apples," she said and, with a wave, left the room. Her parents exchanged a smile. She was such a joy and always had been.

Noelle was born with what Kenna called "an old soul." She hadn't cried when she was born or when they placed her on Kenna's chest, still connected to the umbilical cord. Noelle looked around, found her father, and then found her mother's eyes and stared. She had been so alert and focused, which was very unusual for a newborn. She did not cry until the nurse took her to the warmer and did what they do to newborns, that is. Then she cried uncontrollably until her daddy picked her up, took her into his arms, and cuddled her to his chest. She immediately calmed and stared into Jamie's eyes. She was such a 'good baby' for which Kenna and Jamie were extremely thankful. Being a young parent to a newborn was so scary, but Noelle made the experience easier. As she grew, her personality began to show itself. Very intelligent with a great sense of humor and a kind heart. She was so caring and loving and aware of how those around her were feeling.

"I'll be downstairs in the office if you need me," Jamie said as he leaned down and gave Kenna a quick kiss, then left the room. Having Jamie working from home was a blessing for them all. They were a very close family, and being able to touch base with each other throughout the day made work and school easier for them all. Kenna continued to clean up the kitchen, then sat down at the counter with a fresh cup of coffee. While sipping her coffee, her mind wandered to this morning in the Grove and the voice she knew she had heard. The more she mulled it over in her mind, she came to the conclusion that it wasn't a scary voice or threatening at all. It was soft and yearning, hopeful, a memory forgotten, tickling the recesses of her mind and making her brain itch, but the more she tried to remember, the further away it became.

Shaking her head and taking the last sip of her coffee, she got up and put her cup in the dishwasher. She then grabbed her headphones, put them on, opened the Amazon Music app on her phone, found her playlist, and began her morning cleaning routine. The girls often teased her about her eclectic taste in music, which was a mix of Harry Styles, Taylor Swift, Lewis Capaldi, Eminem, Mumford & Sons, Ed Sheeran, Maroon 5, Imagine Dragons, Linkin Park, and Nirvana, to name a few. Ember said she was like the head-banging mom on Monsters University, the scene when the mom was in the minivan waiting for her son and friends to come back. The mom is rocking out to headbanger music while they're getting chased and into trouble. Kenna chuckled at the memory, then lost herself in the music and sang along. She briefly forgot about the incident in the groove.

After an hour, Kenna was done with the chores and took a cup of hot tea to the back patio, Lucy trailing behind her. Sitting in one of the lounge chairs, she set her tea on the table next to her and leaned back, putting her feet up on the ottoman. Lucy laid down next to her chair, sighing heavily, making Kenna chuckle. Gazing up at the Grove, she again thought about the voice she heard this morning. She knew the Grove held magic because when she entered it, she could feel it run up through her feet to her head, like a soft buzzing. She never broached the subject with Jamie, feeling silly for thinking there was real magic in the world, but sometimes Kenna wondered if Jamie felt it too. She would often catch him gazing at the Grove with a strange expression on his face.

As she was gazing thoughtfully up at the Grove, she caught a glimpse of movement out of the corner of her eye to the right. Turning her head quickly, she saw a misty dark figure moving among the trees towards the Grove. The figure looked to be sheer, see-through, and oily black. Kenna didn't move; she was so surprised. The Black Tourmaline and Amethyst bracelet on her right wrist began to feel warm against her skin, almost hot. She felt fear like she hadn't felt it in years, moving down her spine. Lucy picked her head up and started growling low in her throat, then she stood up and moved in front of Kenna in a guard position. She was staring right at the dark figure as it floated towards the Grove, so Kenna knew she wasn't imagining it.

As Kenna stared at the figure, she felt as if something were trying to invade her mind. It was a pressure in her brain that felt cold and dead but full of anger and hate as well. Her bracelet got hotter, and she jumped up and yelled, "Hey! You're trespassing! Get off our land now, or I'm getting my rifle." She felt silly saying this to a see-through figure, but she was scared and didn't know what else to do. Lucy let out a few loud barks, and suddenly, the figure disappeared. She let out an explosive sigh and sat down hard on the chair, her arms wrapping around Lucy, who moved close to Kenna and allowed her to hug her. Lucy laid her head on Kenna's shoulder and stood there until Kenna was able to move again. "Thank you, sweet girl. You're such a good doggy; you scared the Bad away, sweetheart," she said, giving Lucy a kiss on her head, causing Lucy's tale to wag like crazy.

Kenna made the decision not to tell anyone about this strange encounter. She didn't want to worry Jamie, and she didn't want the girls to be scared to go to the Grove with her today. She also didn't want them to look at her as if she were crazy. She knew what that was like from her childhood. Giving a huge sigh, she sat back in her chair again, picked up the tea, and drank it down in one long gulp. "I wish there was a little whiskey in that tea," she whispered to Lucy. She continued to watch the Grove for a time, but the Bad was gone; she was sure of it because she couldn't feel it anymore.

Chapter Four

L ater that day, in the Grove, surrounded by the natural beauty and quiet, three figures lazed on a large blanket with a few pillows scattered around for comfort, protected by the long graceful branches of the old Birch tree. The two girls, Noelle and Ember, had sketch pads and colored pencils in front of them, with a spray bottle of water between them. Their mother, Kenna, sat facing them, with plants, flowers, and leaves scattered in her lap as she sorted them into piles. "I really like these pencils, Mom," Noelle said as she continued to draw. Then, she sprayed the water and applied strokes to the paper with a tiny brush. She was painting the Tree, including the foreground of early autumn grass and late summer flowers. "Can I have a few petals and twigs for my art project? I'd like to incorporate some texture into my watercolor," Noelle asked her mom. Kenna replied, "Of course! What colors do you want?" "A few petals of each color you have would work," Noelle said. "I really like how portable and easy they are to use," Ember chimed in, then yawned hugely. She was painting Lucy, who was lounging at her feet.

"How late did you stay up last night, Ember?" Kenna asked, adding a flower petal to the growing pile of pink, yellow, and white. Biting her lip and giving her mom a side-eyed glance, Ember responded, "Just past midnight. I didn't want to stop in the middle of the chapter, so I read to the end of that chapter. Then I just got caught up in the story and kept reading," Ember shrugged and continued, "It's such a good book; I can't wait until they release the next one." "I understand. I don't mind you staying up late as long as you're keeping your room cleaned up, doing your chores, and keeping up on your schoolwork. Also, you need at least eight hours of sleep, no exceptions," Kenna said, watching her. Ember gave her a smile and said, "Well, I slept till 9:30, so I got my eight hours in." Noelle laughed and said, "Yeah, but have you looked at your side of the room lately? Looks like a bomb went off in there, but only on your side." Ember gave Noelle a playful glare and said, "Mind your own business, brat." "It is my business; I have to live in that room too," Noelle replied, giving Ember a raised eyebrow and soft smile.

By their own choice, the girls had always shared a room, even though the house contained four bedrooms. They were nine and eight years old before they finally slept in separate beds. Thus, the bedroom designated for Noelle became their "lounge," where they could game on their computers, play the Switch, engage in art activities, do 3D printing, and complete their schoolwork. And, of course, they could have some time away from the 'parental units, ' as they sometimes referred to Jamie and Kenna. Noelle was born on January 14th and Ember on January 13th, one year apart, so for one day each year, they are the same age. When they were younger, they were often mistaken for twins at first glance because they looked so much alike. Both have curly cinnamon-red hair with strands of gold and copper, complemented by a snow-white streak like their mother's. They both have very fair skin; Ember's has a slight hint of gold undertone, while Noelle's is alabaster. Their eyes are dark green, with a striking gold ring in the center inherited from their father. Both possess beautifully arched brows, with Noelle's slightly thinner and Ember's fuller. Perfectly shaped full lips, dimples, and a cleft chin like their father's complete the similarities. The major difference between them is their height. Noelle is 5'10", while Ember stands at 5'3". Noelle is long, lean, and strong like her father; Ember is shorter and curvier but lithe like her mother.

"Stop bickering, please," Kenna said before it became something bigger. Mom, we're not fighting; we just banter like this, you know that," Ember said. Kenna sighed. "I do know. I just don't want to hear it right now," their mother replied, then whispered, "Let's enjoy the peace of the Grove."

Ember watched as her mom glanced around more than normal, staring at the Tree with a contemplative look in her green eyes and then looking around the Grove as if expecting to see someone. "Are you ok, mom?" Ember asked, gazing at her mother, then exchanged a glance with Noelle. The girls were very sensitive to their mother's moods and could sense when she was upset or when a fleeting sadness came over her. When she showed signs of being sad, the girls could always bring her back to the present. Even though Kenna had tried to keep it from them, they knew of their mother's childhood and the abuse she had endured. "Yes, I'm fine," Kenna replied, taking a deep breath and slowly exhaling. She looked at the Tree and examined it again. Then she looked around the Grove again and tilted her head as if listening to something.

Kenna looked up at her girls, who were both watching her with slightly amused expressions. "What's so funny, girls? Do I have paint on my face or something?" she asked, touching her cheek. The girls continued to watch their mother. "You seem like you're a million miles away, Mom," Noelle stated, setting her pencil down. Their mother sighed and glanced around, head tilted again as if listening for something again, then asked, "Have either of you ever felt a presence or heard voices while you were here in the Grove? Have you ever felt scared to be in the Grove?"

The girls exchanged another amused look, then both smiled and nodded, but then they shook their heads no. Ember said, "Yes, we do hear the Grove speaking, but no, we never feel unsafe or scared in the Grove; it's a special place." Then, turning to her sister, she said, "Noelle, do you think our mother has finally opened up enough to listen?" Noelle smiled and replied, "Hmmmmm, Yes, I do believe you may be correct, Ember." "What in the world are you girls going on about?" Kenna asked, laughing. The girls put their painting supplies away into the tote, sat up, and moved closer to their mother. Sitting in front of her, they each took a hand. "Did you finally hear the voices of the Grove?" Noelle asked quietly. "We've been waiting for you to hear them," Ember said.

They sat there, holding their mother's hands, watching as expressions of confusion, worry, surprise, and then amazement quickly crossed Kenna's face. "You've both heard the whispers in the Grove? I thought it was just me and my imagination," Kenna said in amazement. "Mom, we've been hearing them since we first moved here, when we were one and two years old," Noelle stated, smiling. "When did you hear them, Mom?"

Ember asked, shifting her position closer, holding her mother's hand in her lap. "I've always heard whisperings in the Grove but could never make out what was being said. Plus, I thought it was just my mind playing tricks on me," Kenna replied, shrugging, then continued, "This morning, when I came up here with Lucy, the voice said, 'We're waiting,' then it called my name. It was very clear this time. I also heard, 'Come Home; we're waiting.' I feel as if I should know what it means, but the harder I try to make sense of it, the more it just flits away, out of my grasp." The girls exchanged an excited look.

"I think it's time, Noelle," Ember whispered, glancing at the Tree. "I think so too! We should take her over," Noelle exclaimed. They both stood up, as did Lucy, who glanced at the Tree, then back at the girls. Her tail gave a wag as she sat at attention, waiting. Kenna, looking thoroughly confused, asked, "What is going on, girls? Take me over where? Does someone live in the Grove?" Both girls gave loud bursts of laughter, then, still chuckling, grabbed their mother's hands, gently pulled her up to stand, and then pulled her towards the tree.

As they moved closer to the Tree, Noelle said, "Mom, we know you have a sixth sense, and you tend to know things before they happen. You just know so many things....like the weather. You're better at weather prediction than anyone because you're never wrong. Your healing touch isn't like other mothers. When we have a fever, a migraine, or a cold, you don't just make us feel better; you take the illness or pain away. We feel your power. Sometimes, you forget to close yourself off, and it leaks through." Noelle took a deep breath and continued, "And we know this because we have it, too. We are always open, though, not having a reason to close it off, always being home with you and Dad. The terrible things you experienced as a child have caused you to try to close it off and bury it. But today, you've allowed it out enough to hear the Tree." Noelle gave her Kenna's hand a squeeze.

Kenna stopped walking and turned to Noelle. "How do you know about my childhood, and how much do you know about it?" she asked, expression cautious and eyes glinting slightly with a sheen of tears. Ember put her arm around her mother's shoulders and hugged her, saying, "We know some mom. We've always known, even though you didn't want us to. We figure when you're ready to share everything, you will." Kenna pulled both girls into a hug, holding them tightly, sniffing back her tears. "I didn't want you to know there was such horror in the world. I wanted to protect you from it," Kenna whispered, closing her eyes. Noelle gave a small laugh, smiling sadly, and said, "Mom, we have internet. We know there's horror in the world. We know what people can do to each other." Ember took a step back and said, "It's time, Mom. It's time for you to remember ALL of your past, not just the bad parts."

Chapter Five

The girls each took one of their mother's hands and turned towards the tree. They moved to the giant old Birch tree, placing their mother's hands on it, palms flat, then placed their own right next to hers. Kenna, with a daughter on each side of her, hands on the tree, asked, "What is going to happen? What are we doing?" "Come on, Lucy!" Ember called quietly. Lucy came over, placing herself between the two girls, right in front of Kenna, leaning against her legs like Bullmastiffs do. "OK, Mom, relax. Take a deep breath and blow it out slowly. Close your eyes. Do NOT take your hands off the tree," Noelle whispered. "Mom, don't open your eyes and keep your hands on the Tree," Ember whispered. Noelle quietly said, "You're going to feel the warmth and hear the wind. It's ok, don't be scared." Their mother simply replied, "Okay." They all three closed their eyes, and then Noelle and Ember spoke softly:

"With whispered words and intentions pure, We call upon the spirits and elements, To guide us through this enchanted door, Into the realm of ancient lore, Where mysteries lie in forests deep, We step into the realm unseen, With roots as our anchor, Branches our guide, Through the Tree's embrace, We journey wide, where the veil between the worlds is space. "

Kenna felt the wind start to increase, picking her hair up and blowing it all around her head. The Tree began to feel warm under her hands, and the whispers of the Grove became louder and more numerous, filling her ears with soothing words. The bracelet she always wore began to vibrate gently against her skin. Kenna felt a sense of remembrance, like a deja vu. She felt as if she'd been here before. No, she **knew** she had experienced this at some other time in her life. After a few seconds, the wind stopped, the Tree cooled to the touch, and the air felt much colder than it had a few minutes ago; it was crisp and cold, like Winter.

"Open your eyes now, Mom," Noelle whispered. Kenna slowly opened her eyes and, taking her hands off the tree, she stepped back. Looking around in wonder, she asked, "Where are we?" Ember said, "In the Grove, mom. Just not in our world." "Another world?" breathed Kenna as she reached down and picked up a handful of snow. "But how?" she whispered, looking around at the snow-covered ground and trees. 'When had it snowed?!' Kenna thought to herself. Examining the snow in her hand and then looking up to glance around the Grove and surrounding area, she realized it WAS the Grove, but in Winter. Looking towards their house, she gasped. Their house wasn't there; absolutely nothing was there to indicate they had lived there. "Where did our house go?! What happened to our home? Where is your father?" Kenna asked the girls loudly, a hint of panic in her voice. "Mom, calm down. It's ok; the house is where it has always been, and Dad is there, safe and sound. We are in another world. We entered it via the Tree. Our world is exactly how we left it and will be there when we go back," Noelle said, grabbing her mother's hands and forcing her to look at her. "Again, we are in another world," Noelle whispered to her mother. Kenna closed her eyes, took a deep, steadying breath, and whispered, "Ok. Another world. It's ok. Just another world." Straightening up and opening her eyes, Kenna nodded her head to indicate she was ok. "Okay. Okay.....does this world have a name?" she asked her daughters. They both smiled at their mother. "Marqueria," they said in unison.

Chapter Six

B ack in their world, 1000's miles from the Red House in the Country and the Grove, a tall, thin woman with short grey hair and a sour look on her face answered the ringing phone. Despite being just past 10:00 pm, she was still awake and fully dressed. "Yes?" she snapped. The voice on the other end stated, "They activated the Tree and have crossed over." The woman's thin lips smiled coldly. "Was it just the two girls again, or did the mother travel too?" she asked the caller. The man on the other end of the phone cleared his throat nervously and replied, "The mother went as well this time." "Good..good... I believe it's time I paid a visit to the mountains of Montana," she said.

She abruptly hung up the phone, then pushed the button on the intercom next to the phone and demanded, "Call the brothers and get the jet ready. We're going to Montana." Turning the intercom off, she stood staring out the window, lost in memories. It had been over thirty years since she last breathed the sweet air of Marqueria, and it showed in her wrinkles and gray hair. But when she returned there, she would regain her youth and beauty. Shaking herself as if to shake off the memories, she turned and walked up the stairs towards her bedroom to pack and again gave a chilling smile. "Finally," she whispered, eyes glinting coldly, "I'm going home, and there's nothing they can do to prevent it."

Chapter Seven

In the snow-covered Grove, in a world far from her own, Kenna wrapped her arms around herself, not feeling the chill but needing the comfort. Her girls were building a snowman, rolling around large balls of snow until they had the proper sizes, completely carefree teenagers. Lucy was running around happily, rolling in the snow and occasionally eating some. Kenna smiled as she watched three of the most important beings in her life frolicking in the snow. They had always been Winter kids, loving the cold and snow more than any other season, just like their mother. Winter was Kenna's favorite season, with Fall following a close second.

"You've been here before?" she called to her girls. Noelle and Ember finished rolling the snowman's head, placed it atop their creation, then brushed their hands off and walked towards their mother. "Please, don't be angry, but yes, we have," Noelle replied. "When was the first time?" Kenna asked. Ember and Noelle exchanged an "uh oh" look, grimacing. Ember put her arms around her mother, hugged her close, took a deep breath, and sniffed Kenna's hair. She loved the scent of her mother; it was the scent of home and love that brought her great comfort. Kenna returned Ember's hug, smiling to herself. "When was the first time?" she asked again. Noelle, standing behind her mother, wrapped her arms around both

Kenna and Ember, somewhat towering over the two. She, too, took a deep breath, breathing in the scent of Kenna's hair. It's something both girls had always done, sniffing their mother's hair. Noelle sighed and whispered, "Not long after we moved in. I was three, and Ember was two." "Wait, What?!!" Kenna exclaimed loudly, "You've been coming here alone since you were two and three years old?! How is that possible?! How did I not realize you were gone, that you were missing?" She shook her head and whispered, "I guess my 'mother's instinct' failed me, huh?"

The girls both stepped back, putting some space between themselves and their mother. Smiling, Ember said, "Mom, time moves differently here. What seems like hours here is only seconds at home. We could spend all day here and only be gone for several seconds up to a few minutes in our world." "You didn't even know we were gone, Mother," Noelle said, "and we always had Lucy with us, well after we rescued her, that is." Kenna asked, "But how did you get through the Tree? You didn't know to ask, did you?" The girls laughed, and Noelle replied, "No, we didn't know how to ask. We were just collecting the crystals lying on the ground around the Tree, like we always do, when I got this strong feeling that we needed to touch the Tree. I grabbed Ember's hands and placed them on the Tree along with my own. Next thing we knew, we were in Winter!" Then Ember said, "It wasn't until we were older, when they felt we were ready, that they taught us the calling, in case we needed to bring someone through the Tree with us."

"Mother, there's more we need to show you," Noelle said, and, reaching her hand out to Ember, said, "Ember, move closer to me." "Are we going to do the Wind Spell for Mom's magic?" Ember asked excitedly. Noelle grinned at the startled look their mother sent them. Nodding, Noelle took Ember's hands in hers. The girls were standing close together, facing each other, holding their hands out in front of themselves, palms touching, matching Tourmaline and Amethyst bracelets softly swaying on their right wrists. The girls closed their eyes and palms touching, they began chanting:

"Oh, gusts of power, gentle and wild, Carry our words, into the Wild, Whisper through the trees, caress the leaves, Bring forth the magic She desperately needs. With each breath you take, a spell is cast, A symphony of whispers, from the distant past, Whirling and twirling, in a mystical dance, Awakening Her spirit, from a magical trance. Swift as the eagle, soaring high, The wind carries secrets, beyond the sky, Unseen and untamed, a force so grand, Invisible hands, shaping the land. Oh, Magical wind, with your ethereal might, Bring forth the wonders, what's hidden from sight, Blow away the doubts and remove Her layers, hiding Her Truth. We call upon you, oh wind of grace, Embrace us in your gentle breeze, Bring forth the magic, let it unfurl, As we ride the currents, in this enchanted world."

As Kenna watched her daughters doing their spell, she felt a gentle breeze begin to blow her curls around her face. Both Noelle and Ember were enveloped within a sheer swirl of gentle snow, their cinnamon-red curls floating about their heads, their bodies giving off a faint silver and green glow. When their chant was complete, they both turned towards their mother and, holding out their hands, beckoned her to join them in the gently swirling tornado of snow. Kenna walked the few steps, took a hand from each girl into her own, and then stepped into the mini cyclone. Immediately, she felt an electric jolt from her toes to her head, and meeting Noelle's eyes, which were glowing a vibrant green and gold, she asked breathlessly, "What is this?" Noelle gave a soft laugh and replied, "It's magic mother. It's a spell to help you remember your past and the lost magic you've buried. Close your eyes and allow the wind to enter you."

Kenna closed her eyes, holding tight to her daughters' hands. Her hair floated around her head, and she felt the warmth of the snow-laden wind seep into her being. She felt it enter every cell, making her feel more alive than ever before. With that feeling, her mind began to unfurl, removing the locks she herself had placed on it. Images raced across her mind's eye of this realm and all it contained. Kenna felt as if all her defenses were being stripped away, replaced by a loving warmth and gentle embrace. She gasped as the wind suddenly ceased, leaving her with a small sense of loss.

Opening her eyes, she found her daughters gazing at her with looks of wonder. "What?" she asked quietly. They exchanged a glance, and then Noelle said, "You're glowing, Mom. Your entire body is glowing." "You're so beautiful, mom!" Ember breathed. Kenna smiled gently at her daughters and spoke softly, "I feel the magic of this world. I can hear the trees and the birds speaking. I can feel the power in the land seeping into me. I remember all of this. I remember this feeling, and my soul remembers this place."

"They taught that spell to us early so we could help you unlock what you've hidden away. It brought down your barriers and will now allow the connection to this world and our own world to flourish again," Noelle said, pulling her mother down into a sitting position on the snow-covered ground. Ember took a seat next to her. and asked, "How do you feel, mother?" Both girls were watching her with curious eyes. Kenna gave a quiet chuckle, then grinned hugely. "I feel amazing! My body is buzzing with energy and electricity," she said, laughing with her daughters. For some time, the three of them sat and soaked up the peace and energy, allowing Kenna to become accustomed to her returning magic. After a while, Ember asked, "Are you ready to continue our journey?" "Yes, I'm actually very energized and excited to see this world," Kenna replied, jumping to her feet. She had no pain anywhere in her body, as if she had never had RA. 'This is amazing,' she thought to herself.

Kenna backed up a step, turned, and began walking back toward the Tree. Despite the snow, she didn't feel cold, which wasn't strange. She and the girls were very cold-tolerant, even sleeping with the windows open at night in the middle of Winter. Jamie was the same, preferring Winter to Summer as well. He was just as fond of the cold as the ladies in his life. Looking around, she was dazzled by the utter beauty of the Grove. The evergreens were covered in snow, their boughs bending slightly under the weight. The aspens were bare, their leaves having already fallen. But the birch tree! The birch tree still had its leaves. The tree was still dressed in autumn splendor, with golden and red leaves. Its white bark blends in with the snowy background yet contrasts with the dark greens of the pines. Kenna stood several feet away from the Tree, contemplatively eyeing her surroundings. As she stared at the Tree, she caught movement out of the corner of her eye. Turning her head, her mouth opened in a small gasp. Standing twenty yards away was a magnificent pale pink and silver Unicorn.

Kenna stood still, unmoving. The unicorn had a pale pink coat, long flowing silver mane and tail, silver hooves, and a long spiral silver horn between her ears. It was a female, obviously. Kenna wanted to walk to it and stroke its luxurious-looking mane, but instinct said she needed to stay where she was and let the unicorn decide. As she waited and watched the Unicorn, she could hear her daughters whispering quietly.

"No, I don't think she's ready to meet them yet. This has been a bit of a shock, and she doesn't even have all her memories back yet," Noelle said. Ember whispered back to her sister, "Well, I do. Mom is stronger than you give her credit for. She can handle it." Noelle gave a sigh, stating, "I know mom is strong. I know she can handle it, but it's a lot to take in all at once. She has experienced a lot today. Maybe we let it all soak in for her, and then we will come back another day and introduce them at that time." Ember growled, "Noelle, they've been waiting so many years. We should take her to them now!"

Kenna quietly called out to her daughters, "Girls, is this something you've seen before?" Behind her, the girls gave cries of joy and walked over to their mother. "Oh yes, mom. She has greeted us here often. Her name is Raina," Noelle replied. "Isn't she magnificent?" Ember asked her mother. "Darlings, she's amazing. Can I go over and introduce myself, do you think?" Kenna asked her girls. Shaking her head, Ember replied,

"Better to wait until she comes to you, Mom." As the girls watched the Unicorn, it began to slowly walk towards them, throwing her head back, silver mane dancing in the breeze.

When it reached the three of them, the Unicorn stood in front of Kenna and stared at her with eyes of silver mercury. Then, she bowed gracefully, her silver horn touching the snow. It arose, and Kenna slowly reached her hand out and placed it on her muzzle, which was softer than velvet. She took a step towards the Unicorn and continued to stroke her muzzle, then her mane. Her mane felt like warm liquid silk. The Unicorn gave a soft whinny and nuzzled Kenna's neck. "She likes you, mom. I've never seen her bow before, though," Noelle said, chuckling softly. "Do you think because mother is someone special to this world, Noelle?"

Ember said, in her "duh" voice. "Are there more like her?" Kenna asked. "Oh yes, many! But she is their Queen," Noelle said. "Hmmm, well, that makes sense, doesn't it? Raina means Queen, in Slavic," Kenna said, nodding. The Unicorn took a few steps back, bowed again, then turned and cantered away into the forest. Kenna stared after her, mesmerized. "That was amazing," she breathed, "I could hear her speaking to me in my mind. She said, 'Welcome home, Princess. We of Marqueria have all missed you. Your return brings much joy to the Land.' But I still don't understand it all. Princess?" Kenna shook her head in wonder.

Chapter Eight

Turning to face her daughters, Kenna asked, "Soooo. Meet who?" They both looked at her in surprise. "Yeah, you forgot about my Mom Hearing," she laughingly said, grinning at their expressions of surprise. "Now, exactly whom am I supposed to meet? Who has been waiting for me 'for years'? And why did the Queen of the Unicorns bow to JUST me? What is this princess stuff?" she asked again, shaking her head and rolling her eyes slightly, expression wry.

Noelle moved closer to her mom and took her hand, holding it in her own, then said, "The inhabitants of this world, that's who. Now is as good a time as any, I guess. As for why the Unicorn bowed to you, I have no idea. She's never done that before. Please, just trust us, mom." "We will need to walk a little before we get to their place. It's through the Grove and down the valley," Ember said and, walking over, grabbed Kenna's other hand, giving it a tug, then continued excitedly, "Noelle, let's get going! Time is wasting! Come on, Lucy!" she called to her dog, who ambled over and stood, tail wagging. There was a faint trail through the Grove, which Kenna hadn't noticed before. They began to follow it, moving single file now, Ember in the lead with Lucy at her side, Noelle second, and Kenna in the rear so she could keep an eye on her girls. This was usually the order in which they hiked around the mountains back home, with Jamie in the lead, of course. Noelle would always argue, "But the two shortest need to be in the middle in case a mountain lion trails us. They always go for the smallest in the group, you know." Kenna, of course, refused to allow her daughter to be the tail end of the group. She had to keep watch from behind and protect her girls. The trail passed by the Tree and deeper into the Grove, away from where their house would've been. 'Where our house should've been,' Kenna thought and gave a quiet sigh.

As they followed the trail, Kenna used the time to examine her surroundings. The Grove was the same as the one in their world, yet different, seeming more alive, fuller, and richer somehow. There were trees here she'd never seen before or didn't remember seeing. They had vibrant pink leaves and deep red trunks, with branches forming a large circle towards the sky. The branches were heavily laden with dark red fruit the size of a small peach. "Can we eat those?" she asked her daughters, pointing to the pink and red trees. "Oh yes! Their flavor is amazing. Like a cross between a sweet peach and a strawberry, with a hint of vanilla and cinnamon," Noelle said.

Walking over to the nearest pink and red fruit tree, Kenna reached up and plucked a palm-sized red fruit. "What are they called?" she asked, examining it closely and holding it to her nose to sniff. There was a faint glow to the deep red fruit. "Fireberry," Ember answered her mother as she, too, plucked one and took a bite. Shrugging, Kenna took a bite. The most amazing flavor burst into her mouth, coating her tongue. There was a hint of strawberry, peach, and vanilla, but the underlying flavor was heat. Just a hint of cinnamon, warm and delicious. "Oh, My Goodness!"

Kenna exclaimed and said, "I could eat these all day, every day." "I know, right?! They're my favorite fruit here," Ember said, "and I absolutely love the colors of the tree. Pink and Red, who knew?!!" Noelle laughed and said, "Pick one for the road if you want, but we need to continue our journey." Grinning at each other, Kenna and Ember both picked another from the tree, then Kenna, smiling teasingly at Noelle, handed her the fruit and said, "Eat something, please. We don't want you to get Hangry." Smirking at her mother, Noelle said thank you and took a bite, briefly closing her eyes to savor it. "Well, come on! Let's get going," Ember said, again taking up the lead with Lucy.

After walking for what must have been another fifteen minutes, the trees began to thin, and the countryside became a little more open. Still forested, with tall mountains in the near distance and meadow openings here and there. A few small creeks flowed down towards the valley, joining to make a small river that flowed through the valley floor. Looking to her right, Kenna suddenly stopped walking. At first, a trace of fear raced down her back, and her heart started pounding fast. Standing just within the tree line, about 50 yards from her and the girls, was a huge beast of a grizzly bear. It was the biggest bear she had ever seen, much larger than the Polar Bears she'd seen on their trip to the Arctic.

"Girls!" she whispered, not taking her eyes off the Bear. The girls stopped and turned back towards their mother, but then, noticing where she was staring, turned towards the Bear. "Ohhhhh, I was wondering if we'd get to see you today," said Noelle quietly to the Bear, smiling. "Don't be afraid, mother. He watches over us whenever we are here. He's our protector and would never hurt us," Ember said, smiling at her mother and giving the Bear a wave. Kenna studied the Bear, taking in his strangely familiar glowing golden eyes, dark brown fur with golden tips, and massive claws. She met his eyes, mesmerized. The Bear continued to stare at Kenna, then gave a gruff snort, nodded his head, and turned away to amble back into the forest. Kenna let out the breath she hadn't realized she was holding. "Oh My God! I've never been this close to a wild brown bear before!" Kenna exclaimed, "I heard him in my head! He spoke inside my mind and said, 'Welcome home, daughter. You have been greatly missed, and your return is a most joyous occasion.' Why would he call me daughter?" she asked, confused. "Maybe because you're a daughter of this land? I don't know," answered Noelle, shrugging. The girls gave their mom an understanding look, and then Ember said, "Come, mother. We need to continue."

Chapter Nine

Cresting a small hill, Ember and Lucy stopped, waiting for Noelle and Kenna to catch up. Moving to Ember's side, giving the dog a rub behind an ear, Kenna looked over the small valley below. She gasped, eyes wide. She couldn't believe her eyes. There was a Castle at the top of the valley. An honest-to-goodness Castle! Where had her daughters led her? She continued to stare, mouth slightly parted in awe. As she gazed at the Valley and the Castle, Kenna began to have a vague sense of remembrance, but the harder she tried to grasp the memories, the quicker they flitted away, which was extremely irritating. The Wind Spell had opened her to the magic, but her memories were like the will-o'-the-wisp. Unable to catch them, the more difficult it was, the more she chased. Kenna gave a quiet sigh and continued to study the castle.

The Castle sat at the far end of the valley, on a hill. The base was a very large circle with a high stone wall surrounding it, which was made of the same white shining stone as the castle. The stone had the look of ice and snow and sparkled in the sunshine as if made of jewels. It was straight out of a medieval fantasy movie, with tall round towers spaced evenly around the circular base. Just like a wedding cake, each layer was smaller towards the top. There were three tall levels in the middle, and the thirteen towers were as tall as the main sections of the

Castle. The windows were long and arched at the top, the doors huge, and from this distance, they looked to be made of wood. The valley, containing a small village at its center with lovely quaint cottages and shops, wasn't very large. Kenna estimated it spanned maybe one mile long and half a mile wide, surrounded by mountains and peaks and a small river to the left of the village flowing down the valley floor, away from the direction of the Castle.

The mountains behind the castle and surrounding the valley reminded Kenna of the Rocky Mountains, back home where their Red House was. The peaks were covered in snow; the slopes were a mix of evergreens, aspens, and several trees she didn't know the names of. She let out another gasp as she spotted something large flying in the distance. 'It couldn't be.' Kenna thought to herself. As the object flew closer, she could see that, yes, indeed, it was. It was a Dragon. A beautiful, fantastical beast of a dragon! This dragon was a deep sparkling garnet red, with silver tips on the wings and claws. It flew close enough that Kenna could see there was a rider on its back. A dragon rider!

Kenna turned to her daughters and asked, "When were you going to tell me about the Dragons?! You know I adore Dragons. I used to dream about dragons when I was growing up." The girls laughed, and Ember said, "Oh, Mom. I forgot to tell you. There are dragons here, and they come in many different colors. Oh, and people ride them." Her mother raised an eyebrow at her and laughed, then said, "Cute, Ember."

The dragon flew out of sight, and Kenna returned her attention to the Valley and the Village. It was a village like she'd never seen before or one she couldn't remember ever seeing.

The Village was arranged in a circular grid, with a huge plaza in the center. Each cobbled street circled around the Plaza and got larger the further from the center they were. There were a few side streets that intersected the circular cobbled streets and reached the outskirts of the Village. There was also one long cobbled road that went from the Village to the Castle.

There were people going about their day, milling around amongst the charming, picturesque houses and shops. In the Plaza, some inhabitants were sitting at tables, enjoying the sunshine, eating, and visiting. The females were attired in long flowing dresses made from a silky gossamer fabric. Their hair, worn down and unbound, came in various shades of blonde and gold, but a few had manes of silver like the Unicorn. Some of the females had curly hair, but most were straight. The males wore long tunics made of the same material as the females' dresses. While the females' dresses just brushed the ground, the male's tunics stopped just short of their knees with soft-looking leggings underneath, made from the same silky-looking material. The garments came in many different colors; dark jewel tones moved among light pastel shades.

On their feet, Kenna could just make out short and tall boots. The footwear came in many different colors, just like the clothing. She turned to her daughters and whispered, "You've been to this Valley? Do you know these people? Have you spoken to them?" Noelle and Ember exchanged a grin, both nodding. "Yes, we have, mom. They're lovely people and have been watching out for us since our first trip through the Tree," Ember responded. "What do you think of the Castle, Mother?" Noelle asked, eyes sparkling with suppressed mirth. Kenna began to laugh, shaking her head. "A Castle. A freaking

Castle!" she responded, grinning at her girls. Ember returned her mother's smile and took her hand, beginning to lead her down the trail toward the Valley. Ember said, "Come. They're waiting for us, Mom."

As they walked through the village, Kenna continued to glance around. It was as if they'd stepped back in time 600 years, straight into Medieval times. While it reminded her of a medieval village, it was vastly cleaner and more charming. 'More like a medieval fairytale village,' Kenna thought to herself. There were white cobbled streets with sparkling jewels embedded into each stone. Beautifully wrought lamp posts dotted the streets, sparkling glass in the windows and doors, and an abundance of trees provide shade and beauty. It had none of the negatives of a medieval village, none of the dirt, grime, or poverty.

Up close, the villagers were stunning. Their garments were exquisitely made, and their faces were ethereally beautiful. As Kenna studied the villagers, she noticed they were all tall and lithe, with just a few petite women sprinkled in amongst them. Their hair was long, even by the males. Some wore tiny braids at the temples, while others let their hair flow freely. Their skin was flawless and glowing and came in all shades.

After a time, Kenna became aware that the villagers were all smiling and waving at the girls like old friends, but most glanced at her with looks of curiosity and some with excitement. Lucy's tail was wagging nonstop, and she received several pats on her head and scratches behind her ears as they walked along the cobbled sidewalk. Noelle whispered to her mother, "Do you notice anything out of the ordinary yet?" Kenna shook her head and laughed quietly, responding, "Oh, you mean like traveling through a Tree, finding an ancient village, petting a Unicorn, and finding a fairytale Castle? Or did you mean seeing a dragon with a person riding it? Or were you thinking of something else, daughter?" Noelle and Ember both laughed. Grinning, Noelle said, "Fair point, mother. No, I meant about the villagers. Look closely at each one."

Kenna returned her gaze to the villagers passing by, looking for something out of the ordinary. "Well, they're all stunningly beautiful. How can one village hold nothing but amazingly beautiful people? Their clothing is exquisite and looks so soft and comfortable. I feel so underdressed in my jeans, sweater, and Uggs," She said, grimacing down at her faded jeans, green sweater, and slightly worn brown Uggs. She shrugged to herself, as she didn't really care what others thought about her clothing. She'd always dressed for comfort anyway. She then said, "Other than that, no, I don't see anything 'out of the ordinary,'" Kenna said laughingly. The girls exchanged a look, then smiled at the mother, "Give it time," Ember said, grinning, "You'll notice it."

Chapter Ten

Ember was in the lead and stopped in front of a small shop. Then she opened the door and said, "Come on. Let's stop here first before we continue on." Noelle teasingly said, "I thought you were in a hurry to get there. You and your appetite!" The girls exchanged grins, and as Kenna followed her daughters and Lucy into the shop, the smell of freshly baked bread drifted towards her. Her stomach gave a growl, and she whispered, "I'm starving."

Ember led the way to a small table in the corner, near the large front window, waving to the petite female behind the counter. Lucy settled next to Ember on the floor, curling up, giving a huge sigh, then closing her eyes. Kenna moved to the seat facing the door, with her back against the wall, as she always sat in public places. Looking around, she felt the warm and welcoming atmosphere begin to soak into her, easing tension she hadn't noticed she was carrying. The decor in this small cafe managed to be comforting yet luxurious and upscale at the same time. The walls were colored a soft, very light, buttery yellow, with the floors a gleaming, glowing dark hardwood. Small jewels were embedded into the floor, around each table and chair grouping, giving off a soft glowing light. The small round tables with cushioned seating were spaced around the interior, with plenty of room to walk between each.

Crystal chandeliers hung from the dark copper ceiling, providing diffused yet sparkling lighting. The aromatic scents emerging from the kitchen in the back made Kenna's stomach grumble again.

After the three were seated, the stunningly beautiful woman brought over a silver tray with a porcelain teapot and three cups with matching saucers. "It is so wonderful to see you girls again. It's been a while since your last visit. I hope everything has been well with you. What has kept you away for so long?" she said to Noelle and Ember, her voice musical and welcoming. Ember replied, "Oh, we've been fine, Angelique, but between school and Muay Thai lessons during the week, we haven't had much time." "We've missed coming here so much; two weeks is too long between visits," said Noelle, smiling at the woman.

Kenna watched the interaction closely, realizing her daughters were very much at home here. The girls turned towards their mother, and Noelle said, "Mother, this is Angelique. She owns this cafe and makes the most amazing baked goods. She has been feeding us since our first trip through the Tree." Then, smiling warmly at the shop owner, she continued, "Angelique, this is our mother, Kenna." Angelique curtsied and bowed her head towards her in greeting. Kenna gazed at the woman, taking in her flawless, ebony skin and deep blue eyes. Her hair was long, wavy, and pale silver. She had pulled the shiny mass back into a loose bun, but strands were escaping at the temples. The combination was so unexpected and lovely. Kenna blurted, "You are so stunningly beautiful! Your hair is silver, actually silver! Like the Unicorn." She then blushed and covered her mouth with her hand, saying, "I'm so sorry. I don't mean to be rude. This is all new to me, and I have forgotten my manners."

Angelique smiled gently at Kenna and said, "I thank you for the compliment. It is nice to finally meet you. We have been waiting for your return for a very long time. So, you met Raina, Queen of the Unicorns?" Kenna returned Angelique's smile hesitantly and replied, "Yes, at the Tree. She came to me and bowed, then allowed me to stroke her mane before cantering away. Pardon me, but I'm a bit confused. What do you mean 'waiting for me'? Why would you be waiting for me? My return? I don't understand." Angelique turned to the girls and quietly asked, "She doesn't know? Why is she here if she doesn't know?"

After taking a sip of tea, eyes lit with excitement, Ember spoke up, "The voices! She heard the voices of the Grove. We knew The Tree would let her pass, and we felt it was time, so here we are." Noelle nodded in agreement, saying, "Plus, Raina bowed to Mother, and the Bear made himself known to her as well, welcoming her home. We are correct that it was time." Then Noelle, smiling at Angelique, asked, "Would you please bring us some soup, rolls, cheese, and fruit? We missed lunch." With one last almost sympathetic glance at Kenna, Angelique nodded and moved back behind the counter to gather the food.

Kenna looked at her daughters, seeing them in an entirely new light. In this world, they seemed so much more self-assured and in charge, even more mature and self-possessed. She watched them sip their tea and said, "You both seem different here. More complete and confident, older than 15 and 16 years." The girls both smiled at their mother and, setting their tea cups down, nodded. Noelle said, "Here, we don't have to hide large parts of ourselves. We can be ourselves entirely." Ember, nodding again, said, "I agree with Noelle. I can be myself here. I can talk to the trees and animals and listen to the wind with nobody looking at me as if I was crazy like the kids at school did before you started homeschooling us." Kenna took one of each of their hands and smiled rather sadly, saying, "I'm sorry you weren't allowed to be yourselves. Your father and I tried to ensure that you could walk your own path and be your own person. I feel as if we failed you somehow." Noelle quickly shook her head. "No, Mom! That's not it. You and Father are the best parents we could have ever asked for. It's not you and dad. It's the world we live in. They have forgotten the magic in the earth and air; they have forgotten their connection to Nature. Magic and Nature are an integral part of us, and being here only makes us stronger," Noelle said passionately. Ember nodded in agreement, smiling at their mother.

"Girls, I'll be honest with you, I'm rather confused right now. How have you managed to keep this secret for so long? I feel as if I haven't been paying attention," Kenna said, brow furling; she finally picked up her teacup and took a sip. The flavor burst in her mouth, covering her tongue with delicious liquid heat that flowed down, warming her to her belly. The base was black tea, with hints of currant, vanilla, and honey, but there was something else she was tasting. "What is that flavor? I can't quite place it. It's familiar but just out of my reach. Honestly, this is absolutely the best tea I've ever had. I see I've been missing out on more than just the animals here. Do you stop at this shop often?" She asked her daughters with a smile, taking another sip of tea.

The girls exchanged a look, somewhat guiltily. "Yes, whenever we're here in this world, and it's Pomegranate you're tasting. Just a hint," Noelle replied as she held her cup in both hands, elbows resting on the table, breathing in the aromatic steam. "And how often is that?" Kenna asked, taking another sip of tea and closing her eyes, enjoying the warmth and flavor. "We try to come every couple weeks or so, sometimes weekly," Ember said, grinning at Angelique as she set a fully loaded honey-colored wooden tray on the table. Kenna opened her eyes. The tray contained steaming bowls of thick creamy soup, luscious warm dark rolls, a small bowl of whipped pale butter, and small bowls of creamy white and pale yellow cheeses, with a bundle of deep purple grapes on the side. "Thank you so much, Angelique! I'm starving," Ember said. "You're always starving," Noelle laughingly said. "Yes, this one has a bottomless stomach," Angelique said, laughing, then winked at Ember. Walking back towards the counter, she said, "You three enjoy your lunch; let me know if you need anything else."

As Kenna and the girls ate their way through the tray of deliciousness, they continued to speak quietly. She asked pointed questions about their trips to this world, and the girls answered honestly. "We didn't want to keep this secret from you, Mom, but we had promised we wouldn't reveal the existence of this world until you were awoken, until the Tree deemed you ready," Noelle said. "They told us it could be dangerous for you if we told you before you were ready," Ember chimed in. Kenna set her teacup down, stared at her girls for a minute, raised an eyebrow, and smirked, then she said, "Yeah, I really don't feel as if any of this is dangerous. My spidey senses aren't going off at all. So far, I see nothing but beauty and wonder." The girls laughed.

"Do you girls experience the same things I'm starting to? Hearing the animals speak in your mind? Feeling the life force of the land? Hearing the trees talk to each other?" Kenna asked as she buttered a hot roll. Taking a bite, she groaned in pleasure, and her girls laughed at her reaction. "I know, mom! The food here is amazing," Ember said, smiling at her mother and then continuing, "And yes, we experience the same thing that you are now. We always have, even in our world. The love and safety you and Dad provided us allowed our magical side to flourish, even in the mortal realm." Noelle smiled at her mother, eyes full of love and understanding, then said, "They said everything would be explained to you when we brought you to them. So let's finish our lunch, then continue our walk to the Castle," Noelle said.

Ember nodded in agreement, took the last bite of cheese, and then washed it with the last of her now-cool tea. "Who are 'they' you keep mentioning?" Kenna asked. Noelle smiled and said, "You'll know soon, mother." Then Kenna's eyes widened, and she whispered, "I don't have my wallet with me! I can't pay for lunch. I don't even know what kind of money is used here." The girls both laughed, and Ember said, "Oh, we don't pay, Mom. We've never paid." Angelique came from behind the counter, carrying a small satchel. "I've prepared a small snack for you, in case you get hungry later," she said, eyes twinkling as she handed it to Ember, then turned to Kenna, bowed slightly, and said, "And your daughters are correct. You will never pay here." Kenna and her daughters stood up, thanked Angelique for the delicious meal, then called to Lucy and ambled out the door, waving to Angelique as the door closed.

Chapter Eleven

The three females and their dog continued their journey to the Castle. Walking along the cobblestone street imbedded with jewels, they passed a few shops filled with the same beautiful clothing and jewelry worn by the village's inhabitants. "Why aren't the streets and sidewalks covered in snow? And are those gemstones embedded into the stones of the streets and sidewalks?" Kenna asked, looking around. The girls giggled, Ember saying, "Magic mother. There's magic here. Snow is not allowed on the streets and sidewalks. And yes, those are protection gems in the stone. If you look closely, you'll see they're in the window panes and floors of the buildings as well." Kenna sighed, "Right, magic, I forgot."

Kenna stopped at a shop window, where a lovely dark red dress with a flowing long skirt hung. There were matching boots next to it, made of the softest-looking suede she'd ever seen. "Oh, this is so lovely. Look at the deep shade of red and the sparkling thread shot through the material. However, did they make this material? It looks like fine spider silk," she exclaimed, one hand on the window as if to touch the dress. "It is beautiful," Noelle said, "But I prefer the clothes I've seen the males wearing. I'm a pants person, as you know. Easier to fight in." As they turned away from the window to continue their walk, Ember laughed and said, "We know! According to

61

Mom, you haven't worn a dress since you were a toddler. And just when are you going to need to fight?" Noelle shrugged and said, "You never know when a situation may turn ugly. Better to be prepared than not. Isn't that what they teach us in Muay Thai? Besides, I like what I like," then gave her sister a grin.

They walked a few steps before Kenna spoke again, asking, "What did Angelique mean by 'you will never pay here'?" The girls both looked at their mother, smiling. Noelle shrugged and said, "We are treated like Royalty here, Mom. They say, "Royalty doesn't pay," and as I understand it, all the shop inventories are supplied by the Royal coffers, so we don't pay." Kenna stopped walking and turned to her daughters. "What exactly do you mean by that? How can we be Royalty here when we aren't even FROM here? As much as it seems I remember this place, I was born in Montana and grew up in Billings. My parents were not from here, and they looked nothing like the lovely people here," she said in exasperation. She felt Ember take her hand in hers and tug her in the direction of the Castle, then say, "Come, Mother. They're waiting. They will explain it to all of us at the Castle. We don't even have the entire story. They told us we had to wait until you 'woke up' to hear it all. That is why they taught us the spell to awaken you." Turning towards the Castle, the three continued their walk.

When they reached the end of the village and stood looking up the hill towards the Castle, Ember groaned, "I hate this part. Why does it have to be built on a hill? You'd think us being 'Royal,' they'd leave a carriage down here for us." Noelle gave her sister a gentle shove towards the hill, laughing, and said, "Exercise is good for us. Plus, the way we eat when we're here, we need this walk." Ember, showing she truly was only fifteen, rolled her eyes at her sister, then took a deep breath and started the climb along the cobbled street toward the Castle, her mother and sister following behind.

Chapter Twelve

B ack in their world, a private jet was getting ready to take off from a small airstrip just outside Rovaniemi, Finland. Seated towards the front of the plane were two giant men, one blonde and one brunette, who barely fit in the private jet's large seats. They had a lethal air about them, which had more to do with their essence than with their huge, muscled 6'5" frames. The two men were seated across from each other, their seat backs reclined, and their legs stretched out in front of them, resting on the ottomans. Their huge arms were crossed over their chests, and they appeared to be asleep, but one couldn't be certain because of the dark pair of sunglasses each man wore.

The thin, gray-haired woman sat in her lush leather seat in the middle of the plane, typing furiously on her phone. Lips pressed firmly together, she quietly snapped at the man seated across from her, "Tell them to take off already. We need to be in Montana before they go through the Tree again." The man, who appeared to be around 30, was tall and muscled with short blond hair and fair skin with just a hint of a golden tan. He gave a quiet sigh, then stood and walked towards the cockpit. As he was approaching where the two men appeared to be sleeping, the hair on the back of his neck stood up, and a chill ran down his spine. Maxim could sense there was something off with these two. He couldn't quite put his finger on what it was; he just knew they weren't like other men. He passed by them to the cockpit, but they didn't stir.

After less than a minute, Maxim left the cockpit, and as he passed their seats and returned to his own, the blonde man's hand quickly snaked out and wrapped tightly around Maxim's wrist. Maxim felt an almost electric shock and stopped, staring down into the blonde's sunglasses and waiting. "What is your mother up to, Maxim?" the man growled, his voice low and gruff. "You'll have to ask her yourself, as she doesn't tell me everything. All I know is this: we're going to Montana in search of my mother's family Tree." Maxim replied quietly and jerked his wrist loose, continuing on to his seat to the sound of the blonde's low chuckle. Reaching his seat, he sat down, latched his seatbelt, turned to his mother, and said, "We take off in 5 minutes, mother." He then leaned back in his seat, folded his arms across his torso, and closed his green eyes.

The woman glared at him for a few seconds, then turned her seat so she was facing away. She stared out the window, expressions of longing, pain, and anger crossing so quickly across her face that one would wonder if they were ever truly there. Her face now composed into a blank mask, she continued to stare out the window, her mind on the tasks ahead, thinking about the plans over and over again, to ensure she wouldn't fail. 'I have to get home soon. I can't stay in this world, or I will cease to exist,' she thought to herself, the fleeting expression of pain crossing her face.

Chapter Thirteen

After walking through the massive open gate of the gem imbedded walls surrounding the Castle and following the path across the courtyard, Kenna and her daughters stood in front of the Castle's entry doors, which were the largest doors she had ever seen. The entry was twenty feet tall, and with two doors, it was sixteen feet wide as well. The wood was a dark, warm golden brown that was smooth. There were copper bands and copper hardware every couple of feet. Within the wood and copper were embedded jewels, which looked to be Tourmaline and Amethyst, just like the matching bracelets all three of them wore. The door was intimidating and gorgeous but somehow welcoming at the same time. Kenna felt a tickle of remembrance in the back of her mind; a memory half-formed began to take shape, but then it flitted away like the mist in the morning air.

Kenna studied the Castle and the round towers, which were spaced at equal intervals around the castle, their height as tall as the Castle itself. Kenna had always loved castles and towers. When she was just a little girl in pigtails, she daydreamed of escaping to a tower and locking herself away from the world and from her parents. "I love towers," she said quietly. Noelle smiled at her mother and said, "We know, mom."

Her girls, one on each side of her and their dog Lucy in front of them, looped their arms through hers and pushed on the door together. Opening the door was surprisingly easy and quiet as both sides swung open on their own, slow and controlled.

As Kenna walked through the entrance into the huge Great Room, she gave a small gasp. Ember and Noelle both chuckled, watching their mother. "It's a Christmas Castle!" Kenna exclaimed. On the far curved wall was a huge set of amazing stairs, which curved up from each side to form a large balcony overlooking the entire Great Room. There were six large Christmas trees in the middle below the balcony and between each large staircase. The circular walls were lined with huge decorated Christmas trees, and there was one massive tree in the middle of the room, soaring 30 feet towards the ceiling. Inside the castle was a Christmas fairytale that had come true. Reds, silver, gold, and copper sparkled everywhere, with a backdrop of green trees and boughs, all this without being gaudy or gauche. "We knew you'd love it," Ember said. "Nobody loves Christmas as much as our mom," Noelle said, grinning.

The two girls continued to watch their mother as she walked around the massive tree in the middle of the room, staring up at it and then at the floor. "The floor sparkles like ice crystals. What is this stone? There are jewels embedded on this floor, too! There is something so familiar about this place," Kenna was speaking quietly to herself as she knelt down, running her hands over the floor. "It's so smooth and warm but looks cold like ice," she continued. She stood up and walked towards the double staircase, admiring the trees in the middle of the stairs. Looking around, she noticed a very large fireplace on the left wall of the Great Room. The fire within was roaring gently, flickering and glowing, radiating heat into the entire huge room. Lucy had made herself at home in the lush green dog bed, which was laid out before the fireplace, 'LUCY' emblazoned on the side in shiny copper lettering.

Kenna raised an eyebrow and shook her head in wonder when she spotted two large dog bowls to the right of Lucy's bed; she then turned towards her daughters, asking, "Are we alone? Who lives in this Castle?" The girls walked towards her, smiling, eyes twinkling with excitement. "We need to go into the Library. I believe they're waiting for us," Ember said, grabbing Kenna's hand and tugging her towards the right side of the room, where a set of large hammered copper doors were tucked in between two Christmas trees. She hadn't noticed the doors before and eyed them with some trepidation. "But HOW do they know we're here? And what do you mean they're waiting in there for ME?" Kenna asked with a note of apprehension in her voice, staring at the doors. She took the few remaining steps to the door, taking a deep breath. "They just know, mom. They are like us but stronger because they're in this world all the time," Noelle said.

Kenna placed her hand on the large ornate copper handle and turned. She pushed the door open quietly, took a few steps into the room, and stopped, her daughters standing on either side of her. She glanced around the large room, obviously a library, as the entire wall at the far end was covered with shelves and books. The shelves reached almost to the very high ceiling, with rolling ladders at each end of the huge curved wall. The curved wall to the right of the door contained another massive fireplace, which was lit and giving off a gentle heat. The room was warm and inviting, with plush green and red upholstered sofas and chairs placed in front of the fire and another grouping at the end, near the books. The floor was dark, warm wood with the ever-present embedded jewels, and to the left of the door, a massive curved wall of windows with rich, deep green velvet hangings covered the entire wall. The window coverings were open, letting in the bright sun reflecting off the snow.

Feeling a tug on her hand, Kenna looked up at Noelle, who said, "Come, Mother. They're waiting." The girls led her further into the room, towards the fireplace and the sofas. She finally noticed the couple seated on one of the deep green couches facing the door, not having noticed them before as their clothing was the same deep green of the curtains and sofas. She stopped and stared at the man and woman, completely overcome. The man had a head of thick, curly, long, cinnamon-red hair and a long, deep red beard. He looked to be in his mid to late thirties and was as tall as Jamie but not as brawny. The woman also had a mass of cinnamon-red curls and very fair skin, but she was tiny next to the man, probably 5'3". She appeared to be around the same age as the man. They had both stood up as the three approached, with welcoming smiles on their extremely beautiful faces. They were dressed in clothing similar to the villagers but in a deep, rich, dark green, and Kenna couldn't recall if any of the villagers had been wearing this color. Ember ran to them and threw her arms around the man, giving him a hug. Then, she turned to the woman, grinning broadly and saying, "I've missed you so much, Papa and Nana!!" Giving the woman a hug as well. They had returned Ember's hug but hadn't taken their shockingly familiar green eyes off Kenna. Noelle, arm through her mother's arm, pulled her closer to the couple.

Kenna stared at them, her mind trying to comprehend what was happening and what she had just heard. "Papa and Nana?" she softly asked her girls, looking at them in confusion. The woman walked the few steps to Kenna, smiling gently. "I understand your confusion. I sincerely apologize for the secrecy we've asked your daughters to maintain," she said in a soft, melodious voice, taking both of Kenna's hands in hers. A gentle surge of electricity sparked where their hands met, startling Kenna. She looked up from their joined hands and studied the woman. Up close, she was even more lovely, with flawless fair skin, large almond-shaped green eyes, and long curly cinnamon-red hair. Kenna felt the world tilt a little as she continued to scrutinize this woman and noticed her snow-white streak of hair. She could be Kenna's twin with the same hair, skin, and eyes. Where Kenna had a small and slender nose, the woman in front of her had a button nose, giving her a cute, impish quality. Even their hair had the same curl and color, and both had a snow-white streak on the left temple. She was just an inch taller than the woman, but they had the same lithe yet curved bodies.

"My name is Maia, and I am your mother," the woman stated quietly, still holding onto Kenna's hands. "The man over there, hogging the attention of our granddaughters, is Bram, your father," Maia continued. Kenna turned her eyes to where her daughters were seated next to Bram, all three watching her. She met his eyes, eyes as green as her own, and shook her head, knowing deep down it was true, even as she was saying, "I don't understand. I wasn't born here. You aren't my parents. My parents were drunken addicts from Billings, Montana." Maia gently led Kenna to the couch opposite her daughters and Bram, guiding her to sit and then taking the seat next to her.

Bram finally spoke up, his voice deep and stentorian; he said, "Kenna, we are indeed your parents. Yes, you were born here, and those sorry excuses for humans were absolutely not your parents." He then smiled sadly at Kenna, eyes full of anger, sadness, and pain, and continued, "Due to the dangerous circumstances in our world when you were three, we were forced to send you to the mortal world to hide you and keep you safe. We sent you with my sister, your Aunt Hilda, who was supposed to raise you in hiding until it was safe for you to be returned to us. We received missives from her weekly, then monthly. After a few mortal years had passed, the messages stopped altogether."

Kenna looked up, her expression guarded, and asked, "How can you be my parents? You are barely older than I am." Maia, seated next to her and still holding her hand, said, "I'm sure you've noticed our world is not like the mortal world. Time moves differently here. We age but at a much slower rate. While you are 35 mortal years, we are thousands of years old. You, yourself, will age no longer while you remain in our world." Ember laughed and said, "Better than Botox, isn't it, Mom?!" Noelle shushed her sister, saying, "Ember, now isn't the time for levity." Bram laughed heartily, a great booming laugh filled with joy and happiness. He said, "It is the perfect time for levity, my sweet. Our daughter has been returned to us. This is the happiest of occasions."

He watched Kenna with eyes full of hope, happiness, and a touch of sorrow, saying, "We didn't want to send you away. It broke our hearts. We thought it was the only way we could protect you. It wasn't supposed to happen the way it did. You weren't meant to be lost. We didn't know my sister was on the side of the enemy, and when she stopped sending messages, we feared the worst. It was then that we sealed the Tree, ensuring that only you or your descendants could open the way. In doing so, we locked ourselves away, but my sister was prevented from ever returning."

Bram stood up, adjusted the gold-handled short sword strapped to his waist, and then walked a few steps to where Kenna and Maia were sitting. He sat on Kenna's other side and engulfed her in a bear hug of an embrace. She sank into her father's embrace, breathing in deeply the scent of cinnamon, peppermint, cloves, and pine. He smelled like Christmas! His hug was warm and welcoming, and Kenna was soaking up the warmth and breathing in his comforting scent when a forgotten memory suddenly slammed into her mind. It was of her, as a toddler with a riot of red curls tumbling down her back, running towards this man. He swept her up and over his head, spinning around as she shrieked with laughter. Then he cradled her in his embrace, saying, "I love you so much, little Kenna! You're my light and life."

Kenna gasped and pulled away, staring into his eyes and said, "I remember you! In this room, you swung me around while I was laughing." Kenna's eyes filled with tears, spilling over, and whispered, "I remember it all, and I remember you both. I was wanted, and I was loved." As her tears flowed down her cheeks, she felt her mother's and father's arms surround her in a comforting embrace. She could hear her parents (her parents!!) making soothing sounds, and it filled her with happiness. The voices of her daughters interrupted her thoughts, "Please don't cry, Mother. It's ok. Are they happy tears?" They sounded distressed, so Kenna untangled herself from her parents' embrace, stood up, and gestured for her girls to come over. They ran to her, almost barreling her over with their enthusiasm. "I'm ok, my sweethearts. I'm ok now." As she held them to her, she said, "Because of you two, I've come home, and I've found my parents."

Chapter Fourteen

"You have raised amazing daughters, Kenna. So intelligent, spirited, and kind," Maia said, rising from the sofa. "The first time they came through, we sensed it and flew as fast as we could to the Tree. Imagine our surprise to find two and three-year-old little girls, the spitting image of our Kenna, playing in the snow at the base of the Tree, with The Bear standing guard." She laughed softly and stroked Noelle's hair. As he stood, Bram said, "We didn't know how you would find your way back, or if you were still alive to try, we could only hope and pray to the Goddess for your return. In the Mortal world, the Tree is on private land and protectively hidden, not easy to find. When the girls came through, we knew you'd survived, and there was hope. That day, Noelle told us you had just purchased the 'Red House in the Country' and the Tree was on your land. So advanced for a three-year-old, she was." He gave Noelle a one-armed hug, then moved away to stand by the fire.

He stood, staring into the flames for a few moments. "If I could change the way things happened, I would, but I can't. I was fooled by my sister, and because of that, you, more than anyone else, paid the price. I am more than sorry for the abuse you endured at the hands of your adoptive parents. Your daughters have told us of your early life in the mortal world.

It breaks my heart and awakens the beast within," Bram said, his voice gruff and growly. Kenna walked to him, leaving her daughters on the couch with their Nana. "Father. May I call you Father?" she asked quietly. Eyes shining, he turned to her and gave her another wonderful Christmas-smelling hug. "That would make me very happy, my Kenna," he said, gently kissing her forehead.

Kenna smiled softly and continued, "If there is even a small chance my adult life would be changed by not having gone through the Tree when I was little, I wouldn't change a thing. If I hadn't gone to the mortal world, if I hadn't been where I was meant to be, my life trajectory would have been changed. I would never have met my Jamie; I would never have had my amazing daughters. I would not be as resilient or as strong as I am now. It was my fate. I have come to accept it." Leaning back, her Father gazed down at her with surprise and wonder. "You've forgiven your adoptive parents?" he asked in amazement. Kenna shrugged and said, "I just no longer give them power over me. I no longer allow the memory of them to have access to my life. I wrote them off long before they actually died. Hilda, on the other hand, I do not forgive. So that she could be free to travel and find a rich husband, she sold me to them. So the blame lies with her and no other." Maia interrupted them, anger in her voice. "She sold you?!!" Kenna nodded her head and softly began, "Yes, she sold me. I was young, but I remember it clearly now since the Wind Spell. They were a couple looking to adopt a child because they couldn't have one of their own. They had placed an ad in the newspaper, and Hilda responded. They paid her $10,000, their life savings, for me. She handed me over to them as I was crying and begging her not to leave me. She took their money and disappeared. The first month with them was okay, and they were nice enough. But then they started drinking. Due to money issues and the stress of not having enough to pay the bills, they turned to drugs and drinking. They began to neglect me and then yell at me, and eventually, it became physical abuse. This went on for years before they died."

Kenna looked up and found all eyes on her, and all of them were crying silent tears. "Oh, please don't cry. I'm okay. Really, I turned out okay," Kenna said and laid a hand on her father's arm. Bram again engulfed her in a giant, warm hug. Kenna heard Noelle ask, "How did they die, Mom?" Kenna stepped back from her father and looked towards her daughters and mother. She took a deep breath, let it out, and said, "I killed them."

Not a sound was heard as they all stared at Kenna in shocked silence. "Kenna, that isn't possible. You are not a killer. What happened? Tell us the tale from the beginning," her father said gently, holding her hand for support. Kenna shrugged and said, "I was ten when it happened. My adoptive father was very drunk that night and probably high on drugs as well. My adoptive mother was drinking, too, and already drunk. I was hungry because I hadn't had anything to eat since I had eaten lunch at school. I asked them what was for dinner, and that was all it took. They both started screaming at me, and he threw a beer bottle at me, which hit me in the head above my eye. It cut the skin, and blood poured down my face. This set her off, and she began screaming at me for getting blood on the carpet. I remember being a little dizzy when I went to the kitchen for paper towels. They followed me, still yelling. I turned around and realized I had made a mistake. I was trapped in the kitchen, and they were blocking the doorway. He was holding a leather belt with studs on it and told me I would be punished. They both began to walk towards me, and I panicked. I shoved my hands out towards them and screamed 'NO!' They both flew back and hit the wall of the front room, slid down to the floor, and didn't move."

Kenna took a deep breath and continued, "I called 911 and said my parents were fighting, and now they weren't moving. It was ruled accidental death due to domestic violence and drugs. I was put into the foster care system and went from home to home until I turned eighteen. That's when I moved to Butte, got a job, and started college. I ended up in Butte because I'd always felt a pull to be there. When I was studying Montana history in school, I just wanted to go to Butte. I felt I needed to be there. So, that is where I went when I was free."

Kenna's daughters came to her and held their mother until they could control their tears enough to speak. Noelle said, "Mom, we had no idea how bad it was. I'm so sorry you had to endure that." Tears were still leaking from her eyes, and she was holding onto Kenna's hand tightly. Ember couldn't speak yet; she just held onto Kenna, shaking her head. Kenna moved her daughters to one of the sofas, sitting in the middle of them and holding their hands in hers. "I prefer not to speak of my childhood, especially since my adult life has been so blessed. I am okay now. It was in the past, and I rose above it. Please don't shed another tear for the little girl I was. She survived and won," Kenna said softly but firmly to her parents and daughters.

Maia, who was sitting across from them, next to Bram, said, "You are an amazingly strong woman, and I will honor your wishes, daughter. I do think we need to have a little break and a snack before your father and I tell you the rest of your history." Suddenly, a tray with a silver carafe, cups, and a plate of pumpkin spice sugar cookies appeared on the table next to the sofas. "Oh, I like this magic thing," Kenna said, reaching over and grabbing a cookie and then taking a large bite out of it. Maia poured hot chocolate into cups and handed them out to everyone. Kenna took a sip and moaned with pleasure. "This is amazing hot chocolate! Girls, eat some cookies and drink your chocolate. It will help you feel better," Kenna said, handing them each a cookie. Turning to her parents sitting across from her, she said, "Now, what else do you have to tell me?"

Maia turned to Bram and said, "We need to tell her the rest. She needs to know it all."

Kenna sighed, and leaning back against the back of the sofa, she asked, laughing, "There's more? I'm sitting in a fairytale Castle, I've communed with the Queen of the Unicorns, I've seen and spoken to the protecting Bear, and I've watched a person riding on a dragon. A dragon! But most of all, I've found my parents. My real parents. Oh, and let's not forget finding out my children have been visiting said parents for over ten years. How much MORE could there possibly be?" Her parents exchanged an enigmatic look, then smiled. Looking at his wife and raising his eyebrows, he cleared his throat and asked Kenna, "What have you noticed about this land? What has stood out to you the most?" Kenna grinned at her daughters, saying, "Well, like I told the girls, other than the magic Tree, the Unicorn, the stunningly beautiful villagers, oh, and the Castle! What else is there to notice?" Her girls laughed along with their mother, obviously feeling better after a few cookies. "Is there more, Papa?" asked Ember, sitting back with her mom's arm around her shoulder. "Yes. Yes, there is more," he replied, laughing his huge baritone laugh.

Chapter Fifteen

B ack in the mortal world, a private jet continued its long journey to Montana. Two of the occupants were having a quiet conversation, trying not to awaken the two large men towards the front of the plane. "What is your game plan, mother? How are you going to convince them to take you through?" the blond man asked the thin, gray-haired woman. She squinted her blue eyes at her son, meeting his deep green ones. "Maxim, I will do whatever it takes to pass through. I will not die in this accursed land. I will NOT wither and fade away here. I refuse to pass into the Other! And what do you mean by 'you' and not 'we'? You're going through with me," she replied. He shook his head sadly and said, "They will never forgive you for what you did to Kenna, and I am not going through the Tree." Then he turned to the window, gazing out at the night sky, eyes full of sadness. His mother glared at him, asking herself, 'How is he my son? He is nothing like me. He is weak just like his father.'

Chapter Sixteen

In the library of the Castle, Bram was asking Kenna, "While you were in the Village, did you notice anything about the villagers? Anything different from us?" Kenna tilted her head, eyeing her father. She turned and studied her daughters, then her mother. Her green then eyes widened in surprised amazement. "We are the only ones with Red hair!" she exclaimed. Her daughters laughed, and then Ember said, "I knew you'd figure it out, mama." "But there's more, mom. Isn't there, Papa?" Noelle asked her grandfather.

Bram gave a booming laugh and replied, "Yes, there is more, my darling. Not only are we the only ones with this hair color, but we are the only ones with green eyes. No one else in this land has red hair OR green eyes. Only our family is born with such, which shows the blessings from the Goddess." Kenna stared at her father, deep in thought. "But if no one else is born with red hair and green eyes, who do you marry?" Kenna asked, confused. Maia laughingly replied, "That is where the Goddess and a little magic come into play."

"Not only are you the first child born to our family in over 2000 years, but you are the first female child EVER to have red hair and green eyes at birth," her father said, then continued with his explanation, "Our line has always been Patriarchally, in each generation just one boy child is born. Sometimes, a girl child is born along with a boy child, but the female is never born with the Blessings of the Goddess. The red hair and green eyes come from my line only. My father is like me, but my mother was born with silver hair and blue eyes. It was only when she married my father that she transformed and became like her husband, my father." Kenna turned to her mother, asking, "So you were a villager? What color was your hair when you were born?" Her mother tilted her head and asked, "Can you not guess?" Again, studying her mother, her eyes were drawn to the snow-white streak at her left temple, just like she and her daughters rocked. "You were born with white hair, weren't you? Were your eyes Blue? Or....?..." Kenna asked. "I was born with silver eyes and snow-white hair," her mother responded.

Bram was watching his daughter and said, "The white streak of hair you four have has never happened. It's something new, and I believe it's due to the tremendous healing power your mother possesses. More of her essence has been passed to you. You being the first female child ever marked by the Goddess, many believe the line of the Patriarch has ended. They believe you are the first in the Matriarchal line of our family, with more of the Goddess' blessing than any other generation." Kenna looked at her mother, studying the white streak of hair. "You're a healer?" she asked Maia, who nodded and said, "Yes, I am. My magic is more closely connected to the Goddess than others, and it manifests as a strong healing magic." Kenna smiled softly at her mother and said, "I do believe I've inherited some of that healing magic." Her two daughters both nodded in agreement, Ember saying, "Mother can make a headache disappear with just a few gentle strokes and a kiss." Noelle said, "Our fevers never last after mother performs her 'light touch therapy' on us." Maia stared at Kenna, a look of confusion on her face, and asked, "But who taught you the healing magic?" Kenna shook her head, shrugged, and said, "Nobody. It was all instinctual. I just knew how to perform it, and I knew it would work." Her parents exchanged startled looks.

Bram looked towards Kenna and the girls and said, "I'm very curious about your daughters, Kenna. I sense great power within them, and although Noelle and Ember get something from their father's side, like the gold ring in their eyes, I cannot sense mortal within them. Not even a little mortal blood. You're sure your husband is a human?" he asked Kenna, who chuckled and nodded yes, saying, "I think I'd know if he were something other than human." Bram shrugged and continued, "It has been puzzling me since they first crossed over years ago. I have no explanation for it." He looked at his daughter, head cocked, and asked, "You mentioned meeting The Great Bear on your journey here. What happened?" Kenna told of her sighting of the Bear and what he had said to her in her mind, then Ember chimed in, "We've been seeing the Bear since our first trip through the Tree, Papa. He met us there, didn't you see him? When you and Nana got there, he turned and left."

"Yes, he's always there when we come through, and when we were very small, he would give us rides on his back to the village and castle," Noelle said, watching her grandfather. "Have we never mentioned it to you before?" she asked him. Shaking his head, Bram stood up and paced to the fireplace, standing in front of the flames, staring. "Yes, I do remember seeing him a few times. The Great Bear. Hmmmmm. I do believe I need to pay him a visit sooner rather than later," Bram said quietly. "With you being in the mortal world, supposedly taking a mortal husband, there's more at play than the magic of the Goddess here, I do believe," her mother said, watching the girls.

Maia exchanged a look with Bram and said, "Tell her the rest, husband." Bram took a deep breath and said, "We are immortal, and we rarely get ill. The girls have told us about your disease, Rheumatoid Arthritis, they called it. If you were in this world, you never would have gotten it. I'm so sorry you've had to suffer, my darling." He then continued, "My parents are still alive but retired, as they say in the mortal world. They are currently traveling the realms, having an adventure. I took over the family business one thousand years ago." Kenna raised an eyebrow and asked, "Family business? What IS the family business? In the village, they referred to us as Royalty. Is that what you are talking about?"

Maia shook her head and said, "No, not that, although yes, we are the leaders of this land, and they call us King and Queen. But can't you guess? Look around you, around this Castle. Look at your father; really look at him." Kenna turned to her father, studying him. She stood up and walked around the library, trailing her hands over the soft velvet curtains and the smooth wood paneling. She then wandered out into the large room, which was the Great Room. Standing there in the doorway, she continued to look around at the beautiful and magical Christmas trees and the ice-like floors. "Noooo. It can't be. Impossible. He's not real. It has to be something else," she was mumbling to herself as she wandered around.

Turning back into the library, she marched over to her father, who was standing by the fireplace now. Hands on hips, she studied him. Then, after a few moments, "Are you Father Christmas?" she asked jokingly and laughed. Her father gave a huge booming laugh, with one hand on his chest, eyes twinkling, and nodded his head. "Oh My God!" shouted Ember, running over to her grandfather. "Our grandfather is Santa Claus, Noelle! He's real! Santa Claus is real!" she continued. Noelle walked over at a more sedate pace, asking, "Are you serious, Papa?" He brought her into a bear hug and said, "Yes, my granddaughter. I am serious. Santa Claus is real, although I was called Father Christmas, and most of what the humans believe about Santa Claus is made up by storytellers. I don't actually travel around the world anymore on Christmas Eve. It's been several hundreds of years." Kenna asked, "But how? In the mortal world, you are depicted as wearing red, with white hair and a beard, and you're depicted as a very overweight father. How exactly does this work?" Laughing, Maia said, "Yes, they got a few things wrong over the years. Father Christmas has always worn dark green, and not one has ever had white hair or been fat."

While Kenna and her daughters stayed in front of the fire, Bram walked over to the sofa where his wife was and sat next to her, throwing an arm around her shoulders. Kenna watched them, amazed at how youthful and beautiful they appeared. Her parents. 'Still trying to wrap my mind around that,' she thought to herself. "I will start at the beginning, then it should make more sense to you," Bram said to his daughter and granddaughters.

"Around 3000 years ago, my father found a doorway to the mortal world through the Tree, which is on your land in the Mortal Realm. It hasn't changed since before that time. He was an explorer and adventurer at heart, so he would visit that world often over the many centuries. Soon, he started interacting with the mortals, interested in their day-to-day lives and how they were quickly advancing. He became aware of their great need for healers and so began to teach some of the humans the healing properties of herbs and plants. He then noticed the humans had little joy in the dead of Winter, as it was all about survival for them. That's when his visits came to be just in the dead of Winter, stopping at every house while they were sleeping. He left them items to help ensure their survival through the brutal Winters, such as dried fruits and nuts, herbs and vegetables, dried meats and berries. Then, because my Father enjoyed carving toys and such out of wood, he soon began to leave those as well to bring a little joy into their lives. That is how the legend of Santa Claus was born."

Kenna and her girls had been listening intently, but now they couldn't hold in their questions. "What about the reindeer? Don't you use flying reindeer?" Ember asked with a look of disappointment. "But how do you get to all the houses in one night?!" cried Noelle, continuing, "It's not scientifically possible, Papa." Her grandfather chuckled at their questions and replied, "No, I don't use reindeer. That is a human fairytale. The bag depicted in the human fairytale is true, but it is a deep green, and it holds everything I need it to due to a little spell woven into the fabric when my father made The Bag. The pagans of ancient England had the appearance of Father Christmas, which was the most accurate compared to others.

As for the time it takes to deliver all the gifts? Again, magic. It is inside me, part of my essence. As you spend more and more time here, all three of you will continue to come into your own magic, and it will grow stronger, although apparently, you girls are extremely gifted to be able to perform the Wind Spell alone."

"Now, however, there really is no more Father Christmas, but the humans have perpetuated the story for the last couple hundred years or so," Bram said, then continued, "We haven't been to the human world to play Father Christmas for over three hundred years. Yet the legend lives on. My time now is spent mostly with the dragons and training new riders."

"You have dragons?!" exclaimed Kenna, then whispered, "I just adore dragons." This made everyone laugh. "Papa, can we ride a dragon?" Ember asked. "Yes! I would love to have a dragon," Noelle breathed. Their Papa stared at them for a few seconds, his expression unreadable, before saying, "I don't know. A dragon has to choose you. It's a bonding process that takes quite a while. We will talk about that later during another visit." His expression was again rather strange.

Kenna led her daughters over to one of the sofas, sitting down between them. "This is a lot to take in. So much information at once." Kenna said, holding her daughters' hands in each of hers. Her parents sat on the opposite couch, nodding. "We realize this has been an information overload. We understand and want you to know that we are here for you, no matter what, and will answer any and all questions you have," Maia said, smiling kindly at her daughter. "You can come and go as you please, but know this: the more you stay in the mortal world, the more you'll age. You will be, in essence, a mortal and at risk for all their illnesses and diseases. To be immortal as we are, you will need to live here full-time. For your disease to disappear, you will need to live here full-time," she continued, expression sorrowful.

Kenna looked devastated, saying, "But my life is there. My husband is there, and I won't just give him up." She shook her head with tear-filled eyes. Noelle sat up, leaning towards her grandparents, eyes glimmering with tears, asking, "Can we bring our father over? Would that be ok? We could all live here together, right?" Her grandparents exchanged a look, and then Bram said, "It might be possible. The Goddess must deem him worthy of passing through the Tree and living here. But you need to understand this has never been done before. A mortal has never passed through the Tree."

Kenna stood up quickly, a look of distress on her face, stating, "I think it's time we went home. I have a lot to think over, but I must include Jamie. Come girls, as much as I don't want to, we need to leave." "Oh moooommm, can't Noelle and I stay? Then you and Dad can have alone time and talk everything over in private," Ember asked, practically vibrating with excitement. "I'm sorry, sweetheart, but no. Not this time. You and Noelle need to come home with me. This is a family discussion," Kenna said quietly. Although disappointed, Ember nodded her head in understanding. Kenna's parents walked her and the girls to the main door, calling Lucy as they walked through the Great Room. They gave each other a long hug and a promise to see each other soon. The three females, along with their dog, started their walk down the cobbled road towards the village, towards the Tree, and the Red House in the country.

Chapter Seventeen

Kenna and her daughters stood next to the Tree, looking down at where their house should be, with Lucy at their side. The journey back to the Grove had been uneventful, except when they had finally reached the Tree. Kenna had caught sight of two huge wolves standing twenty yards away as if waiting for their arrival. Though both were bigger than any wolf she had ever seen, the male wolf dwarfed his female companion. He was humungous! She grabbed her daughters by the shoulders to stop them. "Girls, stop. Are they friendly or......?" Kenna asked her girls. Noelle shrugged and said, "I don't know, Mom. We've seen them on several occasions, but they've kept their distance from us." The wolves stared at the three females, unmoving. Kenna said, "I can hear them in my head. They said, 'Welcome home, Princess. We have long awaited your return. Go in peace and return soon.' They mean us no harm." In unison, the wolves both bowed their heads and then turned to leave, melting into the trees.

Kenna and the girls turned from the view without a house and walked to the Tree for their return home. 'Is it even home anymore?' She thought to herself as she laid her hands against the warm bark of the Tree. The girls performed the chant to pass through the Tree, and they were home again.

Even though they had been in the other world all day, only minutes had passed in the mortal world. It was almost noon, and Kenna could see Jamie through the kitchen window, preparing lunch as he always did when the females in his life spent time in the Grove. Taking a deep breath, she urged her girls to continue down the trail to their house, with Lucy leading the way.

"How were your lessons in the Grove?" Jamie asked as the three walked through the doorway, Lucy pushing past and heading for her water bowl. Kenna walked quickly around the counter and wrapped her arms around Jamie, burying her face into his chest and breathing his scent in deeply. This calmed her immediately, and she held him tightly, saying nothing. The girls stood just inside the doorway, watching them with solemn faces.

Jamie looked at his daughters' expressions and immediately knew something was wrong. "What happened? Girls, why do you look like you're going to cry? Kenna, look at me!" he demanded, leaning back and placing a finger under her chin, gently lifting it so he could see her eyes. Asking quietly, "What has happened, my love?" Kenna, eyes filled with tears, said, "We need to go sit down in the living room. We have something important to discuss with you." She stepped back, held her hand out to her girls, then, taking Jamie's hand in hers, led them into the other room to tell him about their day.

Kenna watched Jamie with some apprehension. He was sitting on the couch, elbows on knees, head in hands, shoulders shaking, but she couldn't tell if he was laughing or crying. "Is he ok, mom?" Noelle whispered. "He hasn't said anything for almost two minutes," said Ember, eyeing her father with concern. Both girls were seated across from their parents, eyes on their father. "Jamie? Are you going to say anything?" Kenna asked tentatively. Jamie finally lifted his head and turned to face his wife. His expression was not at all what she had expected. He was glowing with happiness! His gold eyes were shining with laughter and happiness.

With a loud booming laugh, Jamie stood up, grabbed Kenna up into his arms, and swung her in a circle. "What has gotten into you?! Put me down! Now, Jamie!" Kenna yelled, but laughing as well. Jamie set Kenna down and turned towards her, holding her face in his hands, thumbs stroking her temples. "I have waited so many years for you to wake up, to remember who you were and where you came from. We can finally go home!" Jamie said, laughing again, then gave Kenna a passionate kiss on the lips. As Kenna melted into Jamie's embrace, she could hear their girls saying, "Get a room! Oh gross, now is not the time, you two!"

Breaking the kiss, Kenna stared at Jamie, his words finally registering. "You knew?! Wait! What do you mean, finally go home?" she asked in amazement. Jamie gave her a sheepish look, pulling her to the couch and down to sit next to him. Holding her small hands in his large ones, he began speaking. "I was sent through the Tree years after you were already here. I was sent to find you and be your protector, and I was supposed to bring you home if I was able," Jamie said quietly, then continued, "I have always known the truth of your origin. I didn't come over until your Aunt had already lost you." "But who sent you?" Kenna asked in confusion. Jamie gave a soft sigh and rubbed his head with his hand. "My father sent me. You do realize, don't you, that there are more magical beings in our land than just your family?" he said, smiling.

Kenna returned his smile and responded, "Yes, I know. I met Raina, Queen of the Unicorns, and I saw a dragon with a rider, Jamie! A dragon! Plus, two huge wolves welcomed me home, and this massive grizzly bear made his presence known to me as well." Jamie gave a start, asking, "You've met Otso?" "Oh, is that his name? I wouldn't say 'met him,' but he made himself known to me and said, 'Welcome home, daughter,' which really confused me. Why would he call me daughter?" Kenna replied. Noelle excitedly chimed in, "But we have, father! We've met him! He's been our protector in Marqueria since we were toddlers. He was at the Tree the first time we crossed through." "Yep! He would let us ride on his back on the way to the village and the Castle," Ember said, grinning.

Jamie stood up and paced to the wall of glass windows, hands in his pockets. Turning and looking at the girls, he said, "Then you have met my father, your grandfather. He is Otso, King of the Forest." Kenna stared at Jamie in confusion. "But, how? How is this possible? How is your father a bear?!" she asked. At this, Jamie grinned and said, "He is a shapeshifter, as am I. He prefers his bear form most of the time, though." Jamie was watching Kenna's reaction. "Well, that explains it then. My father said he couldn't sense any mortal blood in the girls, and it greatly perplexed him. So, my father didn't know Otso had sent you?" she asked Jamie, who shook his head and said, "No, your father doesn't know. Not knowing if there was a spy around your father and knowing your aunt turned out to be the enemy, he believed it best if it was kept a secret." Jamie, sitting next to her and taking her hands in his, continued, "I want you to know this: Our marriage is real, our love is real. The moment I laid eyes upon you in computer class, I knew you were meant for me." Kenna leaned in and softly kissed his lips, whispering, "I know, husband."

Ember chimed in suddenly, "I'm starving! Can we finish this over a snack?" Kenna briefly closed her eyes and sighed, then stood up. "This has been one Hell of a day, and it is only two in the afternoon. I need a break from all this....all this magic stuff. Why don't we go into town now and have a late lunch/early dinner? We can put what you have already prepared in the fridge to eat later," Kenna said. Noelle jumped up and yelled, "I'll be in the car, and I'm driving!" Then raced out of the room. Ember was laughing as she followed her sister out to the garage. Jamie walked over and enveloped Kenna in a warm, soothing embrace, holding her quietly and saying nothing. With a sigh, Kenna stepped back and said, "It's ok. I'm ok. Let's go have our family burger date. We can talk about this later." Together, they walked towards the garage entrance.

Chapter Eighteen

T he family entered the new restaurant, which was rather crowded for a weekday afternoon, and found a booth. The girls sat on one side of the booth, and their parents sat across from them. Picking up the menu from the menu holder, Noelle and Ember quietly discussed what they were going to order. Kenna was looking around the new restaurant, nodding at the few people she recognized. A new eatery opening up in Butte was a big deal, and for the first couple of months, the place would be crowded and do a booming business, but eventually, it would even out after a while. Kenna noticed a booth with four teenage boys staring in their direction and chuckled. Noelle and Ember were oblivious to how beautiful they were, and having the opposite sex stare was a common occurrence. "Kenna. Kenna. Earth to Kenna," Jamie said and took her hand in his. "I'm sorry, I guess I spaced out for a minute," Kenna smiled at him and said, "Shall we order?"

As Noelle was downing the last of her strawberry shake (Yes, she strayed from her usual chocolate) and making slurping noises through her straw, Ember asked her father, "So the gold ring around our eyes, we got from you, and you got your golden eyes from your father?" Jamie ate his last French fry, chewed and swallowed, then replied, "Yes, that is correct. Our family of Bear shifters have golden eyes." He took a sip of soda and then said, "At first, I was unable to shift in this world, but after a time and with practice, I could eventually. I just needed to learn how to access the magic in this land. As for you two girls, I don't know if you'll ever be able to shift. The mixing of magic species actually isn't done in our world." Noelle stopped slurping her milkshake and stared at her father. "Do you mean there is no intermarriage in Marqueria?" she asked, concerned.

Jamie shook his head and said, "No, there isn't, as far as I know. The bears stay with bears, the wolves with wolves, and the elves stay with elves. That is until we happened." Ember leaned forward and excitedly said, "Wait, what?! Elves?? There are Elves? Weird, we haven't seen any of those while visiting the other world." Jamie gave a loud laugh, attracting the attention of a few people near them, including the booth full of teen boys. Lowering his voice, he said, "Just who do you think your grandparents are? They're Elves. And yes, there are Wolf shapeshifters, too. They are very secretive and keep to themselves most of the time. They allowed you to see them today, though. Interesting." The three females stared at him, stunned. "We're half-Elf?" asked Noelle. "But we don't have pointy ears!" exclaimed Ember. Jamie chuckled quietly and said, "That is another human fairytale. Elves don't have pointy ears." Kenna said nothing, continuing to munch on her French fries, deep in thought, a small frown between her brows.

"Are you ok, my wife?" Jamie asked Kenna, stealing one of her fries. She turned to him and growled, "Hands off my fries, mister." Then, giving him a wink and a soft smile, he said, "Yes, I'm ok. It's been an exciting, information-overloaded day. I've just been thinking about what my father said. My father.

Oh man, 'my father'. It seems so natural and weird at the same time." Shaking her head in wonder, she continued, "Anyway, he said that if we were to live there full-time, my disease would disappear. I've been thinking about it, and there are so many advantages to living in Marqueria. Today, I had no pain while we were over there. Absolutely none. And I could hike and move with no difficulty at all. I don't know. I love our life here, our red house, and the Grove so much. This is a decision we must make together, all four of us."

They all remained silent for a bit. The girls had been watching their parents as they spoke. Noelle was the first to break the silence, smiling and saying, "I would love to live there full time. As long as they have cheeseburgers, that is." Laughing, Ember said, "Of course they have cheeseburgers! Papa and Nana served them to us a few times, remember?" Noelle rolled her eyes and said, "Yes, I was making a joke. You know, I'll live anywhere as long as there are cheeseburgers, get it?" "What do you think, father?" Ember asked her dad. Jamie gave a sigh and took Kenna's hand in his. "I love our life here too, and I love our Red House and the Grove. That being said, I do believe we belong in the other world. It is our homeland," he said, turning to Kenna and whispering in her ear, "We can always come to the red house for little getaways." Then he gave her a wink and smile. "We can still heeeeaar youuuuu," sang Ember, rolling her eyes. Her parents laughed and started stacking the trash from their meals on the tray in front of them, getting ready to leave.

As the family of four walked out of the restaurant, it wasn't only the booth of teenage boys who were watching them. They didn't notice the man who had been watching them the entire time they had been there. When they had driven away, the man pulled out his cell phone, made a call, and said, "They're back but talking about going through again."

When they returned home, the girls headed straight to their lounge to do some gaming on their laptops while Jamie and Kenna sat on the back patio, enjoying the evening air. It was starting to get darker earlier, with the sunsets happening sooner. Taking a sip of iced tea, she asked Jamie, "Will we be accepted in the other land? Will our marriage be an issue? Will our daughters' mixed heritage make them a target?" Jamie turned away from staring at the Grove and met Kenna's eyes, saying, "I don't know, honestly, I really don't. I hope it doesn't. With two of the three most powerful species on both sides, it should create a cushion. They shouldn't hear or encounter any prejudice. My father is friendly with the pack leader of the Wolves, and I believe the wolves will accept us."

Jamie's voice had taken on a low, growly quality, which sent a shiver down Kenna's back. He growled, "I want to protect them from such hatred, too, my dear. I won't let anything happen to them or you. Over there, I'm more powerful and able to do just that." Kenna smiled, then said, "I don't know how much protection they need, Jamie. They've been traveling to the other world since they were toddlers. Our girls are fearless and quite capable. I mean, Christ! They rode astride a grizzly bear on their first visit there! When they were practically babies! They climbed onto a bear!" She shook her head in amazement, took a deep, steadying breath, exhaled, and then said, "While we were over there, I was surprised yet impressed by their total independence. They are more self-possessed over there and more confident." Jamie said, "Yes, I can imagine, but my Father was there to protect and watch over them. They were never in any real danger with him there."

"Please tell me about your father, Jamie," Kenna said, watching Jamie as he turned his gaze to the Grove again.

"He is called Otso; He is the Spirit Bear, King of the Forest and its animals. Were-bears that is what we call ourselves, or just Bear. We mostly keep to ourselves, living in the forest on the outskirts of the elven civilization. There are small villages where we live, where mothers raise the cubs, and where females and males come and go as they please. It's like any other village. Contrary to human myth, we are not made by an "infection" but are born. Same with the werewolves. They too are born, not infected, and we are a separate species, just like the Elves and humans," Jamie said, glancing over at Kenna, giving her a small smile, then continuing, "My father is gruff, but was very affectionate when I was growing up. He doesn't speak much, but when he does, it is profound. In his human form, he is very large. Taller than I am by a head, broader and stronger. He has a wild head of deep brown hair and gold eyes like my own. He is the most honorable man I know and cares deeply for his subjects. When he discovered you had been lost in the mortal world, he sent me to find you. To protect you and bring you home when it was safe to do so. Imagine my surprise: after years of searching for you, I walked into class, and there you were." Jamie reached over and stroked Kenna's hair, smiling with eyes full of adoration. "How did you know it was me?" Kenna asked, taking his hand in hers. Jamie laughed and gently tugged her white streak, saying, "You've always had this, even when you were little."

"What about your mother? What is her name?" Kenna asked. Jamie smiled softly and said, "My mother is called Tati, the Goddess of the forest, hunting, druids, and wanderers. She has strong magic and is a seer; that is to say, she has visions. Prophesies are shown to her by the Goddess." Suddenly, Kenna sat up and turned towards Jamie, confusion marring her face. "How can we be almost the same age now, and yet you knew me as a little girl when you were older than I was then?" "I was wondering when you'd come around to that. When you were three years old, I was older, almost a man. When you came to the mortal world, you began aging faster than I. When I crossed through the Tree, I began to age as well, but by then, we were the same age." Jamie said. Kenna cocked her head, saying, "But my father closed the Tree to anyone but me and my line. How did you get through?" Grinning, Jamie said, "Your family isn't the only one the Tree or Goddess listens to. My family has the ear of the Goddess and is just as powerful as yours," Jamie said, then groaned and covered his face briefly with his hands.

"What?!" Kenna asked, startled. Jamie groaned, "Our girls. I wonder just how powerful our girls are going to be when they are on the other side full time." Kenna chuckled and said, "Judging from how they are now, I'm guessing off the charts. They performed the Wind Spell to release my inner magic and help me remember." Kenna paused, taking a deep breath and continuing quietly, "So, there has never been a pairing of Weres and Elves?" Brow furrowed, Jamie shook his head, saying, "No, not that I'm aware of. Ours is probably the first. We have no idea just what abilities our girls will inherit and how they will manifest themselves."

They had both turned their eyes up towards the Tree. Kenna sighed, and Jamie squeezed her hand, whispering to her, "It will be ok, babe." Turning towards her husband, Kenna asked, "Jamie, why didn't you ever tell me about our past? If you were able to get back through the Tree, why didn't you tell me and take us back?" Kenna sat, gazing into Jamie's eyes. There was silence as the two stared at each other. Then Jamie took a deep breath and said, "At first, it was because I didn't know if it was safe on the other side. I wasn't sure the enemy had been defeated. Then, I didn't want to leave here. I didn't want you and the girls exposed to the possible dangers on the other side of the Tree." Jamie's eyes misted with a slight sheen of tears, and he said, "I didn't want to risk our peace or your lives."

Kenna stood up and moved to sit in Jamie's lap, wrapping her arms around his neck. Kissing his soft bald head, she said, "I understand, but what exactly is this enemy? What exactly happened when I was little? Why did my parents need to send me away in the first place? They really didn't go into much detail." Jamie, arms wrapped around Kenna's waist, tucked his face into her neck and breathed deeply. He loved her scent; it was intoxicating and calming at the same time. "Ever since your grandfather found the pathway through the Tree, some three thousand years ago, there has been a faction of elves who believe we need to conquer the mortal world and rule over the humans. These elves practice dark magic and believe that humans should be subjugated. Your family has kept the peace and protected the mortal world by protecting the Grove and the Tree from the others. My father and the pack leader of the Wolves entered into an agreement with your father for the protection of the Mortal realm. But when you were born, a rebellion started. Your father, my father, and the pack master of the Wolves formed an alliance to prevent them from passing through the Tree into the Mortal world. There was outright war, and many lives were lost, but we never discovered who the leader was. Due to a prophecy being whispered about throughout the realm, your parents began receiving threats aimed towards you."

Jamie sighed and continued, "Because of this, your parents made the decision to send you through the Tree with your aunt Hilda until the leader of the traitors could be flushed out. Unfortunately, they didn't realize it was your aunt who was the leader of the dark practitioners. After a few years, one of the elves they had sent to infiltrate the dark faction of elves was able to send word to your father with the information on your aunt. It almost broke him. His guilt was great, as much as his grief over losing you. Everyone else figured your aunt had murdered you in the mortal world, but my father, for some reason, didn't. Probably something my mother had seen in a vision." Jamie shrugged and continued, "When I was the appropriate age, he sent me through to find you." Kenna sat in Jamie's lap, soaking up his warmth and comfort. She then whispered softly, "No, she didn't murder me. She just sold me to a horrible couple for $10,000. Then they tried to destroy me but couldn't. As hard as they tried to make my life Hell, they still couldn't destroy me. In the end, I destroyed them." Jamie held her a little tighter, and Kenna gave a sigh. Then, she asked, "What did the prophecy say?" Without hesitation, Jamie began,

"From the realm of Marqueria, a stolen child shall arise, with fiery red hair and emerald green eyes. Taken from her rightful place, a fate unforeseen, But destiny shall guide her to where she's meant to convene. Born with a spirit untamed, she'll grow strong and bold, A beacon of hope, a story yet untold. To the mortal realm, she was forcibly taken, but her purpose lies in Marqueria, where her powers will awaken. With every step she takes, they shall tremble, As her presence unravels the darkness that assembles. Her red locks shall symbolize her fiery heart, Burning with determination, she'll play her part. Through many trials and hardships, she'll find her way, Harnessing her gifts to bring light, come what may. Her green eyes shall see through deceit and lies, Bringing truth and justice, as the prophecy implies. With her gentle touch, all wounds shall heal, And in her presence, hope shall reveal. She'll unite the divided, bridging the gap, she'll bring harmony to Marqueria's map. Her stolen past shall not define her fate, For she'll rise above and conquer the weight. With compassion and love, she'll break the chains, And peace shall flourish where darkness once came. So let the prophecy guide you, hold it to be true, For the stolen child shall bring peace anew. With red hair ablaze and green eyes so bright, Marqueria shall bask in her guiding light.

"Well, no pressure there. They think this is about me?" Kenna asked, shaking her head and leaning back to look at Jamie's face. He reached up and held her face in his palm, thumb stroking over her lips. He said, "It is about you, sweetheart. As much as you don't want it to be, it is." She cuddled into Jamie, sighing and putting her face in the crook of his neck. They sat in silence for a few minutes, then Kenna gave a gasp and sat up, turning to face Jamie. "Oh my God! I just had some flashes of memories from my childhood. I remember doing something, something that had to be magic! I was very small and must have been around four years old. My adoptive father was screaming at me for something, pulling his hand back to hit me. I yelled 'NO!!', then shoved my hands towards him, and he flew across the room, hit the wall, and fell to the ground. I remember after that happened, they would use surprise attacks to get to me," Kenna whispered, then said, "I've had flashes like this before, but I always thought they were dreams like the night my adoptive parents died. That wasn't a dream either, was it? None of it was a dream; they really happened, didn't they?" Jamie was nodding and said, "Yes, your protective magic was manifesting. Kenna, it was self-defense when your adoptive parents died. You were a child, and it was the only way you could protect yourself." He was watching her, a quizzical look on his face. "What?" she asked. "Sweetheart, I believe you have been using your powers all your life, your entire time in the mortal world. I think you're incredibly strong and gifted to be able to perform protective magic at such a young age, plus the handicap of being in the Mortal world," Jamie said, looking at her in wonder. Kenna chuckled and said, "Yep, that's me. Super Elf, daughter of Father Christmas, Savior

106

of the Realm." Jamie gave her a quick kiss, then stood up, still cradling her in his arms. "Come, my super Elf. I'm taking you to bed. It's been a long ass day, and you've had a lot thrown at you. We both need some sleep." He said, carrying Kenna through the patio doors, then slid it shut with his foot and headed to their bedroom.

Chapter Nineteen

The wheels of the private jet touched down at the small airport in Butte, Montana. Sitting in one of the plush leather seats, the grey-haired woman was on her phone, her expression chilly. "I don't care how long it's going to take you. Get it done." She ended the call with a growl. Glancing towards the front of the plane where the two large men were seated, making sure they hadn't heard her, then looking towards the young man across from her, who was watching her with sad, reproachful green eyes, Hilda said, "Oh, don't give me that look. You're going to benefit from this, too. It's necessary for our return to Marqueria." Then she stood up and moved towards the door. The young man gave a heavy sigh, saying, "Your world has never been my world. I was born here, and this is where I belong." He, too, stood up and then followed her, shaking his head as he walked.

Chapter Twenty

The sun had just peeked over the mountains surrounding the Red House in the country. A fine foggy mist hung in the valleys, creating a quiet, cool environment for the four hunters dressed in camouflage, who were creeping towards an opening in the trees. The fog and crispness of the morning slightly muted the bugles and mews of the Elk herd in the clearing. The tallest hunter, with a grunt tube slung across his chest, signaled for the others to advance in front while he dropped back and blended into the trees. The three remaining hunters spread out in a straight line 50 yards between each of them, using the surrounding brush and trees for cover.

Kneeling down on one knee, each hunter nocked an arrow, preparing to draw back the string if an elk should come within shooting distance. Behind them, some distance back, the tall hunter made a loud, long bugle with the reed in his mouth and the grunt tube in his hand. It sounded exactly like the call of a bull Elk and caught the attention of the large bull on the other side of the clearing. The bull lifted his nose to detect the scent of the intruding elk in the air, then came charging towards the group of hunters hidden within the trees. When the bull stopped 60 yards from the tree line, the hunter in back gave a few cow mews. Again, the bull lifted his head and curled his lips, tasting the air, then gave a loud, aggressive bugle. Another bugle sounded from behind the three hunters near the tree line, enraging the herd bull further.

He was intent upon preventing his harem of cows, many of whom were in heat, from being stolen by rival bulls, so he charged towards the sound of a challenging bull but stopped just 10 yards from the tree line, giving short, aggressive grunts. He was nearest the hunter furthest to the right, who had already drawn the string of their bow back, waiting at full draw. Suddenly, the bull gave a jerk and turned back towards the herd. The hunter had loosed the arrow, which had flown true and found its target, the heart and lungs of the bull. The mortally wounded Elk stopped in the middle of the meadow, stumbled a few steps, and then fell down on its side, its last dying breath leaving its body. The herd left the meadow within seconds, and everything was quiet.

Coming from behind, the tallest hunter walked to the shooter, who the other two hunters surrounded. Jamie said to Ember, "Nice shooting, daughter. This should feed us for the Winter." He gave her a one-armed hug, grinning at Kenna, who was standing just behind Ember. Smiling proudly at his family, Jamie said, "Come, we need to say the blessing and field dress the animal." Kenna, Ember, and Noelle followed Jamie to where the majestic animal lay. They all knelt beside the bull, each placing a hand on its large antlers. Jamie began the Prayer of Thanks, his voice low and rumbly.

"Thank you, Majestic one, for this honorable hunt. My family shall honor your sacrifice by feeding from your flesh, which will provide us nourishment through the harsh Winter. The delicate balance of nature and the interconnection of all living beings shall be honored by us. May your spirit roam free amongst our mountains, and may your herd be many. The memory of your last day will forever be a part of us as we honor you in the retelling of this Hunt. Goddess, we ask that you embrace the spirit of this creature, in honor and love. We ask for the blessing of this hunt and the blessing of this sustenance for our family and friends. Roam free Majestic one, Roam free."

All four said, "Goddess Blessed Be," and proceeded to field dress the animal, working together efficiently and quickly, as they'd done many times before. Two hours later, the animal was hung up in the walk-in cooler in the lower garage of the Red House, and the hunters were having breakfast at the breakfast nook. "I was shaking so much after I shot," Ember was saying, "Is that normal father?" Jamie gave a quiet chuckle and said, "Yes, it is. No matter how many animals I harvest, I still get the adrenaline shakes afterward. Today was a good hunt; you did well, my girl." Noelle said, "I was watching the Elk come closer and closer and had to take deep breaths to help calm myself. I was getting so excited. When it veered towards where Ember was, I was actually so relieved." She laughed and said, "Congratulations, Ember, he is a beautiful animal, and I can't wait to have some Elk burgers." "Thanks, Noelle. My first Elk!!" Ember said, glowing with pride and excitement.

Kenna was watching them all, a soft smile on her face. She took a sip of coffee and then said, "Remember, the hard part is coming in a few days. We need to cut and wrap the meat for the freezer." The girls groaned in unison, making Jamie and Kenna laugh. "Do you hunt in Marqueria, Dad?" Noelle asked. Ember turned to her father and asked, "If you do hunt, do you hunt in Bear form, Dad?" Jamie had been gathering the dirty dishes from the table and paused to look at his daughters, saying, "Yes, we hunt in Marqueria. Shifters hunt in either form, depending upon whom they are hunting with. We have all the animals the mortal realm has and a few more not found here." Ember said, "Good. I don't want to give up hunting. It's almost like a drive within me, enjoying the chase and being out in the trees and mountains. I much prefer mountains and trees to being in town." "Hmmm. It might be your shifter blood causing the hunting drive. We all have it," Jamie said, studying his daughters. Kenna stood up and, giving each of her girls a hug, said, "Come on. Let's get the kitchen cleaned up so we can start weeding out what we leave behind for the move."

Chapter Twenty-One

The next morning, Kenna and Jamie were sitting at the kitchen counter, sipping coffee and discussing 'the move' as the girls had dubbed it, essentially making it into an event. "We can leave everything we don't need or want to take with us. Make this house our 'Vacation' home," Kenna said. Then, she took a large drink of coffee and sighed. Turning to Jamie, she asked, "Is it always Winter in Marqueria?" Jamie turned to face her, draping his arms around her neck and pulling her in for a soft kiss. Pulling back, he said, "No, at least it wasn't before you were lost to this world. Before your aunt took you through the Tree, we had all four seasons. Then, the year you were lost, Winter never left, and it's been Winter ever since. I don't know if it will change once you're over there for good or if it will stay Winter. I guess it remains to be seen."

"Well, as much as I love Winter, four seasons is nice to experience. So, yes, I hope I break the curse," Kenna said, then leaned in for another kiss. From behind them, Ember's voice said, "Come on, guys! It's too early for this." They turned to see their grinning girls standing in the arch between the kitchen and living room. "It's never too early in the morning for affection," Jamie said, kissing their mother again. The girls laughed as they made their way into the kitchen.

Reaching up into the cupboard, Noelle grabbed two coffee mugs, set them on the counter, grabbed the coffee carafe, and proceeded to fill both cups. "Ummm ... since when do you two drink coffee?" Kenna asked, watching them with a faint smile. "We used to drink it all the time with you when we were little," Ember said, picking up the cup and grinning. She took a sip, grimaced and shuttered, and asked, "How can you drink this stuff?!" Laughing, Kenna said, "When we had our little coffee parties, there was more milk and honey in your cups than coffee." Tilting her head, Ember said, "Well, looks like we need some milk and honey. Noelle, will you grab the milk? I'll grab the honey." Walking into the pantry, she called to her mom, "Where's the honey, Mom?....oh never mind, I found it."

Ember came out of the pantry carrying a jug of honey, which they got from their neighbor up the road. Every year, they drop off six large jugs of honey from their hives, and in return, Jamie gives them one of the elk they have harvested. Their honey was the sweetest, richest tasting honey around. As the girls fixed their cups of coffee, milk, and honey, Jamie said, "We were discussing the move before you girls came in....." Both girls interrupted, laughing. "Yeah, that's what you were doing," Ember said laughingly. Jamie, smiling and shaking his head, continued, "Anyway, as I was saying. We were discussing 'the move'. We think you should bring what you want, but pack light. Just the items you don't want to live without. Clothing isn't really needed unless you want to bring a few items you just can't leave behind from this world. It's really your choice."

Both girls nodded, taking sips of their coffee. "Wow. This is delicious! I'm going to drink this every day from now on," Ember said. After taking another sip, she continued, "I have a few clothing items I'll bring, but I want to wear the dresses and boots. They look so soft and comfy." Noelle took a large swallow of her coffee, then said, "I'll try the clothing over there, but the tunics and leggings are what I want to wear. Dad, as a female, would that be frowned upon? Although to be perfectly honest, it doesn't matter to me if they like it or not; I'm still going to wear the leggings and tunics." Her father laughed, then said, "You can wear the tunics and leggings. Many females do." Jamie grinned at his girls and said, "They have no idea what's coming their way, do they?" "Who? Papa and Nana? Oh, they know. I think they get a kick out of Ember and me. Papa calls us 'A breath of fresh air,' and Nana says we're the most stubborn girls she's ever met, but that we're entertaining," Noelle said, laughing, then said, "I can't wait to meet your mother and father. What should we call them?" Jamie smiled at his girls, saying, "In our Bear clans, the grandmother is called YaYa, and the grandfather is PawPaw."

Ember walked around the counter to her father and stopped just behind him. She leaned in and gave him a hug, resting her head on his back. "I'm sorry we didn't tell you we were going through the Tree. I don't like keeping secrets from you, Dad," she said. Jamie turned around and wrapped his daughter in a big hug, kissing her on the head. "It's ok, baby girl. I've known the entire time that you and Noelle were going through the Tree," he said. Kenna quickly turned her eyes towards Jamie, saying, "What?! You knew they were traveling through?!" Ember, hands on her hips, stepped away from Jamie and stared. Jamie laughed and, ruffling Ember's hair, said, "Yep. I watched them the first couple of times, but they always came back happy and healthy. Listening in on their conversations, I figured out your parents were taking care of them." The three females in his life stared at Jamie, stunned. "So, I have been the only one in the dark these past several years? Nice!" Kenna said, rolling her eyes and shaking her head.

Kenna stood up from her chair and walked around the counter and into the kitchen. As she started to clean up the morning dishes, Ember cried, "I have some laundry to do," and quickly left the room. Rolling her eyes at Ember's avoidance of the dishes, Noelle started to load the dishwasher. "Mom, are you really okay with everything?" she asked Kenna, closing the dishwasher and facing her mother. Kenna looked up from the counter. She was wiping down, smiled at her daughter, and then said, "Yes, I am. I really am. It feels surreal sometimes, well, most of the time when I think about it, actually. But, more and more memories are coming back to me, both from the time before I traveled through the Tree and after. In this short time, I've become so much more comfortable with everything." She laughed loudly, then said, "Almost as if I were born to it!" Noelle shook her head and laughed with her mother. Jamie chuckled, then said, "I'll be down in my office if you need anything. I need to wrap up a few loose ends before we make the move." He walked over to Kenna, bending down to give her a soft kiss on her lips. "I love you, wife," he said, then kissed the tip of her nose. "And I love you, Husband," she replied, smiling as she watched him walk away. Noelle sighed and said, "You guys are so cute."

Chapter Twenty-Two

L ater that day, Kenna was sitting on the front deck sipping a hot cup of tea and watching the herd of deer near the rock pile up on the hill, Lucy at her side. The girls were in the house, going through their belongings and deciding what they wanted to take with them. Noelle had asked if her laptop and games would work over there, and her father assured her they would, in fact, work and probably work better due to the magic. Ember was excited about all the new animals, the exotic plants, and the new places we were all going to explore together on the other side of the Tree, in Marqueria. They both wanted to continue their Muay Thai training, and both wanted to bring their bows with them. Their father told them the bows could stay home, as Elven bows were far superior.

Kenna smiled as she remembered the look of excitement that crossed over their faces. Taking another sip of tea, she noticed a car she didn't recognize turn up their 3/4 mile long driveway. Lucy suddenly stood up, raised her hackles, and started growling low in her throat. Setting her cup down on the table, Kenna stood up, too, startled. Lucy had never reacted this way to visitors. She loved people... well, except for that one UPS guy a few years ago. Much to his chagrin, Lucy wouldn't let him get out of his truck, and he eventually had to change routes. Kenna never finds out what it is that Lucy has taken objection to.

As the car moved slowly up their driveway, Kenna heard Jamie come out onto the deck. Turning to him, she said, "I don't know who this is, but Lucy doesn't like them." Jamie said, "I felt it; that's why I ran up from the office. I felt the presence of another from the other side, and there was only one person I knew from there. Your aunt Hilda." Kenna gasped, moving closer to Jamie. Lucy stood in protector mode in front of both of them, looking fierce. Opening herself up to her magic, she too felt the faint difference coming from the passengers of the car.

As the black vehicle moved closer, Kenna was able to see there were two occupants in the front, but blacked-out windows in the rear prevented her from seeing into the backseat. She sensed four occupants, though. The car was a luxury model SUV, rarely seen along these mountain dirt roads. Reaching the end of the driveway, the SUV maneuvered onto the concrete parking pad in front of the attached three-car garage. Jamie moved to the end of the deck and closer to the garage, Lucy at his side, Kenna trailing close behind.

The SUV stopped, and the engine turned off. The two men in the front seats had opened their doors and stepped out, moving to the back doors. They were dressed in black suits with white shirts, black ties, shoes, and black sunglasses. They looked like copies of The Men in Black agents, and Kenna gave a quiet laugh and said, "Oh my." Jamie glanced back at her, chuckling, indicating he was thinking the same thing. Turning back to watch the SUV, Kenna moved to stand next to Jamie, and Lucy moved to block her from walking further than his side. She laid a hand on Lucy's head and said, "SShhh, Lucy. It's ok. Good girl." Lucy briefly leaned her body against Kenna's legs, then moved out in front of both Jamie and Kenna, growling low. Kenna looked at the two men again. She couldn't help it, she gave another soft laugh, and Jamie quietly said, "I know, right?! I think they've been watching too many movies."

The two men, one with white blonde hair and the other light golden brown, each opened a back car door. A tall, thin older woman with short grey hair climbed out of the door closer to Jamie and Kenna. She was dressed in an expensive-looking pantsuit, low-heeled black leather pumps, and carrying a black Louis Vuitton handbag with gold hardware. Kenna rolled her eyes at the expensive handbag, not understanding the allure. On the other side of the car, out stepped a tall blond man who appeared to be around thirty. He, dressed in an expensive business suit as well, walked around the car to stand next to the older woman.

The woman removed her designer sunglasses and made to walk closer to the deck. She stopped suddenly when Lucy increased the volume of her growling and bared her teeth. Glancing nervously at Jamie and Kenna, she asked haughtily, "I have something to discuss with your family; it will be worth your while to listen. Are you going to call off your dog and let us come in for this important meeting?"

The wind gently blowing her hair across her face, Kenna tucked a strand behind her ear, crossed her arms over her chest, and leaned her hip against the deck railing, laughing, then said,

"Yeah, that's not going to happen. I suggest you get back into your car and leave." The woman gave Kenna a cold look, then turned towards the two men and simply said, "Shoot the dog."

Before the two men could even twitch a hand, Noelle and Ember glided out from behind their parents, standing side by side. Each girl was holding a bow, arrows nocked and at full draw. "I have the one on the right," Ember murmured to Noelle, then continued, "Now, get back in your damn car and leave! You heard my mom." Ember stood still, bow steady, not taking her eyes off the men. "You make one move towards your weapons, and you'll have an arrow through your eye," Noelle added. Their hair was floating gently around their heads, and a faint glow was coming from their skin. The two 'men in black' hadn't moved, but on seeing the girls with their floating hair and glowing skin, they exchanged a glance and then lifted their noses slightly into the air as if they were trying to catch a scent. Jamie and Kenna exchanged glances, eyebrows raised, and Jamie said, "Girls, while we appreciate your fierce protection, your mom and I have this under control. Please un-nock your arrows and move behind us." Both girls lowered their bows but left the arrows in place. They moved carefully to stand behind their parents, shuffling to the left of them further out on the deck so they still had a good shooting lane.

Kenna chuckled quietly, gave her girls a smile, then turned back to the unwelcome visitors. The two wanna-be-men-in-black had relaxed their stances, and both were leaning against the side of the SUV, arms crossed over their chests and watching the family. Kenna's aunt Hilda shot them an angry look and turned to the blond man beside her. "Maxim, take care of the dog since these two seem to be most intimidated by two young girls." Turning towards the two men in black, she said, "I hired you to obey orders. You have proven to be useless and won't be receiving the agreed-upon fee. I won't pay for cowardice, and I'll make sure you'll never work again as bodyguards." She said it coldly, with no heat in her eyes or voice. The two men exchanged an amused glance, shrugged, and continued to casually lean against the SUV.

The man, Maxis, stared at Hilda in shock, shaking his head, and said, "Mother, No. I will not harm their dog. Is this really the way you want to handle things?" Hilda gasped, obviously unused to having her orders disobeyed. Kenna turned to Jamie, raised an eyebrow, and mouthed, "Mother?" Jamie shrugged, shaking his head to indicate he hadn't known she had a son. Kenna then spoke up, "We can have this conversation you so desperately want right here, where we stand. You are not welcome here, so you need to speak. The sooner you say what you need to say, the sooner you can remove yourselves from our land." Kenna was standing casually next to her husband. Their body was loose and relaxed, yet there was a sense she was ready to pounce; there was a restrained energy about her. Jamie's stance was a mirror of his wife's, but his aggressive energy was more tangible. The men in black, leaning against the SUV, watched Jamie through their sunglasses, never taking their gaze off him, sensing his lethalness. Every once in a while, they'd lift their noses to sniff the air like an animal would, and this last time, they looked at each other and gave a nod. Lucy hadn't given ground and was still in front of Kenna and Jamie, occasional low growls emanating from her throat.

Hilda looked at Lucy, then turned her gaze to Kenna; hate flashed quickly across her face before she could compose her features into a mask again. Tilting her head and smiling slightly, Hilda coldly said, "You know who I am, I'm guessing? Ahhh, yes, I see that you do. Well, then, I won't pretend this is a loving reunion. I'll cut straight to the point and the reason I'm here." Hilda paused briefly, then boldly said, "I want to pass through the Tree and return to Marqueria." There was a moment of silence from all present; one of the men in black nudged the other with his elbow, and then Kenna burst out laughing, shocking her aunt.

Glancing at Jamie, Kenna raised an eyebrow and said, "She's serious, isn't she?" Jamie smiled faintly and, nodding his head in amazement, said, "Yes, I believe she is." Mouth opened slightly, and with a look of wonder on her face, Kenna turned her head to stare at her aunt. Then, she asked Jamie, "Has she always been so arrogant and narcissistic?" Jamie responded, "I myself have never personally had the pleasure of meeting your aunt. I have just seen her from afar, but the rumors about her were not kind. She had a reputation of being extremely haughty, with a huge sense of entitlement." "Yes, yes, I can see this for myself. Does she seriously think we're going to let her pass through after what she did?" Kenna asked her husband, shaking her head slightly.

Noelle and Ember both quietly laughed, enjoying their parents' banter and its effect on their great aunt, who was quaking in suppressed anger. "Do not speak about me as if I am not standing right in front of you! How dare you?! I am a member of the Royal Family, and I demand passage through the Tree, now!" Hilda shouted angrily, nostrils flaring, face flushed, and hands squeezed into fists at her side.

The change in Kenna was immediate and very noticeable. She went completely, eerily still. Then suddenly, her curls began to float softly around her head, and a soft glow emanated from her skin and stunningly green eyes. Seeing this, the two men in black stopped leaning on the SUV, stood up, and took a step closer to Kenna. Kenna very slowly turned her head, gaze turning to her aunt, who took several steps back, a look of fear crossing her face. Kenna said nothing, just stared at her aunt for a few more moments, then softly said, "You demand? You DEMAND?? YOU?! You have no rights here. I should end you here and now for what you did to me. You were supposed to care for me and return me to my parents when it was safe. Instead, you sold me. You SOLD me, your niece. You sold me to two of the most rotten, horrible people you could find." Kenna's eyes never left her aunt.

Kenna took the two steps down from the deck to stand at Lucy's side on the concrete pad, then said, "Get into your car and leave our land. Do not return. If I see you again, I will not hold back, and you will not survive the encounter." Jamie watched his wife, his expression fierce and full of pride. Behind him, their daughters were whispering between themselves. "Oh my goodness! She's magnificent! I hope she kicks great aunty's ass," Ember whispered. "Ember, please don't cuss. But yes, I agree. Mother looks like a warrior goddess, doesn't she?" Noelle whispered back. Jamie chuckled at the exchange between his daughters and his eyes, never leaving his wife; he moved down the steps to stand at her side.

"You heard my wife. Leave now and don't come back. You will never be allowed to pass through the Tree," Jamie said, his voice low and growling as the Bear surfaced, his golden eyes giving off a soft golden glow. The wind had switched direction and now blew towards the group of strangers, carrying Jamie's scent with it. The two men took off their sunglasses and looked between Jamie and Kenna.

The blonde one said in a low, growly voice, "You are Bear." Jamie looked at him in surprise, glowing eyes intensely studying both men. Then, he took a deep breath into his lungs as if scenting them. Jamie nodded and said, "As are you both. You look familiar to me." "Yes, we are. We weren't aware there would be another of us here, or we wouldn't have approached your house in this manner," the brown-haired Bear stated. "I believe she wasn't completely honest about our mission here," the blonde said, cocking his head and continuing to study Jamie. Suddenly, the blonde gasped, then knelt down on one knee, head bowed. "My Prince. Please, forgive us, we didn't know," he said, head still bowed. The brown-haired Bear studied Jamie, then he too quickly knelt beside his companion, head bowed, saying, "My Prince."

"Ummm, dad, what's going on?" Noelle asked from behind him. "Duh, Noelle. They're Were bears and Father is their Prince. Pay attention," Ember said in a tone of voice that only a fifteen-year-old girl could master. "Stow it, Ember," Noelle responded quietly, watching the exchange between her father and the two men. By this time, their mother had noticed there was something happening beside her, and her hair slowly returned to normal, with glowing red locks gently floating down to lay upon her shoulder and down her back to her waist.

Then the glow from her eyes dimmed slightly, and turning towards Jamie, Kenna asked, "There are more of you in this land? I thought you were the only one." Jamie said, shaking his head in some confusion, "So did I. I wasn't aware of others like me in the mortal realm."

Turning back to the two kneeling men, Jamie said, "Please rise. Then kindly explain how you came to this world and why you are in the service of this woman." The two men stood up, and exchanging a grimacing glance; the blonde said, "We were sent over by your father shortly after you left Marqueria. Our mission was to keep an eye on you and ensure your safety. Unfortunately, we couldn't find you. This world is nothing like ours, and the sheer number of people made locating you rather difficult. It was as if you'd just vanished. Disappeared." The blond gave a sigh, shaking his head. He then said, "My Prince, I am Tai, and this is my brother Kai. We are yours to command." Jamie nodded his head in acknowledgment and said, "Yes. I remember you. You couldn't find me because I didn't want to be found. I was cloaked. I had to be to prevent Hilda from finding me by mistake." Jamie inclined his head toward Kenna's aunt, Hilda. Kai, the brown-haired Were, smiled and nudged his brother, saying, "I told you, brother. I knew it wasn't our abilities." Then turned to Jamie and said, "That explains why two of your father's best trackers couldn't find you." Jamie nodded, then asked, "And how did you come to be employed by this woman?" His tone had become slightly chilled.

The blonde, Tai, rubbed his hand over his face and through his hair, sighing. He said, "She and her son are the only ones with the blood of Marqueria that we have come in contact with. We met in Finland while we were searching for you. She contacted us a few days ago, saying she had a job for us, acting as her security during a meeting. We knew she was Bram's sister. Although this information she never shared with us, we knew." Nodding in agreement, Kai smiled and said, "If we hadn't taken the job, we wouldn't have found you, Prince Jamie. It was meant to be."

Hilda, who had stepped back several feet while Kenna was confronting her, took a few steps forward and cleared her throat. She stared at Kenna and sneered, "You mated with a Were?! Have you no pride? What is your father going to say when he finds out you dirtied our bloodline by mingling it with an animal? Disgusting." Hilda was shaking her head and had a look of utter disgust on her aging face. She then sarcastically said, "While this reunion of yours just warms my heart, it's not what is important right now. I need to pass through the Tree and meet with my brother. It's of the utmost importance that I meet with him. Our world is in danger."

They all had turned towards her, facing her. Now it was six to their two. Kenna, shaking her head, said, "In danger? You're saying that Marqueria is in danger? And you want to save it?! Yet you, yourself, are the one who put it in danger all those years ago. No, you're not passing through the Tree unless my father says you can, and I really don't think he's going to allow it after what you did to his only daughter. I will deliver your message to him myself. But for now, you and your son will get back into your SUV and leave immediately, as I said before." Hilda started to open her mouth to say something, the look on her face bitter and angry, but her son Maxim laid his hand on her shoulder, giving it a squeeze. She looked at him, and he shook his head. He said firmly, "No, mother. You will stop this now. You have asked, and they have replied with their answer. Leave it at that." Turning towards Kenna and Jamie, he said, "I apologize for my mother's behavior today. She received some unsettling news from her physician in Finland last month, and it has made her desperate. I will take her to Butte, where I have booked rooms for us at the Copper King Hotel. You will find us there when you feel ready to talk more. Here is my cell number."

Maxim held out a small, thick business card, embossed with copper writing, towards Kenna, and she took it hesitantly. Then he looked at Kenna, saying, "I would really like to speak with you soon without my mother present. You and your daughters are the only blood relatives I have left, other than my mother. I have heard stories of the other world all my life, but I have always dreamed of having more family. I am not my mother and do not have her desire for power." He looked very sincere, his dark green eyes slightly pleading. Kenna stared at his eyes, gasped, and then said, "Your eyes are green! The exact color as my own and my parents'." Noelle and Ember, having set their bows down on the nearby table, pushed their way between their parents to have a closer look at Maxim's eyes. "Oh my goodness!" exclaimed Noelle. Ember said, "Damn! I guess he is family, right mom?" Noelle rolled her eyes at her sister's use of the curse word, but her father laughed softly, shaking his head at Ember's colorful language. Kenna was studying Maxim, but she touched Ember's shoulder and said softly, "Ember, cool it with the language."

Looking confused, Maxim asked, "Why do my green eyes surprise you so much?" Stunned, Kenna turned towards Hilda and asked, "You didn't tell him your entire history, did you?"

Hilda scowled, shaking her head and saying coldly, "Why should I mention that? The only way one can rule in Marqueria is with Green eyes and red hair? It's a ridiculous rule the Goddess imposed. I was first born and the blooded sister of Bram, yet I didn't receive the gift from the Goddess! But your mother did, didn't she? A lowly Villager gets the mark of the Goddess while I am denied? It's not fair; it's not right. And then there's you! The first female child ever, born with the Goddess' blessings. You will be the first female to rule in your own right. Bah! Of course, I didn't tell him about the eyes or hair. Why should he get the green eyes of the Goddess when he is half-human?!" Hilda's face was a mask of bitterness and hate.

Staring at his mother in distaste and shaking his head, Maxim turned away from her, saying in a voice full of quiet anger and hurt, "Get in the car now, Mother. We're leaving." Turning towards Kai and Tai, he said, "I trust you can find your own way from here? I apologize for my mother's subterfuge. I will personally transfer your payment when I get to the hotel. I don't agree with what she has done in the past and don't agree with her plans for the future." They both nodded, Kai saying, "Don't worry about it, Maxim. It's not your fault. But you might want to consider distancing yourself from your mother; she's nothing but poison." Maxim stared at the Bear with a frustrated, sad expression, then shrugged, walked to the driver's side door, and got in, barely waiting for his mother to shut her own door before he put it in gear and started driving down the driveway and into Butte.

The two Bears exchanged sheepish looks, then turned towards Jamie. Jamie laughed and held up a hand, stopping whatever they were about to say, and said, "You can bunk here while we sort this all out, but on one condition. Please tell me you have a change of clothing; this Men in Black look won't cut it here. Why this choice of clothing, if you don't mind my asking?" Both Bears flushed in embarrassment, and Kai said, "It was Hilda's idea. She insisted we dress like this, saying it would help to intimidate you." Everyone laughed; Noelle spoke up, "If you don't have anything, I'm sure Father has something you can wear." Jamie nodded in agreement and said, "Come, we welcome you into our home." Jamie put his arm around Kenna's waist and turned to walk back into the house. Their girls followed close behind, bows slung over their shoulders, and quietly talked about what had just happened. Kai and Tai watched their Prince's very interesting family for a few moments, then exchanged amused looks and followed them inside.

Chapter Twenty-Three

L ater that evening, the six of them were sitting around the fire pit on the patio, roasting marshmallows and making s'mores. The Bear brothers were wearing borrowed clothes, such as jeans, flannel shirts, and Doc Martens from Jamie. They looked much more comfortable than they had in the black suits. The atmosphere around the fire was relaxed and full of laughter as the two Bears told of their adventures in the Mortal world and all they had experienced over the past several years. Tonight was also their first s'mores ever, and taking his first bite and chewing, Kai's eyes widened, and then he exclaimed, "How have I not known about these amazing little treats?" Noelle laughed and said, "They're better when you slightly burn the outer part of the marshmallow. That's how my mom likes them, too."

Kai inclined his head with respect and smiled at her, "Thank you, Princess." "Wait!! What the shit?! We're Princesses, Noelle! Holy Hell!" cried Ember, speaking very fast in an excited, sugar-fed voice. Laughter burst out of the two visiting Wares, although they tried to muffle it. "Not with a potty mouth like that, you aren't," said Noelle, shaking her head before biting into the oooey gooey mess in her hand. Her parents smiled, shaking their heads. Kenna said, "Honestly, Ember. Every sentence doesn't have to contain a swear word."

She turned to Tai and Kai, saying, "She's been expanding her vocabulary and has recently ventured into the use of swear words. She says they make life more colorful and interesting." Shrugging and smiling hugely, she continued, "I can't say I disagree with her, but we get so many disapproving frowns when she uses them in town around other people."

"Mom, you know I don't care what others think of me. All the kids at school thought I was weird anyway. I guess it's not normal to speak to the plants and animals," Ember said, shrugging, a note of sadness at the last. Noelle put her arm around her sister, pulling her close to her side, and quietly said, "That's ok, Ember, we're weird together. We don't need them." Jamie and Kenna smiled at their daughters, proud of their loving bond and the way they cared for one another. "You're in good company then," Kenna said, tossing another bag of marshmallows to the girls and saying, "One more each, and then it's time to go up to your rooms, brush your teeth, and settle in for the night." Both girls nodded as they put another marshmallow on their roasting sticks and stuck them over the fire.

Jamie was watching the two other Bears across the fire, his expression unreadable. "Did you know Hilda was an Elf when you met her?" he asked Kai and Tai, then took a sip of his beer. Kai looked up, about to take another bite of what must have been his twelfth s'more, and cocked his head to the side. "There was something about her, a weak scent of magic. But by that time, she had aged enough to be basically human. We thought maybe somehow, though highly unlikely, there was an elf in her family tree way back. Then we discovered her name and connected the dots," Kai said, shrugging.

"When she mentioned coming to Montana, searching for her family Tree, we both knew what that actually meant and that there was more to the story. She had no idea we were Bear, or she wouldn't have approached us. We knew the Grove and Tree were in Montana, so we decided to play along with her plan until we had a better handle on what she was up to," Tai said, then took a swig of his beer, washing down the last of his s'more. "We sure never expected to find another Bear, let alone our Prince," he continued, tipping his beer towards Jamie. Jamie nodded and took another drink from his bottle of beer, then asked, "What is her son like? Maxim? We didn't know she had a son, so that was quite a surprise." Kenna had been watching the interactions between the Weres and listening quietly. Now she spoke up and said, "He doesn't seem to be like his mother. He refused to shoot Lucy, and that goes far in my book. I also didn't detect anything evil in him. He seemed kind and rather sad."

Tai looked at Kai questioningly, and he replied, "He's alright. I listened in on their conversations on the jet when they thought we were asleep, and Maxim doesn't hold his mother's belief system. From what I could gather, he doesn't want to be a ruler and would rather stay in this world and run his deceased father's companies. He wants to improve 'the human condition' as he calls it." Tai said, "I grabbed his wrist as he was passing by me. While I couldn't read any evil in him, he does contain quite a bit of magic, much more than his mother. What's interesting is he's not even aware he has magic, and neither does his mother. I sensed sadness and loneliness, but there was nothing deviant or threatening."

Jamie nodded in understanding, eyes flicking to Kenna, then said, "She can't pass through. She obviously has no magic here, so she won't be able to activate the Tree herself." He took Kenna's hand and brought it to his lips, placing a soft kiss on her palm. She leaned over and gave him a kiss before standing up and calling to the girls. "Come, my teenage Princesses. It's time to go in for the night. I will walk you up and tuck you in," Kenna said. Ember replied with her teenage attitude, "Mother! We're not babies anymore. We don't need you to tuck us in at night anymore." "It's not for you; it is for me. I need to tuck you in tonight, ok? I need this," Kenna replied softly, herding them before her into the house as they yelled their goodnights to their father and the Bear brothers.

Kai, who had been watching the three females enter the house, leaned forward and turned to face Jamie, then asked, "Does your father know about your family, my Prince?" Jamie gave a quiet chuckle and grinned, then nodded. "The girls have been visiting him since they were barely toddlers when they found their way through the Tree. He has been meeting them at the Tree on the other side every time they crossed over," Jamie said, shaking his head again. Tai laughed quietly and said, "Your daughters are a force unto themselves. I sense great power in them. In your wife as well." Jamie nodded and said, "Kenna found out a few days ago who and what she is. Or rather, I should say, she remembered who and what she was. The girls performed a Wind Spell for her when they brought her through the Tree to Marqueria, much to her immense surprise. She has been remembering more and more every day."

The two Bear brothers stared at Jamie in surprise. Tai asked, "Your daughters performed the spell alone?" Jamie nodded and said, "Yes, King Bram and Queen Maia taught it to the girls when they were younger, in preparation for the day the Tree deemed Kenna was ready to remember." Kai said in awe, "Such power is in those who are so young. But why did Princess Kenna forget who and what she is?" Jamie replied, expression dark, "She had blocked the early memories from her childhood and the memories from before she passed through the Tree due to trauma she'd endured growing up in this world. Hilda has a lot to answer for." Jamie growled, the expression in his eyes murderous.

Kai looked up with a dangerous look in his eyes and asked, "What did she do to your wife?" Rubbing his bald head a few times, Jamie sighed and then began to explain, "Not long after coming through the Tree, Hilda sold Kenna to a couple from Billings who were looking to adopt a child but were not approved. She took the money they paid her and disappeared. Kenna's adoptive parents were very abusive. They beat her and starved her, mentally and verbally terrorized her. Unfortunately for them, she had protective magic and would use it unknowingly. One day, when she defended herself, the couple didn't walk away. The authorities ruled it an accident, and Kenna was put into the foster care system, then bounced around for the next couple of years from home to home. When she turned eighteen, she aged out and was free. She moved to Butte, got a job as a waitress, and started college. That's how we met; we both took the same computer science class."

On hearing Hilda's crimes towards Kenna, the other two Bears growled low in their throats, expressions equally as murderous as Jamie's.

"We are yours to command, my Prince. In defense of your family, anything you ask of us, we will do," Kai said, his brown eyes hot with anger. Tai said, "For what she has done to the Princess of the Realm, she must pay for her crimes." Jamie studied both men, then nodded, saying, "I appreciate your loyalty. I will think upon how best to utilize you." Thinking to himself, 'I will use them as I see fit; I'm just not sure yet what I want to do.' His number one priority was the protection of his wife and daughters, and second was the Tree and Marqueria.

Chapter Twenty-Four

"We need to go through the Tree and talk with our fathers. Plus, I'm sure Otso would love to see you after all these years. I just don't want to leave the Tree unprotected while we're gone. I don't trust Hilda," Kenna was saying to Jamie as the two sat at the kitchen counter, drinking coffee in the early morning light. Sighing, Kenna took a large drink from her cup and then set it down, turning her chair towards Jamie so they were facing each other, knees touching. Jamie, his hand at the back of Kenna's neck, pulled her closer and then leaned in to plant a soft kiss on her forehead.

Taking her small hands into his massive ones, he said, "I have that part figured out, babe. Tai and Kai will stay here and patrol the land. Remember, time passes differently in Marqueria, so we won't be gone for very long. Nobody will mess with the Tree, and they will keep your aunt away. Let's go change clothes and go through now while it's early." "Do you trust them?" Kenna asked softly. Nodding yes, Jamie said, "With my life, as you should too." Kenna scoffed loudly, then jumped off the tall chair. "Not likely. My circle is small, Jamie. I keep it small for a reason," she said as she walked quickly towards their bedroom. Shaking his head, Jamie chuckled and followed after her.

"Damn it! No way are you going without us!" Ember was almost yelling at her parents, with a look of frustration on her face. She was standing with her hands on her hips on the patio in front of her parents, trying to block them from going. Her green eyes were faintly glowing, and her hair was floating softly up off her shoulders. Noelle was right next to her, with the same pose and the same expression, and green eyes glowing softly as well. "Parental units, we would be safer at your side than to leave us here with total strangers and the threat of that snake, Hilda," Noelle said heatedly, then turned to Tai and Kai, whispering, "No offense," before quickly turning back to face her parents. Tai and Kai were sitting at the patio table, drinking coffee and casually watching the family drama unfold. They had faint smiles on their faces, but one could tell they were straining very hard not to laugh out loud. They both bowed their heads to Noelle, indicating they were not offended, and said together, "No offense taken, Princess." The brothers looked at each other and grinned broadly before turning back to watch the outcome.

Jamie and Kenna exchanged exasperated glances. Raising independent free, thinking daughters had come back to bite them in the ass, Kenna thought to herself. "OK, you can come with us. You should probably officially meet my parents anyway," Jamie said, shaking his head and grinning, then rubbing his hand over his bald head. Sighing, he turned to the two Bears who were laughing quietly at the table. "Yeah, laugh it up, guys. One day, you'll have cubs," Jamie said; the two brothers paled, and deep pain flashed across their faces; then Jamie continued on, "You can make yourselves at home while we're away, which actually shouldn't be more than five minutes if we don't stay overnight. I've shown you the security cameras and how to check them; other than walking the perimeter every once in a while, there shouldn't be much you have to worry about." Kai chuckled and said, "No worries here, Prince Jamie." Tai, nodding in agreement with his brother, said, "This will be a cakewalk, as they say in this world. Hilda won't try anything this soon."

Ember, who was already halfway up the hill, yelled to her dad, "Dad, come on and hurry up!" Then she stopped and waited impatiently for Kenna, Jamie, and Noelle to catch up. Kenna felt it was best to leave Lucy home this trip; extra security for the Tree on this side, she said. Lucy was sitting between Tai and Kai on high alert while the two Bears watched the family disappear up the trail toward the Tree. "That's a family worth guarding, wouldn't you say?" Kai asked Tai. Tai nodded and said, "This will be one of our more entertaining assignments, to be sure." Exchanging an amused glance with each other, they stood to go start their rounds, Lucy joining them.

Chapter Twenty-Five

When the family arrived through the Tree to Marqueria, there were four figures waiting for them. Bram, Maia, Otso, and another female Kenna didn't know. Noelle and Ember quickly walked to their Papa and Nana, giving each of them a hug, both talking excitedly about their experience yesterday. "I had my arrow aimed right for his eye," Ember said proudly. "And I had mine on the other one's eye," Noelle said, just as proud. Bram and Maia looked at the girls' parents with concerned expressions; Bram asked, "What is this talk of an almost battle? What has happened?"

Kenna walked forward, gave her parents each a hug, and then stepped back to stand next to Jamie. "Kenna, has something happened?" Maia asked again. "We will get to that in a minute, Mother. For now, I'd like you to meet my husband, Jamie," Kenna said, threading her arm through Jamie's and smiling up at him, eyes shining. Jamie smiled lovingly down at his wife and said, "And I'd like to introduce you, my love, to my parents." Introductions were made all around, with Ember and Noelle relaying their exploits to Jamie's parent, who were in their human forms. Jamie's father was a bear of a man, with hugely muscled arms and legs, barrel-chested, with a long flowing beard and hair the color of mahogany. His voice was deep and growling, but he spoke gently to his granddaughters.

Jamie's mother, Tati, was tall for a female, standing at 6'1", and while she was muscled, it wasn't in the way her husband and son were. She was long and lean, with defined muscles, yet feminine in face and form. Strength emanated from her, but so did an unexpected gentleness. She shed a few tears when she met her granddaughters, engulfing them in hugs right away.

"You did more than watch and protect, I see," Jamie's father said, laughing low in his chest as he gazed at Kenna and Jamie. "It was inevitable once we met. I refused to live without her," Jamie said, tugging Kenna into his side, his arm around her waist. Kenna laughed and said, "I had some say in this, too, husband." Otso said, "It is a good match. Your daughters are warriors at heart; they are fearless. Have they shown any signs of shifting? Or any Elven powers?" Otso turned to watch the two girls, who were making another snowman under the tree. Bram had walked over at this point, overhearing the questions. He said, "I sense great power in each of the girls. It will be interesting to see how these powers manifest due to their mixed parentage." He, too, was gazing at the girls as they played in the snow, their two grandmothers watching them, their eyes filled with love and pride.

Jamie cleared his throat and said, "They have shown a few talents. They can speak with animals and plants and make plants grow in the winter, and their archery skills are incomparable. As for transforming, neither has shown signs of it yet, although they are both amazing trackers and hunters. Plus, they are able to access the Goddess in the mortal world, as is Kenna." Bram beamed at Kenna in pride; Otso smiled and nodded his head. Kenna asked, "Will the girls be ostracized due to their mixed heritage?" Bram and Otso both shook their heads, Bram saying, "No, No, I do not believe so. Your daughters have been coming here for years and are truly loved by all." Then Otso said, his voice deep and growling, "There may be a few who believe in keeping the species separate, but they will not speak out. Who would dare challenge two of the most powerful rulers in this land?" Kenna took a deep breath and quietly said, "I hope you're right."

The eight of them were seated around a table ladened with a magnificent smorgasbord of delicious foods and treats. It had appeared out of nowhere while they had been visiting, much to Ember's delight. "This is amazing! I was so hungry," Ember said, then took a bite of a buttered roll and chewed happily. "You're always hungry," Noelle said, laughing, then taking a huge bite of her cheeseburger and closing her eyes in bliss. Jamie and Kenna chuckled as they watched their girls enjoying the food and the company of their four grandparents. Looking around the table, Kenna smiled and squeezed Jamie's hand. This is what she had always wanted growing up. Parents who were loving and wanted her and all of them wanting to spend time together as a family.

"What are we going to do about Hilda and her son Maxim?" Kenna asked her father, then took a bite of chocolate cake. It was the most delicious cake she'd ever had, and she quickly took another bite, much to Jamie's amusement. "I knew you'd enjoy the food here, especially the desserts," he said quietly, reaching over with his fork and stealing a bite. Kenna continued speaking to the group about Hilda, "Maxim says she received some concerning news a few weeks ago from her doctor. I believe that is the drive behind her desperation to pass through the Tree. She has aged significantly as well. She looks to be seventy-five years old, old enough to be your mother. Yes, she's much older looking than you are, father. Her hair is a dull grey, and she is quite wrinkled and thin." Bram, his expression tinged with sadness, said, "Yes, you're probably correct as to the reason she is so desperate. She has been in the mortal realm for far too many years and has lost her connection to the Goddess. She will pass into the Other soon, I believe, if she doesn't pass through the Tree."

Otso nodded his head, and his voice raised so all could hear; he said, "We need to deal with her. She must not be allowed to come through the Tree. Hilda is a danger to our granddaughters and your daughter. She has never accepted that she wouldn't be the ruler, never accepted that The Goddess didn't choose her, Bram. It is a deep-rooted bitterness and poison within her soul. Yes, it is a poison. As for Maxim, I'm not sure. Tai and Kai seem to think he is not like his mother." Bram, nodding his head, said, "While I agree with you that Hilda must be dealt with, I'm not convinced about Maxim. I need to meet the man before I will make a decision on him. Hilda, on the other hand, no. She will not be coming through the Tree. We will need to discuss this further, Otso, on how to ensure it doesn't happen."

Maia spoke up from the end of the table, saying, "Kenna, my daughter. The girls said you tapped into your magic while in the mortal world. Your hair was floating around, your skin glowed white, and your eyes emanated a green glow. Is this correct?" Kenna felt herself blush slightly and, nodding, said, "Yes, I guess so. I wasn't aware it was happening at the time. I was concentrating on Hilda and keeping her from my family. It just all happened so quickly; I wasn't even aware my eyes were glowing." Shrugging, she picked up the glass of wine in front of her and drank a deep drink. Jamie smiled with pride at Kenna and said, "You were magnificent. The power coming off you yesterday was immense. I'd never felt anything like it before. The fact that you and the girls can tap into the Goddess' power while in the mortal world is amazing and unheard of."

"Then she is the one in the prophecy. The one who will save us all," said Tati quietly, staring at Kenna with eyes full of hope and a touch of sadness. "Wait, what?! What prophecy?" asked Noelle, looking at her mother with a slightly worried expression. "There's a prophecy about mother? Really?" exclaimed Ember; she, too, looked at her mother but with excitement. Jamie and Kenna exchanged a look; neither had wanted their daughters to know about the prophecy just yet. "Can we hear it, Mom?" asked Noelle quietly. The adults at the table all exchanged looks before Kenna sighed and said, "Yes, you two can hear it. Keep in mind, it's just a prophecy; it doesn't necessarily have to be about me." Jamie raised an eyebrow at his wife and smiled, shaking his head. "Babe, you know it's about you. You felt it the night I recited it to you," he said to Kenna. Kenna rested her elbows on the table, head in hands, and sighed. Jamie put his arm around her and pulled her to his side, leaning down to whisper, "It's going to be alright. I'm here with you, and I will help you through all of it if it comes to fruition." Kissing her temple, he looked at his mother and asked, "Will you please recite the prophecy, Mother, since it was you who made it?" Kenna's head snapped up, and she looked at Tati with surprise. "You made the prophecy?" she asked Tati quietly. "Yes, it was I," she replied simply.

Tati began reciting the prophecy, her low voice and melodious.

From the realm of Marqueria, a stolen child shall arise with fiery red hair and emerald green eyes. Taken from her rightful place, a fate unforeseen, But destiny shall guide her to where she's meant to convene. Born with a spirit untamed, she'll grow strong and bold, A beacon of hope, a story yet to unfold. To the mortal realm, she was taken, but her purpose lies in Marqueria, where her powers awaken. With every step she takes, they shall tremble As her presence unravels the darkness that assembles. Her red locks shall symbolize her fiery heart, Burning with determination, she shall play her part. Through many trials and hardships, she will find her way, Harnessing her gifts to bring light, come what may. Her green eyes shall see through deceit and lies, Bringing truth and justice, as the prophecy implies. With her gentle touch, wounds shall heal, And in her presence, hope shall be revealed. She'll unite the divided, bridging the gap and bringing harmony to Marqueria's map. Her stolen past shall not define her fate, For she will rise above, she will conquer that weight. With compassion and love, she'll break the chains, And peace shall flourish where the Darkness once came. So let the prophecy guide you, hold it to be true,

For the stolen child shall bring peace anew. With red
hair ablaze and green eyes so bright, Marqueria shall
bask in her guiding light.

There was complete silence from those seated at the table.
Noelle and Ember stared at each other, expressions worried.
Turning towards their parents, they found them returning their
gazes. "Mom, you have to save Marqueria? But how?" asked
Noelle, brow furrowed. Suddenly, Ember exclaimed, "You're
like Harry Potter, mother!" Then she grinned. This broke the
tension, making Kenna and Jamie laugh. "Oh yes, Ember has
told us about this Harry Potter character," said Bram, nodding
his head and smiling at his granddaughter. "Mother is not like
Harry. Mother is a Princess and an Elf. Harry was just a wizard
and half-human," said Noelle, frowning at Ember and
continuing, "This isn't a good thing, Ember." Ember returned
Noelle's gaze, and understanding dawned in her eyes. "Is there
an evil wizard you have to defeat?" Ember asked her mother
with a worried expression.

Smiling softly at her girls, then shaking her head, Kenna
said with a small frown between her eyes, "I don't think there's
an evil wizard, but I do think there's evil. I felt a small part of it
the other day. I felt as if I were being watched. It felt cold and
dark and made my body feel as if someone was trying to invade
it. I saw a shadow figure gliding towards the Grove and yelled
at it. It turned towards me, and Lucy growled and barked at it,
and then it just disappeared. But that was back in the mortal
world, which is really confusing me now." This caught Jamie's
attention, and he quietly asked, "When was this? Where did it
happen? Where was I?" Laying a hand on his, she smiled and

said, "The morning when I first heard my name called in the Grove. I was sitting on the back deck after cleaning the house and before going to the Grove with the girls that day," Kenna said, then shivered. She continued, "It was a chilling feeling. Someone was watching me, but I couldn't tell from where. This was before the girls performed the Wind Spell on me, so I wasn't as in tune with the energy around me as I am now."

Jamie turned to his father and Bram, asking, "Do you think it's possible there are more from Marqueria who have passed through the Tree? Or is there another passage to the mortal world?" Frowning, Bram rubbed his hand over his beard and then said, "In over 3000 years, I've not found another way through. I suppose it's possible there's another way, but I doubt it." Otso grimaced and said, "If there are more from here who have passed through, it's not one of ours. Everyone is accounted for. Maybe a wolf or elf has managed to get through the Tree?" Looking at Bram questioningly. Bram said, "I will have a gathering of Elves and do a census. As for the Wolves, it's been several moons since I've met with them. I will send a missive to the Alphas. We journey together tomorrow, Otso?"

Otso nodded his agreement, picking up his cup of mead and drinking deeply, his eyes on his son Jamie. Otso asked, "Jamie, you'll be joining us tomorrow when we meet with the Wolves?" Jamie, turning to Kenna, asked, "You don't mind, do you, love?" Kenna raised an eyebrow, her expression wry, and said, "Not if you don't mind my tagging along, love." She then grinned at Jamie and waited. Otso, Bram, and Jamie all looked at one another, Jamie smiling and chuckling softly. Then, turning to Kenna, Bram said, "We would be honored if you'd accompanied us, but be warned, the Wolves are not as amiable as the Elves and Bears. They are very solitary and prefer to stay out of the politics of the Realm." She smiled at her father and said, "I can handle it, Father. I am, after all, The Savior of Marqueria." She then shook her head and laughed. "I will never get used to saying that. Anyway, I'm very interested in meeting the Wolves. There were two at the Tree the other day when the girls and I were returning to our Red House," she said.

Kenna looked up to find the men staring at her, two in stunned silence. "What?" she asked. "What did they look like? You never did say," Jamie asked, voice a little growly. Kenna shrugged and said, "Huge, gorgeous wolves. Black as night, with golden eyes similar to Jamie's. I heard their voices in my mind. They said, 'Welcome home, princess. You've been missed. Hurry on your return journey.' Or something like that. Why?" Otso chuckled and said, "You have met the two Alphas of the Wolves and received their blessing on your return. This will make things easier tomorrow."

Kenna turned towards her mother and Jamie's mother, asking, "Can the girls stay with you tomorrow while we are away?" Both women smiled hugely, eyes shining, and nodded. "I would love to spend the day with our granddaughters and get to know them better," said Jamie's mother, Tati. Both girls were bouncing in their chairs excitedly. "Hot Damn! We get to spend the day with our grandmothers!" said Ember, grinning broadly. Noelle rolled her eyes and said, "Language, Ember. You're a Princess and need to start behaving. No more potty mouth." Ember shook her head at her sister and said, "I've always been a Princess. A few cus words aren't going to change that." "Girls," said Jamie, raising an eyebrow at his daughters. They both said, "Sorry, father."

Jamie and Kenna stood up, signaling the end of their lunch and time for them to leave. As the others stood and walked away from the table, it and all it held, along with the chairs, disappeared. Kenna laughed and said, "I could really get used to this type of cleanup very easily." Then the girls both said their goodbyes to their grandparents, and with the promise of returning in the morning, Jamie and Kenna took their girls' hands and walked to the Tree to pass back through to their Red House in the Country.

Chapter Twenty-Six

In the mortal world, in the town of Butte, Hilda and Maxim were having lunch in the restaurant attached to their hotel. Hilda had a sour look on her face as she looked around the restaurant, which was a regional chain steak house, then turned towards her son and said, "This town leaves a lot to be desired. There are no upscale shops, and the decent eating establishments are slim." Her son, Maxim, shook his head and replied, "I find this town to be quite charming. I've never had a better steak anywhere in the world than at the place we ate last night. What was it called? Casagranda's? Yes, that was it. Their food was simple and delicious. Also, I've heard of this handheld pastry filled with meat and potatoes; I'm interested in trying that. A Pasty, I believe they call it."

Maxim took a large drink of coffee, then continued, "There is no better backdrop either. We are at the top of the Rocky Mountains, Mother. 'A mile high and a mile deep,' I believe, is one of the sayings in this tough little town. It really is rich in history. Though a mere 160 years old, it has been at the forefront of so many issues in this country and in the world, for that matter. Did you know they were one of the first towns in the western United States to have electricity? I also read that the Union is strong here, and it is called the Gibraltar of Unionism due to the citizens forming unions during the mining rush. It has a very rich and varied history, and I look forward to exploring this area." Maxim took a sip from his cup, then continued, "I may even lay down some roots myself. There is a large Finnish population, and they emigrated here in the past to work in the mines. Many of the families still remain. There was even a FinTown full of Finlanders."

His mother stared at him for a few moments, then sneered and said, "You think I care about this dirty little town? Do you think I care if they got electricity before anyone else? Well, I don't. You think so small. What is 160 years of history compared to the tens of thousands of years of my heritage? Why would you want to settle in this little place when I can give you so much more in my world?" Maxim sighed, setting down his coffee cup. Leaning closer to his mother and lowering his voice, he said, "I have told you many, many times before I do not want what you want. While I admit to some fascination with seeing Marqueria, I do not want to live there. My father was human, I am half-human, and I want to work on making human existence better for all. The world could be a much better place for everyone. It could be more like my homeland of Finland. I want to educate people and give money to those causes I deem worthy. I do not want to rule, especially a place I am not from and have little connection to." Shaking his head, he stared at his mother in disappointment and disgust he couldn't hide. "You need to ask forgiveness from those you have wronged, especially Kenna. What you did to your own flesh and blood disgusts me. I am ashamed to call you mother. You need to atone for your sins against your family," he said.

Hilda stared at her son, stunned at his impertinence. He had become bolder since arriving in this wild west little town. Lowering her own voice to a whisper yell, she leaned forward, arms on the table, and said, "How dare you speak to me like that?! I am your mother, and I demand respect. If your father hadn't left everything to you, I'd have disowned you and let you find your own way. You will show me respect, if for no other reason than the fact I AM YOUR MOTHER!" Maxim gave a quiet chuckle and said, "You do realize that when you demand respect for being a mother, you actually needed to have earned said respect, right? You gave birth to me. You weren't a mother. I was fostered off on the nanny, the maids, and anyone else you could find. If not for my father, I wouldn't have known the love of a parent. All I am to you is a means to the throne. You have some crazy idea that you can put me on the throne of Marqueria, and how you think you can accomplish that, I have no idea. I want no part in your plots and hunger for power. Leave me out of it."

His mother sneered at him and said, "Your father was weak too. It wasn't hard to make him fall for me; I was young and beautiful 32 years ago before this world sucked all my magic away. Now, they say I am dying? Bah! I will pass through the Tree and regain my magic, my youth, and beauty. Nothing you do will deter me." She stood up, threw her napkin on the plate, and stormed off toward their suite.

Maxim sighed. 'Why do I feel responsible for her?' He thought to himself. Was it because his father had asked him to take care of her? Towards the end of his life, his father accepted that his wife had never loved him. She had just wanted a rich husband and a cushy life. The son she gave birth to was a way of tying herself to him. In truth, their marriage was a sham. For the first twenty years, Hilda kept up the facade quite well. Her husband had no idea she was using him, but as their son grew to manhood, his father was forced to admit to himself that his wife was not the person he believed her to be. She was a cold, calculating, somewhat evil woman. While on his deathbed, his father admitted to his son that he understood what his marriage and his wife were really like. Even knowing this, he had asked Maxim to care for her after he was gone. Shaking his head again, he signed the bill, leaving a generous tip, and headed after his mother.

Chapter Twenty-Seven

The next morning, Kenna, Jamie, their girls, and the two Bear brothers were standing in the Grove near the Tree. They were discussing how the day was to progress in Marqueria. Jamie was saying, "I'm sure the Tree will be safe while we are all in Marqueria. There will be guards posted on that side to ensure no one passes from this side." Tai and Kai nodded in agreement, but Kenna looked unconvinced. "I think I should call and speak with Maxim. Ask him to keep his mother busy and away from here," She said, holding the business card Maxim had handed her. Jamie said, "If that would make you more comfortable, I'm ok with it." "As if I was asking your permission, husband," Kenna said, giving him a mock angry look and then laughing at his expression. "I would never expect you to ask my permission, wife," he said quietly. She reached up and gave him a soft kiss, saying, "I know, my love."

Kenna pulled out her cell phone and quickly dialed the number on the card. Maxim answered rather quickly, and she explained what they were asking him to do. He readily agreed, saying he would keep his mother occupied. He said that it should be easy since she had an appointment at the nearby medical facility, which should take most of the day anyway. After hanging up, she relayed the conversation to the others, her expression thoughtful. "What's that look? What's concerning you, love?" Jamie asked his wife. Kenna said, "She must really be dying. That completely explains her desperation to pass through the Tree. If she were to go to Marqueria and stay, would she be cured of whatever it is that ails her?" The three Weres exchanged guarded looks, and Jamie said, "Kenna, don't let Hilda manipulate your kind heart. If she passes through the tree and stays in Marqueria permanently, then yes, whatever damage there is to her cells will be repaired. She would eventually return to her prior self. But are you willing to take that risk knowing she hungers for your father's position? Knowing she abandoned you in the worst way possible?"

Kenna bit her lower lip and sighed, her expression troubled. "I will discuss it further with our fathers today. I'm not impulsive, as you know," Kenna replied to Jamie. "The many, many gnome statues in the garden by no means support that statement, my love," Jamie said, laughing loudly. Kenna faintly blushed and said, "What? I happen to think gnomes are adorable. Let's get going; the day is wasting." From behind her, Kenna heard, "Gnomes?! Here? Crap!" whispered by Kai. Kenna laughed and raised an eyebrow at her husband, shaking her head. Jamie reached down and lifted her up into his arms, laying a loud kiss on her lips, and said, "I'd have you no other way, wife. You're perfect the way you are." From behind them, the girls yelled, "Oooh, get a room!" "Now is not the time!" Everyone laughed and walked closer to the Tree, laying hands on it. Lucy ran up to Noelle and Ember, squeezing in between them just as they began to recite the chant together, asking the Tree for passage. When they passed through to the other side, they were greeted by a dozen men and women unfamiliar to them. There were six Bears, three of each gender, and six Elves, again three of each gender. Standing in the center of the twelve were Jamie's and Kenna's parents.

The girls walked over to their grandparents, giving each a hug, then stood next to their Nana and YaYa, excited about their planned day together. The six Elves and six Bears all bowed to Kenna and Jamie with reverence. A tall male Elf to the right of Bram took a step forward and said, "It is with joy we greet you this day, Prince Jamie and Princess Kenna." A tall female Bear took a step forward and said, "We, too, greet you with respect and joy, Prince Jamie and Princess Kenna." Again, they bowed their heads, then stepped back to join their comrades. Kenna felt her face heat, and she looked to her husband for directions. Jamie said, "We thank you for your kind greeting and are very happy to be back in Marqueria." Kenna looked towards the group of Bears and Elves, finding their eyes on her in curiosity, with expressions of hope and kindness. "Thank you. I appreciate your welcome more than you can know. I am still finding my way in Marqueria after so long an absence," Kenna said, smiling slightly as she met each guard's eyes in turn. Suddenly, Ember was next to a female Elf with braided silver hair, asking her excitedly if she could hold her bow. The Elf laughed and smiled down at Ember, asking, "Do you know how to use one?" Ember smirked and said, "I've been known to shoot around a bit. Damn, that's a beautiful bow! May I hold it?" The twelve guards all laughed out loud at Ember's use of the curse word, then looked to her parents, who were shaking their heads with faint smiles.

The female Elf asked Kenna, "Is it ok, my princess, if your daughter examines my bow?" Kenna nodded her answer and watched as Ember took possession of the beautiful bow. She examined it carefully and, with reverence, then asked for an arrow. The Elf looked surprised and looked to Kenna again, who nodded her head again, showing she was ok with it. Ember proceeded to nock the arrow, then turned to find something to shoot at. One hundred yards away was one of the red and pink fruit trees. Ember took aim and let the arrow fly. Everyone was watching as the arrow flew true and pierced one of the low-hanging fruits. With a shout of triumph, Ember then handed the bow back to the Elf and ran towards the tree to retrieve her prize and the arrow. "She has many talents with the bow for one so young," said the female Elf, then continued, "Does she have an elven bow yet?" Kenna shook her head and said, "No, she does not, as yet. Something we obviously need to remedy." "I am the Elven archery instructor and Creator. I would be honored to create a bow for the Princess if you would allow it," the Elf said, watching Ember saunter back towards the group. Noelle walked out to meet her, saying, "Nice shot, sis!" Ember handed one of the pieces of fruit to her sister and said, "Thanks. You'll have to try these bows. Dad was right. They're far superior to the ones we have back home." The archery Elf turned to Kenna, asking, "They both practice the art of archery?" "Yes, they've been shooting since they were quite young. We hunted near our home, and they've been very successful," Kenna replied, smiling at her daughters as they returned and munched on their fruit.

Bram cleared his throat loudly and said, "As entertaining as my granddaughters are, it is time for us to depart for our meeting." Otso was nodding in agreement and stepping forward towards his Bears; he said, "You six will stay here and guard the Tree along with the six from the Elven faction. No one is allowed through. Tai and Kai, you are to come with us." The brothers nodded, moving closer to Jamie and Kenna. Maia and Tati moved to stand with their granddaughters, and Tati said, "Come, my precious girls. Your Nana and I have an entire day planned for you."

The two grandmothers started to lead the girls and their dog toward the path to the Village, but both girls suddenly stopped and ran back to their parents, throwing their arms around them. As the four of them stood in their embrace, arms around each other, Lucy pushed her way into the center of their family hug, much to the amusement of the surrounding Elves and Bears, who were watching the affection with approval. Noelle said quietly, "Please be careful and take care of each other." Ember whispered, "Come back to us." Jamie and Kenna hugged their daughters tightly close to them. "We will always come back to you, my daughters," Jamie said, kissing each one on the head. "I would never leave you alone, sweethearts," whispered Kenna, a slight sheen of tears in her eyes. With a last kiss on the head, Kenna pushed them gently towards their grandmothers and said, "Now, go have fun with your grandmothers. Try to control the potty mouth, please, Ember." This comment elicited a chuckle from all present and caused Ember to roll her eyes as she backed up from her parents. "Love you!" The girls shouted at their parents as they and their dog joined their waiting grandmothers for the walk to the Village.

Otso was gazing after the four females and the dog as they made their way down the trail. He turned to Kenna and Jamie and said, "Those girls are the future of Marqueria, and we couldn't ask for better. They are truly remarkable young women, and you've done well by them." There were nods all around. Kai spoke up and said, "I've had the honor of observing the princesses in action. They are fearless, brave, intelligent, and powerful. They didn't hesitate to take Tai and myself on when they perceived a threat." Otso chuckled low and said, "Ahh, yes, they told us of your encounter. Judging from Ember's shooting, you'd not have walked away had they decided you were a threat." The Were brothers both laughed, nodding their heads in agreement.

Bram spoke up, saying, "Come, it is time for us to go. We have agreed upon a meeting place not far from here, but we need to leave now, or we will be late." The six followed a trail in the opposite direction of the Village, and looking back, Kenna saw that the twelve left behind had formed a shield around the Tree. Every other one facing the Tree, every other one facing out. She felt better knowing the Tree was protected and turned back to follow Jamie, with Kai in the front of the group and Tai in the rear.

Kenna was so busy oohing and aaahing over all the new types of plants and animals on their way to the meeting spot that she ran smack into Jamie's back when he stopped. Jamie turned around and caught her before she fell on her butt, laughing and asking, "Have you been daydreaming on our stroll through Marqueria?" Kenna joined in on his laughter and said, "No, I've been examining all the new plants and animals, some of which I vaguely remember, most I don't. I think I even saw a few fairies! There are fairies here, right? Tiny, about 6 inches tall, have wings and can fly, come in all different colors? Sounds like a fairy, right?" Kenna sounded very excited about the idea of fairies. Jamie pulled her into his arms, hand behind her neck, and pulled her in for a soft kiss. Pulling slightly away, he said, "Yes, those are fairies." There was the sound of someone clearing their throat; Jamie and Kenna turned their heads to see Tai standing there, grinning widely at them. "If you're done, your Highnesses, might we continue on to the meeting place?" Tai said, barely suppressing his mirth. Jamie and Kenna laughed and turned back towards the trail, continuing to catch up with the others.

Tai, following behind, spoke up and asked Kenna, "Do you really think Gnomes are cute?" Kenna looked back at Tai and said, "Of course! Don't you?" Tai was wearing a rueful look and shook his head, saying, "Pardon my language Princess, but I think they're little assholes. Always stealing things or hiding them from me, pilfering our pantry. No, not cute at all." Kenna stopped and stared at Tai. She breathed out softly, "They're real?" Jamie and Tai laughed loudly, and both nodded. Jamie said, "Yes, they exist, and yes, they are little assholes." Kenna grinned and said, "Well, then. I like them even more." Then she turned around and continued walking.

When they joined Bram, Otso, and Kai, they were standing on the edge of a large clearing, which had a small creek flowing slowly through the middle. The meadow was dotted with red and pink fruit trees that Kenna adored. Underneath one stood the pale pink unicorn with a silver horn, mane, and long flowing tail, grazing peacefully; Raina had come too. In this meadow, the grass was a deep shade of blue instead of green and spotted with melting snow here and there. On the far side of the meadow, under a massive tree with blood-red leaves and snow-white trunk, there were six men and women seated at a large round table made of dark honey-colored wood laden with food and drink. Kenna said, "Oh good! Believe it or not, I'm starving." She then started across the meadow without waiting for the men in her group.

Behind her, she heard her husband laugh, making her grin to herself. Kenna appreciated the fact that she had changed into Marqueria's clothing before this encounter. The material was exquisitely created, extremely soft against her skin. The clothing was form-fitting yet unrestrictive and not tight at all. It stretched and allowed her to move as she wanted and needed. Kenna smiled. Noelle was correct about the tunic and leggings being the better choice to fight in, and she thought that one never knows when a fight will present itself. She strode across the meadow, jumping the small creek, her long cinnamon curls blowing in the breeze and shining like dark fire in the sun. The sparkling dark green material of her clothing was stark against the blue and white of the ground. The six men and women assembled at the table suddenly stood up and moved to stand in a line in front of it. Kenna didn't slow down; she strode sure and strong. She continued walking until she was ten feet from the group.

She had to wait briefly before her husband, father, father-in-law, and the Bear brothers joined her. While she waited, she eyed the Wolves across from her. It was obvious who the leader was and who his mate was. She studied them as they studied her. Kenna could detect a hint of amusement in the female leader's eyes as she reached out with her magic to get a sense of the group. "You must be Kenna, the long lost Princess returned to us." Purred the female Alpha, looking her up and down with a faint smile. Kenna returned the perusal, finding her utterly stunning. Long, straight, dark brown hair flowed around her like liquid silk. Her eyes were the same shining gold as Jamie's, and her skin had a dusky hue. She was at least six feet tall and had long bones and strong, lean muscles. Powerful. That's the word that entered Kenna's mind. "My name is Luna; I'm the Alpha female of the Wolves. This is my mate, Ulric, our Alpha male," Luna said in a husky voice, indicating the tall man next to her. Kenna turned to study him, finding the male version of Luna. Taller, stronger, more muscles. Thick black hair braided in the back, same gold eyes, and dusky skin. Ulric also had a short, manicured black mustache and beard. Smiling at them both, Kenna nodded her head and said, "I am pleased to officially meet you. I do remember you from the Tree a few days ago."

Suddenly, Jamie slid his arms around her waist and pulled her back against his chest, kissing the top of her head. Kenna briefly closed her eyes and leaned her head back against Jamie's chest, breathing in his scent as it enveloped her, comforting her. Jamie said, "It's good to see you again, Ulric, Luna." Nodding his head to both. "You're looking older, cub. Last I saw you, you were passing through the tree and barely old enough to be on your own. You've grown up strong, Jamie," Ulric said, laughing, then continued, "And I see you found the lost Princess." Eyeing Jamie's arms around Kenna. Lifting her head up from Jamie's chest, Kenna said, "And I made him marry me." Giving the Wolves a wink, she turned her head and smiled at her father, who was looking at her with twinkling eyes. "You seem to be in a hurry today, daughter," he said softly. Kenna laughed and said, "I'm just excited to explore the land and try to remember everything I've forgotten." She lowered her voice to a whisper and said, "Plus, I'm starving, and they have food." She eyed the table behind the Wolves speculatively. Luna laughed out loud and said, "Oooh, I'm going to like her. She's feisty. Come, let's sit at the table and break bread together while we discuss the issues at hand." Luna grabbed Ulric's arm and tugged him to the table.

After they'd all taken a seat and served themselves, there was a brief period of quiet as the feast before them was consumed. Kenna groaned around a mouthful of pasta with cream sauce and chicken. Beside her, Jamie laughed softly. On the other side of Jamie, Otso let out a deep, loud laugh and said, "My daughter, by marriage, enjoys good food, but you should see how their younger daughter can put away a meal. That girl has a bottomless stomach; she does." Luna smiled at Kenna and Jamie, then said, "I have seen your daughters over the years and watched them grow into strong, brave, and kind young ladies. You and Jamie have raised them well." Kenna took a small sip of wine, then asked Luna, "Do you and Ulric have any children?" Ulric and Luna exchanged a loving look full of pride, and then Luna said, "We have three young ones. Two boys and a girl. The two boys are your daughters' ages, and our daughter is thirty."

Kenna stared at them, stunned, and said in surprise, "But you're so young! How can you have a daughter who is thirty?" Luna laughed and said, "We are similar to the Elves in longevity, so we're older than we look. Our daughter is named Ulrika. She's unmarried and hasn't found her mate amongst Marqueria's wolf packs. Our older son is Blaze, and our youngest is Alaric." "We should have our children meet soon. Noelle and Ember will need friends here," Kenna said, smiling at Luna and Ulric. They both nodded in agreement.

Otso stood up and said, "It's time we discuss the issue of Hilda and her son." Bram, seated next to Kenna, said, "Yes, you are correct, Otso." Then, with a wave of his hand, the table was cleared of food and drink. Kenna smiled, thinking she'd never get used to this easy cleanup. While the two Alphas, Otso, Bram, Jamie, and Kenna, remained seated, the other Weres stood up from the table and moved to form a circle around it, facing out. Tai and Kai placed themselves behind Kenna and Jamie, facing outward towards the other side of the Meadow. Ulric turned towards Kenna and said, "We understand Hilda made her presence known to you and trespassed on your land, attempting to gain access to the Tree?" Kenna nodded, saying, "Yes, that's correct. Her son Maxim mentioned in passing that she had received some unfortunate medical news prior to her coming to Montana. I believe she is dying and wants to pass through the Tree to regain her magic, health, and youth."

There was a brief period of silence as everyone digested what she had said. Luna asked, "What is her son like? Maxim, right?" Kenna sighed, shrugged, and said, "I don't feel that he is like his mother. He has no desire to rule. He's half-human, and I feel his ties are to the mortal realm." Otso turned to Jamie and began to speak, "Do you think...." Suddenly, the ground began to tremble, and Kenna began to glow. She was sitting eerily still, head tilted to the side as if listening to something. Quickly, she turned to Jamie and said, "Our daughters need us. We must get to the Castle now! There is an evil hunting them." Everyone stood up and moved to Kenna's side of the table. Kenna, still glowing, turned to her father and asked, "Is there a way we can get to the Castle instantly? I feel as if there is." Bram was nodding, his face showing deep concern, and said, "Yes, there is, but you're not trained yet." "Tell me what to do, and I know I can get us there!" Kenna demanded loudly, "Please!"

Bram said, "Yes, daughter, I will. Everyone who is going, please form a circle, grasping the hands of the ones next to you. You must not break the circle." The two Alpha wolves, Tai and Kai, Otso and Bram, and Jamie and Kenna, formed a circle and joined hands. Bram said, "Now, Kenna, you must picture the Castle and where you want to bring us exactly. Then reach down deep for your magic and let it flow through you and into those around you. Everyone must follow Kenna's lead and allow the magic in." Kenna said, "OK. I've got this. We go now!" She closed her eyes, her hair began floating about her head, her body's glow brightening to an intense white, and then they disappeared.

There was a pop sound, and suddenly, the group was standing on cobbled stones. Kenna broke out of the circle and sprinted towards the back of the Castle, calling her girls' names as she ran, Jamie at her side. When they rounded the corner and entered the rear garden, Kenna and Jamie stopped in their tracks, stunned by what they were witnessing.

Chapter Twenty-Eight

"This land is alive with magic, our life force, and that of the animals and plants. Reach down and feel the magic and power flowing through her as the rivers and streams flow upon the land," Tati was saying to her granddaughters, who were seated on the ground, hands buried under the snow, fingers dug into the ground. They had returned to the Castle but were outside in the gardens, both their grandmothers giving lessons in the ways of magic and nature. Noelle exclaimed softly, "I feel it! It's a gentle buzzing warmth." Ember said, "I, too, feel it. Noelle, if you close your eyes, you'll be able to see the actual flows of magic. They are like our rivers and streams. Why are they different colors, YaYa?" Tati smiled at Maia, who was seated next to her on the ground, and replied, "Each color represents an element. Dark blue is for liquid water, green represents plant life, brown for the earth and rocks, white signifies snow and ice, red is the fire within the land, silver signifies air and wind, and pink is for the Spirit."

Suddenly, Lucy started growling low in her throat and stood up from her spot under a tree. She walked to where the girls were on the ground, standing in guard mode, a low, rumbling growl emanating from her. Noelle, with her eyes closed, suddenly sat up straighter, head tilted to the side and a small frown between her eyes. "What does black represent,

YaYa?" Maia let out a small gasp and asked, "Do you see black, Noelle?" Her expression was very worried, and meeting Tati's gaze, she slowly shook her head. Ember whispered, "I see it too, and I don't like it. It feels cold and malevolent and as if it's searching for something." Noelle said quietly, her voice shaking, "I think it's looking for us. It's coming closer to us! Ember, stop touching the ground and disconnect now!" Noelle and Ember quickly pulled their hands up and opened their eyes, jumping to stand up. Their grandmothers rapidly followed suit. Lucy positioned herself before them on alert.

"Can it be, Tati? Is it back?" Maia asked, voice quiet and very worried. Tati turned to Noelle and Ember, saying, "This is very important. I need to know exactly what you felt and saw, please." The girls were pale and shaking slightly, but they moved closer to each other. Noelle wrapped an arm around Ember's shoulder and pulled her in tight. Ember took a shaky breath and said, "I spotted it in the distance shortly before Noelle asked you what black represented, and it was then that my bracelet started to feel hot on my skin. It was a misty, inky black, not like the streams but more like a fog, but also more solid. It was slowly moving around as if searching. When I reached out for it, it felt cold and wrong. Not the cold of ice or snow, but....." Ember trailed off, unable to put into words what she felt. Noelle whispered, "Death. It felt like death and nothingness, but yet hate and anger were mixed in with it as well. My bracelet got hot, too. Why?" Maia said, "Your bracelets and your mother's matching one are made from protection gems, which are spelled to detect evil and protect you from it when it is present. It was working, and that is why the evil couldn't find you at first."

Exchanging a worried look and a nod, Tati and Maia each quickly grabbed a girl and gently guided her into the nearby circle, etched deeply into the white stones, each stone imbedded with Black Tourmaline and Amethyst. Lucy stood between the girls, growls increasing. The grandmothers then put their arms around their granddaughters, forming an inner circle the girls held within their embrace. Tati and Maia began to chant softly:

In the depths of darkness, evil does its search
Reaching towards our most precious adored.
We cast this circle of protection to hold.
With perfect light and perfect love
We call upon the Spirits above
We call upon the Earth below
We call upon the Air surround
We call upon the Water that flows
We call upon the Fire Within
To ward off the shadows and banish the dark.
We raise a shield, protection assured
With each verse we weave, a barrier is formed
A sanctuary of light, our loves, it enfolds
By the power of Earth, Water, Air, Fire and Spirit
We cast this circle of protection to hold.

Within the embrace of their grandmothers, Noelle and Ember felt the power emanating from the two women. The sisters felt the barrier form around them with a popping sound at completion, and then a fine silvery film formed over their heads, creating a bubble from the circle etched into the ground to a few feet over their heads. The wind began rushing about, lifting their curls and throwing them around their heads. Dark clouds instantly covered the skies and blocked out the Sun. Then lightning shot across the sky, and thunder boomed loudly, and the ground trembled beneath their feet. "Nana?! YaYa!! What is happening?!" cried Noelle, her arms holding Ember tightly to her. Ember laid her head against Noelle's chest, fearfully watching the sudden storm raging violently around them. Tati said, "Sshhh, my child. It will be ok, my darlings. We have worked a protection spell and are within the circle. We are safe. Just breathe." Maia added, "Do not leave the circle, sweethearts. The inlaid protection spells around the Castle will repel the evil. The black you were seeing when you touched the magic is pure evil, and it is hunting you both. I have sent a message to your mother; they should be here soon, but the entity will most likely be gone by then."

Their grandmother's arms still encircling them, and their arms encircling each other made the girls feel safe. But then a flicker of anger sparked deep within them both because they hated feeling weak and vulnerable. So, without a verbal word spoken between them, they moved in tandem. Their arms dropped from around each other, and then Noelle said, "Nana, YaYa, please let go of us. We are fine, but we need some space." Maia and Tati exchanged a glance, both worried, but then lowered their arms and took a step back, freeing the girls. All of them still remained within the circle, as it was very large at fifteen feet across.

When their grandmothers had released them, Lucy moved to stand beside them, and then Noelle and Ember placed their hands in front of them, palms touching, and closed their eyes, facing each other. Their bodies began to glow, and their hair of fire floated gently around their heads, untouched by the violent winds around them. Maia and Tati both gave a gasp of surprise but didn't interfere. Together, the girls began to chant,

By the power of the Goddess and Sacred Light

We banish you, Darkness, from our sight

return to the shadows from which you came,

To be devoured by the Eternal Flame.

Begone, Darkness, we banish you.

Into the dark, we will pursue. Begone!

The brightness emanating from the sisters became blinding, yet the heat was comforting and warm. At the last word, which was spoken in such a commanding tone, a shockwave burst outward from the circle, and the evil was gone. Suddenly, the sun shone brightly, and the breeze gently danced. The girls opened their eyes to find their grandmothers watching them with amazed looks on their faces. "How did you do that? How did you know to do that?" asked Maia in awe. "Our granddaughters are very powerful, it would seem," said Tati, shaking her head in wonder. Noelle shrugged and said, "We just knew. It felt right. We heard a voice telling us what to do, and it felt right. Oh, and I can talk to Ember in my head now." Grinning, Ember said, "Yeah, you can't keep secrets from me anymore, Noelle." Noelle smiled and gave her little sister a hug, saying, "As if I could ever keep a secret from you." They all laughed at this, their relief palpable. Lucy gave a happy bark, tail wagging.

Suddenly, their parents were there right next to them, enfolding them in their arms, holding them tightly. Saying nothing. Lucy squeezed her way into the middle of them, and the five of them remained in the embrace until Kenna leaned back and asked, "Are you ok? Were you hurt?" Her eyes examined them both for injuries and found none, and she breathed a sigh of relief. Jamie asked, "What happened? Why did you need to cast a circle?" Then, he glanced at his mother and mother-in-law as the grandfathers entered the circle, anxious to see their loved ones and confirm for themselves that they were indeed safe. "It was evil, Daddy, and it was hunting us," said Ember, eyes wide. Her father pulled her back into his arms, hugging her tightly.

Noelle put an arm around her mother's shoulder, cuddling close, then said, "We were practicing our magic and touching the elementals which flow within the land when we felt and saw the black evil. It was searching for us, and I could tell when it found us. It made a beeline straight for Ember and me, and our bracelet got hot. We disconnected, and then Nana and YaYa set the circle and did a protection spell." Noelle then glanced up at her parents and grandparents, noticing two adults she didn't know standing with Tai and Kai a few feet away. Glancing down, she bit her lip, looking a little ashamed, and then said quietly, "I got angry, I got so angry. I couldn't help it. I hated feeling helpless and threatened. So, I connected with Ember's mind, and we suddenly knew what to do. It was instinctual. We drove it away together." Her father laughed and said, "Yes, we saw what you did. We arrived just in time to witness your amazing magic."

Chapter Twenty-Nine

Kenna disengaged herself from the family group hug and stepped to the outer rim of the circle, examining it. Lucy followed her over and sat at attention, eyes alert and scanning the surrounding area. Kenna knelt on her knees at the edge and laid her hands on the ground, pushing through the snow and touching the soil beneath, feeling for the magic in the land and the evil that was hunting her daughters. Her hair began to float softly about her head, her skin giving off a faint glow. Closing her eyes, she searched with her mind and magic, soon finding the retreating darkness. It felt cold and dead but was emanating hatred and anger; Kenna didn't like the way it felt. She sent a blast of pure white magic towards it, melting it into nothingness. The darkness could no longer be felt, but she had a feeling there was more out there hiding somewhere.

Standing up and stretching, giving Lucy a scratch behind the ears and a kiss on the top of her head, Kenna turned back to find all eyes on her. Blushing slightly, she said, "That piece of darkness is no more, but I feel there is more hiding out there somewhere. It was just a scout of sorts." Maia walked to her daughter and, taking her hands into her own, asked, "How did you know how to destroy that piece of darkness? How did your daughters know such a powerful banishing spell?" Maia's expression was puzzled but held a hit of pride as well.

Kenna shook her head slowly, a look of consternation on her face. She said, "I don't know. There was a female voice in my head. It instructed me on how to perform the spell. I hear her sometimes; I have over the years. Especially when what I was experiencing was horrible and painful." Kenna looked up to find everyone watching her with expressions of awe and wonder. She blushed again, asking, "Did I do something wrong?" Maia suddenly wrapped Kenna into her warm embrace and said, "No! No, my dear, nothing wrong and everything right. You have been blessed by the Goddess, and she has been with you all your life. She is the voice in your head, She is your guiding light, She has been teaching you all these years." Maia rubbed her hand up and down Kenna's back in a soothing way. Kenna soaked up the mother's love she had been denied most of her life, eyes prickling with unshed tears.

Noelle and Ember walked to their mother and Nana, Noelle quietly saying, "We hear her too, Mom. She has been talking to us since we moved into the Red House. She has been guiding us as well. She told us how to banish the Darkness." Ember nodded in agreement and said, "She is everything good and filled with love and light unless we are threatened, and then I feel she is wrath. We have learned so much from her." Kenna gave each of her girls a hug, and while still holding their hands in her own, she turned towards the crowd of watchers. "Girls, there are a couple of new faces I'd like to introduce you to," Kenna said. Ember piped up, "Oh, you mean the Wolf Alphas? Yes, while we haven't officially met, we have seen them around often." Lucy was at her side, and Ember walked to the Wolf Alphas and stuck her hand out. They stared at her hand, then looked at Jamie for understanding. Jamie laughed and said, "She is introducing herself; shake her hand." Ember reached out and grasped the Alpha female's hand and pumped it up and down. "Like this," she said. "Oh! Yes, of course. We do this, though," and the Alpha female grasped Ember's forearm with her hand and told Ember to grasp her forearm. Then she said, "Well met." Ember said, "I much prefer your greeting."

Lucy gave a quiet bark, tail wagging, and sat waiting for the Alphas to acknowledge her. This brought laughs from all around, and then the two Alpha Wolves knelt down and touched foreheads with Lucy. Luna said, "It is an honor to finally meet the guardian of the two Princesses. We have witnessed your bravery over the years, sweet Lucy." Lucy gave Luna a doggy kiss, then turned to Ulric, who quickly stood up and said, "I do not need a kiss, Lucy. But yes, you are a fitting companion for the Princesses." Lucy gave another quiet bark, then returned to Kenna's side.

The Alpha female said, "I am Luna, and this is my mate, Ulric. We are pleased to finally meet you both, Princesses." Ember said, "I am Ember, and this is Noelle, my sister. Don't let her fool you; she is older than I by a mere twelve months, not the ten years she'd like you to believe." The Alphas both chuckled and inclined their heads towards Noelle, smiles on their faces. "We have watched you often over the years. I watched you as you became amazing young ladies, brave, strong, and kind. We have two cubs your age and would love to introduce you to them when the time is right," Ulric said, her voice low with a slight growl to it. Noelle replied, "We look forward to the introduction. We don't have any friends in the Mortal world where we were born, and there aren't any elves our age around here to hang out with."

It was then that Kenna interrupted the introductions, firmly saying, "Now, is someone going to tell me exactly what it is that is hunting our daughters? This is more than a faction of Marqueria residents who want to take over the mortal realm. I realize now you've been telling me half-truths, and I need all of it so I can protect my daughters." Her expression was stormy, and her green eyes gave off a faint glow. Jamie walked over and laid his hand on her shoulder, saying, "Calm, my love. Bram, if you do not mind, we can all go inside the castle and have the entire tale shared by those in the know." His eyes were cold and hard as he looked around the group of leaders, continuing, "Because my wife is correct. There will be no more half-truths from any of you."

Chapter Thirty

Everyone was assembled in the library except for Lucy. She had decided to lie in front of the fireplace in the Great Room and sleep in her comfy bed. Kenna, Jamie, and their girls sat on a green sofa across from Bram, Maia, Otso, and Tati. The Wolf Alphas sat on a sofa placed in the space between the other two sofas, the sofas making a U shape, with the giant fireplace at the open part of the U. Tai and Kai placed themselves behind Jamie, Kenna, and the girls having assumed the positions of bodyguards again. Ember turned around and gave them both a huge grin and a wink before turning back to face her grandparents. Kenna spoke softly but firmly, "I will not accept anything but the entire truth from any of you. If we are to bring our daughters here to live, we need all the information, no matter how dark it is. We need to have all the tools available to us for the protection of our family." She met every gaze in turn, not backing down.

Bram was the first to break the silence, saying, "I apologize, daughter. It was never our intention to withhold information; we just believed we had time to let you adjust to all the changes before we burdened you further. Apparently, we were wrong." In her fifteen-year-old smart-aleck voice, Ember said, "Ya think?" Jamie turned to Ember and gently said, "Ember, be respectful. You have a voice here, sweetheart, but it will be used respectfully. Do you understand, daughter?" Ember blushed lightly and said, "Yes, father. I apologize for my tone. But I need you all to understand I am very, very upset as well. Noelle and I were the ones being hunted. We felt the evil that was in search of us. It was the worst feeling I've ever felt," she sighed, then continued, "But, you're correct, and I will be more respectful. As long as they are 100% honest with us." This last was delivered as she stared at her grandparents with hard eyes. Noelle put an arm around Ember's shoulder and pulled her close, saying, "It's ok, Ember. We're ok. The Goddess was with us and showed us how to protect ourselves. I'm sure our grandparents didn't mean to put us in harm's way." But Noelle, too, stared her grandparents down.

From the direction of the Wolf Alphas came a muffled laugh, making Kenna turn towards their sofa, eyes twinkling with mirth, trying to suppress her laughter as well. She and Luna exchanged a smile, Luna giving Kenna a nod and a wink. Kenna turned back towards the grandparents, seeing that all four had rather sheepish looks on their faces. Otso ran his hand through his hair, sighed, and said, "Never have I ever felt as small as I do now, with these two young cubs chastising us with just a look and a few words. We apologize to you both as well, our granddaughters. We never intended for you to ever be in any danger. Yes, you all will hear the entire tale of the Darkness."

Otso then let out a booming laugh, turning to Jamie and saying, "As I've said before, you have done well, very well by these girls. But I do not envy you the battles to come with these two formidable cubs as they continue to grow and test boundaries." There were chuckles all around, which broke the tension. Maia turned to Tati and said, "Why don't you start the tale? Since it was you who had the prophecy and you who saw the beginning of the Darkness." Tati gave Maia a small smile and inclined her head in agreement.

"Marqueria had always been a land of light and harmony, where all species coexisted in peace. That is until Bram's father found the entrance to the Mortal Realm. Over a millennium of traipsing through the Tree and around the Mortal world allowed something to slither into our world. At first, we didn't notice, as it kept going to the shadows. But soon, discord began amongst the species. The Wolves moved further into the forest, away from the Elves and Bears. The Bears kept to themselves more and more, forgetting age-old alliances. Then, among the Elves, infighting began, and it started with Hilda. She wanted to do away with following the Goddess altogether. She believed that because she was the firstborn, she should rule, regardless of whether the Goddess chose to bless her or not. And The Goddess chose not to bless her. This jealousy and desire to rule is believed to have come from the Mortal world when the Darkness snuck through the Tree. Hilda was taken with it; she sought it out and began to practice in secret, soon recruiting others who thought the same way she did. All this we found out later, of course, after she had taken you through the Tree."

Kenna stared at Tati, and with surprise on her face, she asked, "Are you telling us that there was no jealousy or evil in this world before my grandfather began traveling to the Mortal realm?" Tati nodded. "That is correct. The evil came from the Mortal Realm," Tati replied to Kenna.

Jamie and Kenna exchanged a glance, both showing surprise. "If the evil originated in the Mortal Realm, then maybe there's information there on how to fight it. On how to eliminate it completely," Kenna said, raising an eyebrow at Jamie. He nodded, then said, "As much as the four of us know about the Mortal Realm, we should be able to find information about it. We can start with the Bible." Noelle spoke up now and said, "There's plenty of information available on the internet and in libraries. Ember and I can help you search, as we are extremely tech-savvy. But the Bible, Dad? Wasn't that just a book written by men way back when? A way for them to control the masses and subjugate women? Isn't it a book of fiction?" Kenna spoke up, "There is a lot of truth in the Bible, sweetheart. There actually was a man named Jesus; he actually existed and traveled around preaching and taking care of the sick and poor. Do I believe he was the actual son of God? I didn't before I was made aware of all this and Marqueria. I'm still not sure, but the Bible is a good place to start for information on combating evil. It's full of stories of good versus evil, Angels, Demons, and the Devil."

"Does this mean we have to delay our move to Marqueria?" Ember asked, a frown marring her beautiful face. Jamie took a deep breath and let it out slowly. Turning to Kenna, he asked, "What do you think, my love?" Kenna looked around at the faces of the leaders of Marqueria; each one turned towards her in expectation of her answer. "I don't think we need to delay our move, but that being said, I want to know what is being done to ensure the safety of Noelle and Ember," she said.

Bram nodded and said, "The Castle itself has enchantments and protection spells built into it. This action was taken soon after we became aware of the presence of the Darkness here in Marqueria. There are circles within circles, within circles of protection. The outer circle surrounds the entire outer wall, grounds, and Castle. The wall itself is a giant protection circle, with protection gems embedded in each stone. Then, there's a large circle inside the wall that surrounds the entire grounds and Castle. Then the Castle itself is round and is a protection circle. Then, within the grounds of the Castle, scattered throughout the gardens and courtyards, are smaller circles, like the one the girls used today. They are etched deep into the stone, with the spells embedded within the stone. Each tower is a protection circle as well. The stones used to build all this are also embedded with protection gems, Black Tourmaline, and Amethyst, which are also placed in the glass of the windows. Once a circle is cast, the Darkness cannot get through. But after seeing the girls in action today, I'd say they can take care of themselves."

Ember asked excitedly, "So we will be living here with you, Papa, and Nana?" Jamie and Kenna exchanged smiles. Maia smiled at her granddaughter and said, "Yes, if that is what your parents want. Your family will have a tower to yourselves." Noelle and Ember turned to the parents, pleading looks on their faces. "Can we? Please?" asked Noelle. Jamie said, "Yes, we have already discussed this and feel it is best to start out here for now." "Yes!" cried the girls in unison.

"Can we access the internet from here, which is in the Mortal world?" Kenna asked. Luna spoke up now, saying, "Yes, you can. Our sons and daughter use it often to study the ways of the Mortal Realm, so they can be prepared for the future in case the knowledge is needed." Kenna and Jamie stood up, pulling their daughters up with them. This signaled to those present that this meeting was over. Jamie said, "We will return to our home and prepare for the move, then. In two mornings, we will come back to Marqueria." Tai and Kai moved to stand with the family of four as they prepared to leave. Kenna asked her father, Bram, "Would I be able to move the six of us and Lucy to the Tree, like I moved us to the Castle?" Bram nodded his head and said, "Yes, you are very powerful and did amazingly well, as if you'd been doing it your entire life. It should be easy for you." Goodbyes were said all around, and then the six returning to the Mortal world joined hands. Lucy was in the middle, leaning against Kenna. They were gone in an instant, leaving the leaders of Marqueria alone to discuss their plans further. The safety of Noelle and Ember was of utmost importance to all present.

Chapter Thirty-One

Back at the Red House in the Mortal world, Kenna and Jamie were sitting at the dining room table, several Bibles scattered over the table, bookmarkers inserted at various passages within the books, as well as books on folklore and Native American oral history. At one end of the table, Noelle and Ember were sitting in front of their laptops, researching the great evils of the world, past and present. From the kitchen came the sounds of cooking activities, an occasional swear word, and the clang of a dropped pan. Noelle and Ember giggled at the sound of the dropped pan and the loud cuss word.

Kenna looked up towards the kitchen with a worried expression, asking, "Should I go help them? From the sounds of things, they seem a little lost in there. Plus, I don't want my kitchen destroyed." Jamie gave a quiet chuckle, shook his head no, and said, "No, stay away. It would insult them if you were to interrupt and take over. They are doing what they believe is their duty to us, protecting and feeding us while we do our research. They are warriors of the Bear clan, and it is ingrained in them to protect and care for their Prince and Princesses, especially the cubs." Kenna gave one last concerned look towards the kitchen and sighed. "Fine, but I'm not cleaning up the mess they're obviously making," she said rather grumpily, returning her attention to the Bible and the passage she was highlighting with a green fluorescent marker.

"I think I found something!" exclaimed Noelle from the end of the table. Her parents stood up and walked to where the girls were seated, peering over Noelle's shoulder at her screen. "See here? This entry is right there. It mentions a great evil that took over the land. According to this, it was over thirty-five hundred years ago. So before great-grandfather found the entrance through the Tree, right?" Kenna nodded, then asked, "Does it say where this evil originated?" Noelle tapped a few keys, then scrolling down, let out a quiet gasp, and said, "You won't believe where it says it originated from!" She turned in her seat to face them and said, "I think it says Montana."

Ember softly breathed out, "No waaayy." Kenna and Jamie stared at Noelle in stunned silence. The silence was broken by Kai and Tai, who yelled from the kitchen, "Lunch is ready!!" "Come and get it!" Ember jumped up, saying, "I'm starving!" Then quickly walked towards the kitchen. Noelle sighed and said, "Let's go eat. We can talk about this over lunch and include Tai and Kai. Although, I'm a little scared to see what they cooked for us." She laughed as she walked towards the kitchen. Jamie and Kenna exchanged amused glances and followed their daughters in to see what they were being served.

When Kenna entered the kitchen, she was pleasantly surprised. It was spotless, but for the breakfast counter, which contained four large pizzas, each one with different toppings, spread across the counter. There was one pepperoni, one veggie, one full meat, and one just cheese. The pizzas looked professionally prepared and smelled amazing. Ember was already placing several pieces on her plate, one from each pizza. "Boys! I'm impressed. I didn't think you had it in you," mumbled Ember, around a mouthful of food. "Ember, manners!" said Noelle as she, too, grabbed one of each, then went to sit at the breakfast nook next to Ember. "Don't talk with your mouth full of food, Ember," Kenna said, eyeing her younger daughter as she crammed another bite into her mouth. Ember nodded in acknowledgment and continued to chew.

Everyone was finally seated around the breakfast nook, munching on pizza, when Noelle told Tai and Kai about the information she had found regarding the evil that was here over three thousand years ago. The brothers stopped chewing and looked to Jamie and Kenna in surprise for confirmation. Tai asked, "Can this be true? Montana? As in here? The Tree? Our Tree?" "I'm afraid so. Apparently, 'an evil emerged from a great tree near the top of the tall mountains.' According to the entry. It's an old Native American oral myth or traditional story, passed down by word of mouth through the generations," Noelle said, then took another bite of the meat pizza.

"You two really know how to make great pizza. Where'd you learn?" Ember asked between bites. The brothers both gave Ember a smile, Kai answering, "When we first traveled through the Tree, we realized we needed to earn some money as that is how this world is set up, but we had no documentation, so we couldn't get hired. The only place that would finally hire us was a pizza joint in uptown Butte called The Vu Villa Pizza. The owner took pity on us and hired us under the table. He also taught us how to make the best damn pizza pie in Montana." Jamie laughed and said, "You've got to be kidding me! Yes, we know the place well. I actually worked there during college until I graduated." Jamie shook his head and said, "Huh, such a small world. I'm amazed we didn't run into you before you came with Hilda."

Kenna, having finished her pizza, pushed her plate away, took a sip of soda, and asked Noelle, "Does it say which tribe this myth comes from?" Noelle nodded, saying, "The myth is found across all tribes. The Evil One is the common name for it. They say, 'The Evil One deceives and preys on the Five-fingered beings.' That is all I could find so far. But from what I've read, it has to be our Tree. 'North of the boiling and smoking land, north of the Burning Mountains, South of the Backbone of the World, the White Tree grows in the Rocky Mountains.' This is what I found already translated." Kenna gave a small gasp and said, "I know where those places are from my Native American studies class. The boiling and smoking land and the Burning Mountains is referring to Yellowstone National Park. That's south of us. The Backbone of the World is Glacier National Park, which is north of us. And, of course, some native Americans called the Rocky Mountains, 'Asin-wati' which means rocky mountains. Which is exactly where we are and where the White Tree is." Kenna leaned back in her chair, shaking her head. "It sounds as if they are saying the evil came out of the Tree and infected the land, doesn't it?" Kenna asked the group.

Ember stood up and began to gather the dirty dishes with Noelle's help. As she walked into the kitchen, Ember said, "Then the evil came from Marqueria and not from the Mortal realm." Jamie and Kenna stared at one another with concerned looks, and then Jamie turned to Tai and Kai. "Do you remember anything about a great evil from three to four thousand years ago?" he asked them. The brothers shook their heads, and Kai said, "We are only five hundred years old, but as far as we know, there are no tales told regarding a great evil, except for the time Princess Kenna passed through to the mortal world thirty-two years ago." Kenna stood up and said, "Please excuse me." And left the room.

"We need to get this information to Bram and Otso as soon as we can. In one hour, we will meet on the patio for a trip through the tree. This can't wait." Jamie said as he finished cleaning off the table, then walked into the kitchen. The brothers followed him, and then he told his daughters, "Girls, go pack and bring everything you think you can't live without. Put it in a backpack." Then Tai said to the girls, "Don't worry about the dishes. We will get them loaded and washed." So, the girls went up to their room to gather what they wanted to take with them and to change into appropriate clothing for the journey. Jamie gave each of the Bear brothers a squeeze on the shoulder, saying, "Thank you. I need to go check on Kenna. She left rather abruptly, and I'm concerned." Jamie left the kitchen to go find his wife.

Chapter Thirty-Two

Jamie finds Kenna in their bedroom suite just as she finishes changing her clothing. She was now dressed in the tunic and leggings of Marqueria, with soft leather light tan boots. This time, she was wearing a pale sage green set, which made her fiery hair seem even more vibrant, and her eyes were greener. "Are you ok, wife?" he asked her as he wrapped her in his arms. Kenna cuddled into his chest, breathing his scent in, calming her nerves. She nodded and said, "I just needed a break from the discussion. Also, I knew you would want to take a trip through the Tree, so I came to get ready. Do you like my new clothing? Luna gifted it to me." Jamie pushed Kenna gently away to look over her new outfit. "The color is amazing with your hair and eyes. How do you like the clothing of Marqueria?" he asked her. "I've never felt material as soft as this, yet it's durable and keeps me warm. I absolutely love them," she replied. He leaned down, gave her a quick kiss, and headed toward their closet. "I need to change as well. We meet on the patio in less than an hour," he said. "Ok. I'm going to give Maxim a call to check in and see if Hilda is occupied," she said as she left the room to find her cell phone.

Maxim picked up on the first ring, sounding a bit frantic, and asked, "Has she shown up there?" "I'm sorry, what?" Kenna asked. Maxim said, "Hilda. Has Hilda shown up at your house? She has disappeared. After her doctor's visit, I left her in her room to rest and went to explore the town a bit. I was gone for two hours, and when I came back, she wasn't in her room. The desk clerk doesn't recall seeing her." "No, she hasn't come here. We haven't seen her. What was her state of mind when you left her?" Kenna asked.

Maxim groaned and said, "She was upset. They want to start chemotherapy, but she refuses. The doctor told her she had just a few weeks at most if she didn't receive treatment. I offered to stay with her, but she refused and practically chased me out of her room. I should have known she was going to make a break for it. I have a feeling she's headed for the Tree." Kenna said, "We're headed to the Tree now. I'll let you know." She hung up and then quickly joined the rest of the household on the Patio. Everyone was already there, wearing full backpacks.

"We have a problem," Kenna said to the group as she walked through the patio door. Jamie saw the look on Kenna's face and asked, "What's wrong? Is it Hilda?" Nodding her head, she explained what Maxim had told her on the phone. They all turned towards the Grove, looking for Hilda. Jamie, starting up the hill, said, "Come on, everyone. Let's go see if she's up there." Kenna, Noelle, and Ember followed Jamie up the hill, and Tai and Kai took the rear position. Looking back, Kenna was surprised to see that the brothers had changed into Marqueria clothing in shades of black and brown, and they were each wearing two short swords, one on each hip. Seeing her eyeing the swords, Tai said, "We came prepared for whatever awaits us, Princess Kenna. We are masters with these, so rest assured, your daughters will be safe." Kenna gave them both a grateful smile and continued up the hill after her daughters.

When they reached the Grove, Jamie was stopped just inside the tree line. He signaled back to the group to stop and wait. Noelle and Ember moved back to stand with their mother, each taking a hand. Tai and Kai separated, with Kai moving around the girls to join Jamie and Tai staying back with Kenna and the girls.

Jamie whispered, "I saw movement and scented something I'm not familiar with, which is concerning." Kai lifted his head and scented the air, then said, "I don't recognize this scent either. It feels wrong, though." From behind them, Tai said, "Ummmm, guys. You might want to look behind you." Turning around, Jamie and Kai were greeted by the sight of Kenna, Noelle, and Ember holding hands in a circle and glowing. Their cinnamon-red hair was floating softly around their heads; their skin gave off a silvery glow, and their eyes were shining green. Kenna said, "We recognize the scent and the feel. The Darkness is here."

"Kai, Hurry! Sketch a circle in the soil big enough for the six of us." Jamie said, then he grabbed the arm of his wife and pulled her and his daughters up to a flat clear part of the Grove, several yards from the Tree. Their backpacks were deposited on the ground just as Kai finished drawing a large, deep circle into the soft dirt, which the six of them entered quickly. Kai had also placed large chunks of many different colored crystals around the circle, just inside the line. Kenna recognized them as the same ones embedded in the stones in Marqueria and some from the ground surrounding the Tree. Jamie, Kai, and Tai formed a circle around the females, facing outward. Kenna, Noelle, and Ember joined hands again and began to chant.

In the depths of darkness, evil does its search
  Reaching towards our most precious adored.
  We cast this circle of protection to hold.
  With perfect light and perfect love
  We call upon the Spirits above
  We call upon the Earth below
  We call upon the Air surround
  We call upon the Water that flows
  We call upon the Fire within
  To ward off the shadows and banish the dark.
  We raise a shield, protection assured
  With each verse we weave, a barrier is formed
  A sanctuary of light, our loves, it enfolds
  By the power of Earth, Water, Air, Fire and Spirit
  We cast this circle of protection to hold.

With a loud "pop," the circle activated, and a film of silver formed over their heads. Kenna, Noelle, and Ember were all glowing like sunbeams, their hair still floating, but their eyes were open, and they were examining the surrounding area. Their glowing eyes moved to the Tree, and Kenna called out, "We know you're there. There's no use hiding from us, so you might as well come out, Hilda."

Chapter Thirty-Three

From behind the Tree, out stepped Hilda, but not Hilda. Her eyes were black, even the portions that were supposed to be white. There was a light mist of dark grey fog surrounding her. She walked towards their circle but stopped twenty yards away. When she spoke, her voice held an echo, as if someone was speaking with her. "You can't prevent me from passing through the Tree, not now that I have rejoined with the Darkness. I will now be strong enough to pass through without your help. If you leave the circle to try and stop me, you will die," Hilda said, low and echoey.

"Where was the Darkness hiding, Hilda? In this world or Marqueria?" Kenna asked, moving to stand in front of the group, much to Jamie's consternation. Hilda laughed an eery deep laugh and said, "You think you can trick the Darkness? Bah! Your Goddess is no match for the Darkness; His followers are many." Noelle and Ember had moved up to stand with their mother, each gripping one of her hands in theirs. Jamie, Tai, and Kai could tell that the mother and daughters were communicating with each other, but no words were being spoken out loud. The three males backed up a step to give the females some room to move, knowing something big was coming.

"Aahhh, I see you've brought your precious daughters for me to feast upon. I've had my eye on them since they first discovered the Tree. So much power in two such small creatures it was difficult for me to deny myself the pleasure of sucking them dry. But, I knew I needed to wait for the right moment, and it seems that moment has presented itself," The Darkness said via Hilda's mouth.

"You won't lay one hand on our daughters. You'll never get the chance," growled Jamie from behind his wife and daughters just as they ignited into a blinding white light. The three had been chanting softly, but now they raised their voices into a crescendo that they could all hear.

By the Light that shines so bright
We banish darkness from our sight
Evil darkness, you must flee
For only Love and Light shall Be.

A blinding blast of light emanated from Kenna, Noelle, and Ember, knocking the Darkness/Hilda to the ground, where It/she lay motionless. The mother and daughters released their hands and left the circle before Jamie or the brothers could stop them. Catching up to his wife and daughters, Jamie said, "Wait! Let me check her first." He moved out in front of the great loves of his life, a drive from deep within needing to protect them. As they approached the Darkness/Hilda together, Noelle and Ember suddenly said, "Stop!" The group stopped a few yards from where the figure lay unmoving. Noelle said, "I still sense the Evil within her. It didn't leave but burrowed deeper into her soul." Ember said,

"Mom, Noelle. Do you hear the voice of the Goddess? She's telling us what to do to hold the Darkness. Listen." The three females again joined hands and closed their eyes.

From behind Jamie, Kai whispered, "I've never felt so useless as I do now." Jamie turned around and said, "I know. This is hard for me to do, standing back and letting my wife and daughters battle where I cannot. But I trust in their strength and magic." Tai nodded in agreement, watching the three Princesses begin to glow again.

The three females moved to stand over the Darkness/Hilda, Kenna at the head and Noelle and Ember to each side of the motionless figure. Suddenly appearing to Kenna's right was a round green cloth containing a small pair of scissors, a jar with a lid, a bottle of water, a shaker full of salt, and a black candle. Kenna moved to the cloth, grabbed the scissors, and leaned down to cut off a chunk of Hilda's hair. She then placed the hair in the jar, along with a pinch of salt and half the bottle of water. Next, she screwed the lid onto the jar tightly and gave it a few shakes. She pinched the wick of the candle, and it immediately caught flame. Holding the burning candle in one hand and the jar in the other, Kenna let the melting wax drip over the lid until it was completely covered in black wax. Then she blew out the candle and placed the jar on the green cloth, returning to her position at the head of Hilda's form. Grabbing her daughters' hands, they began to chant again.

By flame and soot and blackened wax,
No longer shall anyone suffer your attacks.
We bind you now from doing harm.
By flame and soot and blackened wax,
No longer shall anyone suffer your attacks.

We bind you now from doing harm.

By flame and soot and blackened wax,

No longer shall anyone suffer your attacks.

We bind you now from doing harm.

The three females were glowing again, with their hair floating around their heads.

By the Goddess, so mote it be

Suddenly, Hilda gave a jerk, and her body arched off the ground. Kenna, Noelle, and Ember all stepped back to the circle, ushering the men before them. When they reached the safety of the Circle, they all turned to watch Hilda. Hilda's mouth opened wide, and a guttural scream issued from her throat. Just as suddenly as it began, it was over. Hilda's body collapsed to the ground, and she lay motionless again. Ember spoke up first, saying, "It's safe to leave the circle. The Darkness is bound. The Goddess froze the jar." They all walked over to where Hilda lay, cautiously gazing down at her.

Kenna leaned over and grabbed the now frozen jar, wrapped it carefully within the green cloth, and said, "We need to place this somewhere safe and keep it frozen." Raising an eyebrow, Jamie stared at his wife and asked, "What exactly did you three do?" Noelle spoke up, saying, "It was a type of binding spell. It will keep the darkness within Hilda's body until we can find a way to destroy it." Jamie looked at Hilda again and asked, "So, does she stay this way? Unconscious?" All three females nodded. "It was the only way we could contain the Darkness," Ember said. Kenna said, "I will take the burden of the guilt for this, my daughters. This is not yours to carry." Ember, eyes on fire, said, "There is no guilt to carry, Mother! She was evil; even without the Darkness, she was evil." Noelle said, "Ember is correct. There is no guilt with this." A tear sliding down her cheek, Kenna wrapped her daughters into her embrace, holding them tightly.

Chapter Thirty-Four

The sounds of someone rushing up the trail to the Grove caught everyone's attention. They all turned towards the entrance to the Grove, the men moving to the front to create a barrier between whoever was coming and the three females. There was movement at the tree line, and after a few seconds, Maxim walked slowly into the Grove, looking around. "Oh Shit," whispered Ember, much to the Bear brothers' amusement.

Maxim caught sight of the group of six and started to make his way towards them. Examining the Grove as he walked, his eyes roamed over the trees, bushes, and the crystals scattered on the ground. When he noticed the Circle, he raised an eyebrow and continued forward. He stopped a few yards from them, saying, "This Grove is amazing. It makes my skin buzz, but I feel so at peace here." He gazed around, a small smile on his face. "You can feel the magic of the Grove?" asked Noelle. "Is that what I'm feeling? Amazing. I didn't think I'd be able to, being only half-Elf," Maxim said, looking awed. Looking at Kenna, he asked, "Have you found my mother yet?" They all stared at him in stunned surprise, then quickly looked over to where they had left Hilda. She was gone.

"Ummmm...where did she go?" asked Noelle, walking over to where they had performed the Binding Spell. Ember joined her and slipped her arm through Noelle's as they stood looking down at the spot. "Did the Goddess take her?" asked Ember softly. "I don't know," answered Noelle. "What is going on? Where did who go? You found my mother?" asked Maxim, joining the group who had all moved to the spot where Hilda had been left.

Kenna looked up and met Maxim's eyes. Eyes so like hers and her parents' and whispered, "Maxim, we found her, or rather she found us. She wasn't herself, though. She had the Darkness inside, and it had taken her over. She, or the Darkness, threatened to drain our daughters and kill us all. We had to do what we did; there was no other choice." Kenna's eyes filled with tears, which spilled over to run down her cheeks. She said softly, "I'm so sorry, Maxim." Maxim stared at Kenna. "Are you saying she's dead?" he asked, running his hand over his face and into his hair. The look on his face was a mixture of sadness, pain, and relief.

"She wasn't a very good mother to me. I'm surprised I feel sad at all. I knew she never really wanted or loved me," he said, then shrugged and continued, "I know she did a horrible thing to you, Kenna. What she did was unforgivable, and she won't be missed, not really." Kenna spoke up, "She's not dead, Maxim, that is, as far as we know, she's not. We performed a binding spell on her and the Darkness to trap the Darkness inside of her. She was still breathing and lying right here on this spot. When we turned to meet you, we left her right here. But now she's gone. She just vanished." "What? I don't understand. Did you bind the darkness inside her? Forever?" he asked, his face a mask of confusion. "Only until we could find a way to get the darkness out of her safely and destroy it," Kenna said, moving to take his hands in her own, she continued, "She was fine when we left her to meet you. We have no idea where she went."

Maxim nodded and looked towards the Tree. "Do you think she went through the Tree?" he asked. As he looked around the assembled group, he realized the thought hadn't even crossed their minds. There were shocked looks from all. Noelle said, "We need to go check. She might have gotten through the Tree." Kenna moved to the Tree and walked around it, examining it closely. "I don't get the impression she has gone through, but I can't be sure," she said, then turning towards the others, said, "Let's all go back to the house and gather what we need, what we left behind like my backpack, then we can all go through the Tree." Maxim spoke up in a quiet voice, "But what if I am unable to pass through? I'm half human, and my mother wasn't exactly good." Ember smiled and said, "If the Goddess deems you worthy, you'll be able to pass. Don't worry. I sense nothing but good in you." Then she headed back down the trail towards their house.

Chapter Thirty-Five

Back down at the house, as the group reached the patio, Lucy could be heard from inside the house, aggressively barking and jumping against the door. "Something has her riled up," said Kai, looking around for anything out of place. Jamie went to the patio door, turned the handle, and pushed the door open. Lucy shot out, running full speed straight up the hill to the Grove. "What the Hell?!" shouted Ember, who then took off after her dog, Noelle, close behind her. Kenna shoved the jar with the frozen water and hair into Jamie's hands, saying, "Freezer!" And then turned and ran after her daughters and their dog. Jamie quickly placed the jar in the nearby freezer, shut the patio doors, and chased after his family, the Bear brothers, and Maxim close behind.

When the men reached the Grove, they found Lucy at the Tree, sitting at attention and just staring. Kenna and the girls were close to her, petting her back and making soothing sounds. When Jamie came within her field of vision, she turned her head to look at him and gave a long whine, then turned back to stare at the Tree. "We found her like this when we got here. She won't budge from this spot, and she won't take her eyes off the Tree," Kenna said, then she kneeled down next to Lucy and gently cupped her head, moving her own face closer to Lucy and meeting her amber eyes with her own green ones. "Lucy. What's wrong, sweetheart? Tell me what has you so upset," Kenna spoke softly, then leaned her forehead gently against Lucy's, closed her eyes, and whispered, "Show me."

Kenna had a soft glow emanating from her skin and remained in that position with Lucy for a few moments before gasping and suddenly standing up. Keeping her hand on top of Lucy's head, she turned towards the group and said, "Lucy says Hilda went through the Tree. The Darkness is still trapped within her but is controlling her." "But how did she get through the Tree? She has no magic left, and she was blocked," Maxim asked, looking confused. Kenna said, "The Darkness has enough magic to get them through. Apparently, the Darkness can move between worlds as he wants. Hilda's body was about to die, so the Darkness pulled her through so Marqueria could heal her. We need to get to Marqueria now!" The backpacks were quickly donned, and Kenna motioned everyone over to the Tree. Lucy moved to stand between the girls, refusing to be left behind this time.

Noelle quietly explained to Maxim how they were going to travel through the Tree and he looked a little apprehensive. "What if I don't travel with you? What do I do?" he asked Kenna. Jamie and Kenna exchanged a look, and then Jamie said, "If for some reason you are unable to travel through, you may return to our house and make yourself at home. It's a good place to wait. But I think Ember is correct; you'll be deemed worthy, and the Goddess will let you pass through." Maxim inclined his head in thanks and followed the directions the girls were softly telling him. When everyone was ready, the girls asked the Goddess for passage through the Tree. The next instant, found them all standing in Marqueria, the ground covered in even more snow than before.

Looking around, Maxim had an awed expression. Then he let out a loud gasp and took a few quick steps back. This caught the attention of everyone, who looked at where Maxim was staring. Thirty yards away stood two huge wolves, two immense brown bears, and Bram and Maia. Noelle and Ember walked to their Nana and Papa, giving each a quick hug. Then they greeted the other four, giving the two huge bears each a hug.

Kenna walked to Maxim and gently took his arm, leading him to where the girls were chatting with Jamie's parents and the Alpha Wolves. Jamie, Kai, and Tai followed quietly behind, all three on alert, their eyes constantly looking around. Lucy ran on ahead and greeted the two huge wolves with a touch of nose. She then went to her girls and sat between them; she, too, was on alert.

When Kenna reached her parents, she said, "Mother, Father, I'd like to introduce you to your nephew, Maxim." Bram stepped forward and held out his arm, grasping Maxim's forearm and saying, "Well met, nephew. I'm happy the Goddess deemed you worthy and allowed you through the Tree into Marqueria. I look forward to getting to know you better, but now is not the time for such a conversation." Maia scoffed and gently pushed Bram out of the way, then wrapped Maxim in a warm, motherly embrace, saying, "Welcome home, nephew. You are to stay with us; we will have rooms prepared for you." When Maxim stepped back from the hug, there was a sheen of tears in his eyes, and he ducked his head, saying,

"Thank you for the warm welcome. I wish my visit was under better circumstances. I'll let Kenna explain what has happened."

Giving both her parents hugs, Kenna stepped back to stand next to Jamie. She raised her voice enough so that everyone could hear her, then explained the events of the day in the Mortal realm. Tati, who was now in her human form, said, "Yes, we felt the disturbance when the Darkness passed through. We quickly phased here to meet you." Jamie asked, "What is the plan, mother?" Stepping forward and giving Jamie a quick hug, she said, "We are to assemble at the Castle and discuss it there, where there are very strong protections built in." Returning to her group of six, Tati reached one hand out for Otso's and one out to Bram, Bram reaching for Maia's hand, Maia reaching for Ulric's and closing the circle, Luna held Ulric's and Otso's hands. "See you at the Castle!" Bram called out as they vanished.

Maxim wore a stunned expression as he watched them all disappear. Turning to Kenna and Jamie, he asked, "Are we going to do that?" Noelle laughed and said, "Yes, we are. It's the easiest way to travel and the quickest." "Come on. Let's form the circle, and Mother can transport us," Ember said as she grabbed her sister's hand, then took one of Maxim's into her own. Kenna reached out and took Maxim's other hand, then one of Jamie's. Jamie took hold of one of Tai's hands, and Tai reached out and gripped his brother's hand; then Kai took hold of Noelle's hand, and the circle was completed. The first few times Kenna had done this, she was nervous, but now she felt like an expert. The next instant, they were standing in the courtyard of the Castle. Maxim gave a laugh and said, "I could get used to this type of travel!"

Chapter Thirty-Six

The group had assembled in the Library next to the roaring fire. The room seemed to change to accommodate the number of people present, so more seating was placed around the area. "So let me get this straight. Are you Father Christmas? And you actually visit human homes on Christmas Eve?" Maxim asked with an astonished look on his face. Bram gave a great laugh and said, "I haven't visited a human home in almost 300 years. It had gotten to be too dangerous, with all the modern inventions and security, not to mention all the weapons people have in their homes now. But, yes. My father and then I played the part of the human's Father Christmas."

Noelle and Ember were sitting with the Wolf Alphas, who were answering the questions being quickly shot at them by the two inquisitive Princesses. "Where is your home? Do you live in a Castle?" Ember asked. The two Alphas laughed, Luna shaking her head and saying, "No, my Princess. We live in a large house made of logs within one of the villages of Wolves." Noelle exclaimed, "A log cabin! Oh, I do love log houses." She smiled at Luna, who returned her smile and said, "I do as well. It's like living within a large tree." "When will you be bringing your children to meet us?" Ember asked. The two Alphas exchanged a quick, unreadable look. Maia, who had been keeping eyes and ears on the girls, spoke up, "Luna, Ulric. While this mess is being sorted out, and if you'd be willing, your children can come here and stay in a tower with the two of you. Tati and Otso stay here until we banish the Darkness and Marqueria is safe again. It would give the girls company, which I'm sure they'd really appreciate." Everyone present turned their gazes to the girls and the Wolves, waiting in expectation.

Luna and Ulric exchanged a smile, and then Ulric said, "It would be an honor to bring our sons and daughter here. We will go fetch them now and return soon." The Alphas stood up, held hands, and then were gone in the blink of an eye. Ember and Noelle both gasped, saying, "I didn't know they could travel like that. I thought they had to be with an Elf." She turned to look at her YaYa and PawPaw, head tilted, and asked, "Do you travel like that, YaYa?" The Bears smiled at their granddaughter, nodded, and said, "Yes, we can all travel like that. It is something we teach our young, but usually, they're not ready to travel alone until they reach adulthood." "Dad, you can travel like that? You don't need a mother to do it?" Ember asked Jamie. Jamie laughed and said, "While I can travel like that, it has been many years, and I would like to practice before I attempt to bring others along with me. Your mother is so powerful; she's able to bring many along."

Bram and Maia stood up and moved to the library door. "Come, we will show you all where you'll be staying," Maia said. The group stood en masse and moved towards the door, following Bram and Maia out. Ember and Noelle found their parents as they walked towards the library door, staying close to them as they followed the crowd.

Following Bram and Maia through the large Great Room lined with Christmas trees, Maxim and the Bear brothers grinned at each other when they saw Lucy next to the fire, asleep in her plush personalized bed. Maxim glanced around the Great Room, taking it all in. When they reached the double staircase, Maia stopped and turned to Maxim and the Bear brothers. She said, "If you three will follow me, I'll show you to your suite of rooms on the second floor of the main castle." Tai and Kai gave each other a questioning look, and then Kai stepped forward, saying, "While we appreciate your kind offer of our own rooms, we would prefer to stay in the same tower with your daughter and her family. Jamie and Kenna are our Prince and Princess, and it is our duty to ensure their safety. We are meant to guard their young, the Princesses Noelle and Ember." Bram moved next to his wife, taking her hand in his hand, and said to the Bear brothers, "We would be honored if you guarded our daughter and her family. We will place you in their tower." Turning to Maxim, Bram said, "Come, I will show you to your rooms and let you get settled. You will find a wardrobe full of clothing which will fit you perfectly. Feel free to rest and freshen up before we meet in the dining room for Dinner with the Alphas and their families." Bram and Maxim moved to the stairway on the left and began walking up.

Maia turned to Otso and Tati, asking, "Would you prefer your own tower, or would you like to stay with Jamie and Kenna and the girls?" Tati looked at her husband and said, "I would love to stay in their tower, my husband. It would give us some time to catch up with our son and his family." Otso chuckled and said, "As you wish, my dear." Then turned to Maia and said, "You heard my Queen. We will stay with the family."

Maia inclined her head and chuckled, then said to Kenna, "It is a good thing we chose the largest tower for you and yours. It seems you will have many to watch over the girls. Come, I'll show you to your tower."

Maia walked to the staircase on the right, the group trailing after her. On the second floor, she turned right and walked down a high-ceilinged and wide curved corridor, lit by soft golden light filtering in from the jewel-embedded windows. At the end of the corridor was one large wooden pocket door. Maia slid the door open and stepped into what looked to be a large elevator. "You have an elevator!" exclaimed Ember, pushing through everyone to jump in next to her Nana. Maia grinned at Ember and said, "But of course. The towers are very tall, and stairs are an inconvenience." Noelle moved in next to her Nana and sister, and then the rest of the group entered. "Each floor is its own set of suites, but connected with a staircase set against the exterior wall, but still inside the tower. This allows you to visit the other suites without leaving your room via the elevator. Each door leading to the elevator has a lock and the ability to add a security charm, so there can be no entry via the elevator. The same is true for the doors to the stairway."

The elevator stopped on the third floor of the tower, and Maia said, "Tai and Kai, this is your floor and suite of rooms. You will find a complete wardrobe for you both in your preferred manner of dress. There is a bedroom for each of you on opposite sides of the tower, a sitting room in the middle, and a bathroom connected to each bedroom. You will find the staircase to the upper floors at the back of the sitting room, on the outer wall. There are protection gems embedded in each stone in this tower, so it is an added level of security." Tai and Kai bowed to Maia and, in unison, said, "You honor us, your majesty. Thank you for your kindness." Then they opened the door to their suite, with Ember yelling out, "See you at dinner, boys!" Much to the amusement of the Bear brothers.

The elevator stopped on the fifth floor so that Otso and Tati could enter their suite of rooms. Noelle and Ember waved goodbye to their YaYa and Ukki, then turned to Maia, and Noelle asked, "Why aren't there any even-numbered floors?" Maia said, "Every suite of rooms has high ceilings, so they are actually two floors tall. The first and second floors are for storage, so the rooms start on the third floor." "Oh, I see," Noelle said quietly. "I have placed you on the top of the tower, the seventh floor, with access to the roof lookout via the back staircase. I believe you will find it comfortable," Maia said, opening the door to the suite of rooms on the seventh floor. Jamie, Kenna, Noelle, and Ember followed her into the rooms. "Oh, mother. This is a lovely space you've chosen for us," breathed Kenna in awe.

The room had soft, welcoming lighting, but Kenna couldn't tell where it came from. There were no lamps or overhead lights. Looking around, she realized it was emanating from the walls. The jewels embedded in the stones were glowing. The white stone floor was similar to the ones throughout the castle, but soft, luxurious rugs were placed at strategic places for comfort. The sitting room furnishings were similar to the Library's. They looked very comfortable and were placed near the large fireplace. To the left of the fireplace was a solid door, which Kenna assumed led to the staircase to the other suites. There was a door on opposite walls of the sitting room, which must have been the bedroom suites.

Noelle and Ember rushed to the door on the right, pushing it open and entering the room, laying claim to it. Kenna heard, "OOOhhhh this is beautiful!" "Look at the mural of the unicorn!" Jamie and Kenna exchanged smiling glances, then turned to Maia and said, "Thank you, Mother. We couldn't have asked for more beautiful lodgings." Maia laughed, saying, "Well, I hope you come to think of them as your home. This is and always has been your home, my dear." Kenna walked to her mother and wrapped her arms around her, kissing her cheek. "Yes, this is home," Kenna said softly. Maia stepped back and stated, "I will leave you to rest and refresh before dinner with everyone. You will find the wardrobes are full of everything you could ask for, as is the one in the girls' room. I love you, daughter. Welcome home." She then exited the room, softly closing the door behind her.

Chapter Thirty-Seven

"**A**re you ok, my love?" Jamie asked as he wrapped his arms around Kenna from behind. She leaned her head back against his chest and sighed. "I think so. It's just been a crazy week, hasn't it? A week ago, I was an orphan from an abusive home. We were the parents of two amazing girls from Montana, where we lived a very quiet life. Now, I'm an Elfin Princess, the Savior of the Realms, married to the Prince of the Were Bears. Not to mention, our daughters and I can wield magic and speak with the Goddess.....But, I think I'm okay," she said and chuckled quietly, turning around in Jamie's arms and resting her cheek against his chest, breathing deeply, needing his comforting scent.

Jamie was rubbing a hand gently up and down Kenna's back, soothing her. "Would you like to take a soak in a warm bath before we go down to dinner?" Jamie asked her. Shaking her head against his chest, then leaning back to see his face, She said, "I want you to carry me into that bedroom and tuck me in for a nap." Her eyes looked exhausted. "You don't have to ask me twice. I'm here to serve you, my wife," he said and swung her up into his arms, moving quickly for their bedroom door.

Jamie and Kenna were lying quietly in bed, cuddled up, half drowsing, and listening to the soft chatter of their girls coming from the sitting room. "Should we wake them up?" Ember was asking Noelle. "I don't know. When is dinner?" Noelle replied. Ember sighed loudly and exclaimed, "How should I know?" Noelle said, "I'm going to try to contact Nana with my magic and ask her." "You know how to do that?" Ember asked. "I think I do," Noelle answered her. There was a short period of silence before Noelle said, "Nana said we should wake them up; the Alpha Wolves are back with their cubs." Ember said, "Let me try it." After a few seconds, Ember said, "That is so cool. I could hear Nana in my head."

Jamie chuckled quietly and said, "I guess it's time for us to get up and dress for dinner." Kenna groaned and sat up and said, "Fine." Then, I got out of bed and walked into the bathroom, looking back and saying, "I'd like to sleep for a week; I feel exhausted. It's strange how fatigued I feel lately." Jamie asked, "Do you need help dressing?" "No, I'm not that tired, like when I was so sick. I'll be out in a few minutes," Kenna replied and closed the bathroom door.

Thirty minutes later, the four of them were assembled in the sitting room, all dressed for dinner in clothing from Marqueria. This clothing was very different than the clothes worn daily. They were more formal, like the formal wear in the mortal world, but still made of the amazingly soft material Kenna had come to love to wear. "Mom, you look amazing!" exclaimed Ember. Noelle said, "You both look like a fairytale royal couple. Oh, wait. You are a fairytale royal couple." Then she smiled wryly. Ember said, "That would make us fairytale princesses, Noelle." She was grinning at Noelle. Noelle shrugged and said, "Yeah, I guess so." Kenna immediately picked up on Noelle's mood and asked her, "Are you ok, sweetheart? I know this has been a lot this past few days, so if you need to talk about it, we are here for you."

Noelle took a deep breath, let it out slowly, then whispered, "I don't know, Mama. When Sis and I were coming here before, I loved this place, and coming here was an adventure, but I never felt unsafe. Now, since Hilda and the Darkness, it doesn't feel as safe. I don't feel as safe here, and I don't like that feeling." Jamie stepped closer to Noelle and pulled her in, holding her tightly, running his hand over her curls. "It's ok to feel this way, daughter. It has been unsafe for you since the Darkness," he said softly, then leaned back, placed his hands on either side of her face, and said, "But know this: You will be protected by everyone in this Realm. Our families are powerful and won't let anything happen to you or Ember. I promise, my dear." He kissed her forehead, then grabbed Ember and pulled her into their family hug, with Lucy coming over and squeezing herself into the middle of the four of them, causing the girls to laugh. "She always has to be in the middle of the hugs," Ember laughingly said, then reached down and patted her head. There was a knock at the door, causing the girls to give a small jump, which in turn made them both blush a little. Evidently, they didn't like feeling afraid; it angered and embarrassed them.

Jamie walked over to the door and opened it to find Tai and Kai standing there. They were dressed in the same finery as Jamie, similar to a Tuxedo, but theirs were a different color, dark mahogany brown, while Jamie's was black. Ember let out a wolf whistle and said, "Damn. You boys sure clean up nicely." This caused Noelle to roll her eyes and say, "Language, Ember!"

making everyone laugh. "Well, thank you, Princess. I hardly recognized you without the smudges of dirt," Kai said. Ember curtsied in an exaggerated manner and then grinned at him.

"We've come to escort you to dinner, your Highnesses. Otso's orders," said Tai, moving aside to allow them to follow Kai into the elevator. Kenna looked at Noelle, noticing she looked more relaxed since the Bear brothers had arrived. 'Maybe I'll have them guard the girls full time,' Kenna thought to herself as she followed them into the elevator.

Chapter Thirty-Eight

F ollowing Tai and Kai into the Dining room, Kenna gave a slight exclamation of surprise. The room was gorgeous! The walls and floor were made of the same white stone as the rest of the castle but with several different colors of gemstones embedded into the individual stones. The room was a dazzling, sparkling mixture of glowing lights, yet muted enough not to be bright on the eyes. The very long and wide table was set with a dark green tablecloth with silver threads shot through, sterling silver candlesticks with dark green candles, crystal goblets with silver rims, and white and silver place settings. The chairs, dark wooded tall-backed ones, were covered with dark green velvet fabric over soft backs and seats. The overall effect was definitely a romantic fairytale.

Glancing around the room at all assembled, Kenna's eyes landed on the Alpha Wolves and the three unfamiliar faces standing next to them. They were a stunningly beautiful family. All five of them were over six feet tall, even the younger teenage boys. They all had the same coloring as their parents, with dark hair, dusky skin, and eyes of gold. Luna caught Kenna's eye and smiled, turning to say something to her mate; then, as one, all five began to walk towards Kenna and her family. When the Alphas reached Kenna's family, Luna and Ulric inclined their heads to them. Luna said, "Prince Jamie and Princess Kenna, we'd like to introduce our young." Indicating the young female next to her, she continued, "This is Ulrika, our firstborn and only daughter. To her left is Blaze, our secondborn. The one at the end is our youngest, Alaric."

The Alphas' young all inclined their heads. Kenna quickly introduced her family to the Alphas' children, and there were 'hellos' and 'nice to meet yous' all around before there was the delicate sound of a ringing bell. Turning towards the sound, Kenna saw her parents standing at the head of the table, smiling at everyone. "If you would all make your way to the table and find your seats, all of which are assigned, we will begin dinner soon," Maia said.

Walking around the table with Jamie, Kenna soon found her place, right next to Jamie and to the right of her parents, who were both seated at the head of the table, side by side. To her parents' left were Jamie's parents, right across from Jamie and Kenna. Next to Jamie sat Ulric, then Luna. Across from the Alpha Wolves sat Maxim and Ulrika. Next to Ulrika, sat Noelle, then Ember. Across from Noelle and Ember sat Blaze and Alaric. Finally, at the end of the table, Tai and Kai sat, with Kai seated closest to Ember. Kenna breathed a small sigh of relief. She was pleased to see the Bear brothers seated close to the girls.

Bram and Maia said together, "Let us eat." Suddenly, the table was filled with food. Gloriously delicious smelling food. There was ham, roast turkey, roast beef, mashed potatoes, mixed salads, freshly baked rolls and whipped butter—platters of Beef Wellingtons with all the accompaniments. There were small silver boats of gravies, and salad dressings placed strategically along the table, along with silver bowls of whipped butter. Roasted carrots and asparagus, bowls of pasta with Bolognese, and pasta with thick creamy Alfredo sauce. A few platters of what looked to be salmon fillets and halibut. There were a couple of different wines, a couple of types of juice for the young ones, and pitchers of water. The dinner was served family-style, with everyone passing the platters and bowls of food off to the person on their right.

The conversation around the table ebbed and flowed as the food was consumed. From the end of the table, Kenna heard a rather loud groan of pleasure and glanced down at her girls. Ember was chewing a mouthful of food, her eyes closed, and she had an expression of bliss on her face. Kenna chuckled and, catching Noelle's eye, gave her a wink. Noelle had a platter of cheeseburger in her hand, which she passed down the table. On her plate were six more and one half-eaten, next to a pile of French fries. Kenna noticed the teen sitting across from Noelle had a plate full of cheeseburgers as well, and she smiled.

Jamie leaned over and whispered in her ear, sending a chill down her back, "What are you smiling at, wife?" Turning her head, she kissed his lips and whispered back, "Look down the table at the burger eaters. If nothing else, they have cheeseburgers in common." Jamie looked down the table to where Noelle was sitting, then, leaning a little forward, saw the plate sitting in front of Blaze, which was piled high with cheeseburgers and fries. He gave a chuckle and turned back to Kenna. "That is hilarious. Didn't think I'd see someone ever be able to out-eat Noelle with cheeseburgers," he said. Next to Jamie, Luna laughed softly and said, "Yes, Blaze is obsessed with cheeseburgers and French fries. He can eat a dozen in one sitting. I've noticed your Noelle is not far behind him." Jamie laughed and said, "Nobody has ever eaten more cheeseburgers in one sitting than Noelle. This will be interesting to watch."

Ulric glanced down the table at the teens, nodded his head, and laughed. Then his face got serious, and looking at Jamie, he asked, "Will you make the castle your home, or will you be returning to your home village with Otso and Tati, Jamie?" Jamie shrugged and said, "We haven't thought that far ahead. Until we can find Hilda and deal with the Darkness, we feel it is safest for the girls to be within the Castle grounds." Ulric nodded and said, "Yes, you are probably correct. If Bram and Maia are amiable to the idea, we would like to stay longer as well. Having our young within the walls of the Castle is a relief and will enable us to perform our duties more easily for our pack and Marqueria."

At the head of the table, having overheard their conversation, Bram spoke loudly to all present, saying, "We open our home to all who want to stay. For those of you who have young, we understand the need to keep them safe, and our home is yours for as long as you want to remain." Next to him, Maia was nodding in agreement, smiling down towards the end of the table where the young were seated. Ember, who was between bites, had kept up a steady stream of conversation with Alaric sitting across from her and let out a shout of "Yes! Someone our own ages to hang out with." This elicited laughs from around the table, with the exception of the Bear brothers. They stared at the two young males seated across from Noelle and Ember with eyes that held a warning. Much to the boys' credit, they returned the stares without flinching, while the girls were oblivious to the undercurrents surrounding them.

Kenna nudged Jamie with her elbow to catch his attention, but he had already noticed the exchange. Turning back to Kenna, Jamie said softly, "I have a feeling we won't have to worry about the girls as long as Tai and Kai are around." Next to Jamie, Luna raised an eyebrow and spoke up, saying, "You don't have to worry about our boys. They will treat your daughters with the utmost respect and kindness. But yes, it will be nice knowing they are all being protected by the two Bear brothers. I've heard they are experts with the short swords, and their Bear form is unbeatable."

Kenna leaned forward so she could see both Luna and Ulric and said, "We did not mean to insult you or your sons. Our daughters are completely oblivious to how lovely they truly are and have ignored the attention of teens in the Mortal Realm. Most of the males were not amiable to being just friends with the girls, and because of this, Noelle and Ember were ostracized at school." Luna nodded in understanding and said, "Our sons are not interested in your daughters in that way. All three of our species mate for life and only with the Mates chosen by the Goddess. They have not met their mates as yet, but they have time. They want only to be friends with the girls." Beside her, Ulric nodded in agreement and said, "Our sons will be a good added protection for your daughters as they too are trained in the art of swords and hand-to-hand combat." Jamie gave a quiet chuckle and said, "From the looks of things, they're not easily intimidated either."

Kenna leaned forward and asked Luna, "What type of hand-to-hand combat do your sons do? Our girls practice Muay Thai and would love to continue the lessons here." Luna's eyes widened slightly in surprise, and they replied, "They, too,

225

practice Muay Thai. New sparing partners would be a welcome break for our boys. Is that okay with you both?" Exchanging a look and quick nod with Jamie, Kenna said, "That would be wonderful! Our girls didn't have any actual friends in the Mortal realm, and while they attended public school for a couple of years, it soon became apparent it wasn't a fit for them. We have been homeschooling them, and they've taken private lessons in town for the Muay Thai and art."

Maia said, "One of the towers is not in use at the moment, and the main floor is set up like a training room. The children are welcome to use it as their own for their training." Luna and Kenna gave Maia huge smiles and nods. Kenna said, "Thank you so much, mother. We really appreciate it." Maia nodded, reached over, and laid her hand on top of Kenna's, giving it a soft squeeze.

Luna smiled at the gesture and asked, "Kenna, if you don't mind my asking, are your memories coming back to you?" Kenna shrugged and said, "Oh, I don't mind you asking at all. And yes, every day, I remember more and more of my life before traveling to the Mortal Realm. Unfortunately, I also remember more of what happened to me while I was there." Kenna's eyes glazed a little as she stared off toward the fireplace at the end of the room. Maia gave her hand another squeeze and said softly, "If I could take away your pain, I would, daughter. Maybe it would help to speak about it, as you remember?" Kenna looked back at her mother and gave her a soft, sad smile. Shaking her head, she said, "Talking about it probably would help me to process what happened, but with everything that has been going on these past few days, I don't feel as if it is the most important thing right now."

Across from Luna, Maxim cleared his throat, his green eyes sad and distressed, and said, "Kenna, I am deeply sorry for what my mother did to you, for her part in your pain. I wish I could do something to ease your burden. That being said, mental health is very important to maintain and address. I am not ashamed to admit that I have gone to a therapist for most of my life. It helped me deal with my mother and the pain she inflicted on those around her, myself included. Talking about your trauma is the first step in healing." Kenna slowly nodded her head and said, "Thank you, Maxim. I know you're right; I just need to find the time." Jamie put his arm around Kenna's shoulder and pulled her closer to his side, leaned down, and kissed the top of her head. "Anytime you need to talk is the right time, my love," Jamie said.

Ulrika laid a hand on Maxim's and asked, "Your mother was unkind to you?" Maxim looked down at Ulrika's hand on his. Blushing slightly, he looked up into Ulrika's golden eyes and said, "Yes, she was. She had never wanted children, and I was just a tool to bind my father to her. She wanted the comfortable and luxurious lifestyle my father could offer her. There was no warmth in her, and I never received a hug, a kiss, or a simple word of kindness from her growing up." He shook his head slightly and said, "But I don't want to bring down the mood of the dinner party speaking about my mother." Ulrika took his hand in hers and said, "Mothers are supposed to love and protect their young. I'm sorry you had to grow up without love in your life." Maxim's green eyes stared into Ulrika's golden eyes, the two ignoring those around them. Kenna leaned forward and raised an eyebrow at Luna, and they exchanged a knowing smile. Ulric cleared his throat and loudly asked,

"Is there dessert after this amazing dinner, Maia?" This broke the silence and also broke the spell, gripping the two across from him, who both blushed deep red and dropped their eyes to their plates. Jamie gave a quiet chuckle and whispered to Kenna, "I do believe there is a romance blossoming over there." Kenna nodded and grinned at Jamie.

Maia answered Ulric, and smiling at his subterfuge, she said, "Well, of course, there is dessert. Our granddaughters would not stand for no dessert." Smiling down towards Noelle and Ember at the end of the table. "Nana, what's for dessert? Is there more than one? If so, can I have one of each?" Ember asked excitedly. This brought laughter to the table and a few. "I'll take one of each too, please," and "Ember, I swear you have a bottomless stomach. You could outeat our entire clan," said Kai, who was grinning like a teasing big brother at Ember. Ember promptly rolled her eyes at Kai, then flipped him the bird, much to Kai and Tai's amusement. "Ember," Jamie said in an 'I will not tolerate that at the dinner table' voice. Ember flushed and said, "Sorry, father. I won't do it again." Jamie nodded his head at her, and under his breath, he said, "Yeah, right."

The two Alphas next to him burst out laughing along with Jamie's and Kenna's parents. Then Ulric said, "That one is most spirited. She would make a fitting partner for our Alaric if we chose the mates of our children, that is." Shaking his head, Jamie said, "She is that and more. As for arranging mates, she is to be only sixteen next month. Time enough for matchmaking far into the future. Besides, let us wait and see if the two young ones even like each other before we decide to marry them off," Jamie laughed and continued, "But, more important than that,

I made a promise to my wife that our daughters will marry only for love. Why would I deny them the opportunity to find their soul mates when I myself married mine?" He turned to Kenna and gave her a soft kiss on her lips, taking her hand in his and laying another kiss on her palm. "As I married mine," Kenna said, smiling up at Jamie. From down the table, their daughters said, "Get a room. OOOhhh, stop already. Now is not the time or place, parents!" More laughter from around the table, Jamie and Kenna shaking their heads.

Suddenly, the table was cleared of dinner and its debris. In its place were scrumptious desserts of many kinds. Mini cakes and pies, puddings and cookies. Kenna spotted several Creme Brûlée and cups of rich, decedent-looking chocolate mousse with the cups made from dark chocolate. "Oh my," whispered Noelle. Kenna sent her a smile and a wink, then reached for one of the chocolate mousses and a Creme Brûlée. Taking a bite of mousse, Kenna closed her eyes in bliss and groaned. She was in Heaven. Beside her, Jamie chuckled and asked, "Any chance you'd share with me?" Kenna whispered, "Get your own buddy, boy." And took another bite. There was a period of silence at the table as the desserts were being eaten, groaned over, and shared.

Kenna did, in fact, share her desserts with Jamie while Jamie fed her a few bites of his Fireberry pie, which was his favorite. Looking down the table at their daughters, Jamie and Kenna laughed at the pile of treats in front of them and the two boys. Tai gave a groan and leaned back from the table. He said, "After almost twenty years in the Mortal world, I had forgotten how amazing the food is in Marqueria. I'm going to have to start training twice a day just to stay in shape." Kai nodded in agreement and, while staring at Noelle and Ember, said, "Same. Seriously though, where do you two put it? How can two such small beings eat so much?" Ember, without looking up from her chocolate cake, said, "We're young; you're old. Your metabolism has slowed, old man. We're in the prime of our youth." She shoved a giant bite of chocolate cake into her mouth and shrugged her shoulder at them. "Get used to it," she said around a mouth full of cake. Noelle rolled her eyes at her sister's manners, shaking her head. The Were brothers laughed, not expecting anything less from Ember.

Chapter Thirty-Nine

Over the next several days, the residents of the Castle fell into a friendly camaraderie and routine. The young ones, or cubs and pups as the adults called them, began to have their daily Muay Thai sparing sessions with each other in the training tower. Much to the surprise of Blaze and Alaric, despite the considerable size difference, the girls won at least half their sparing matches with the boys. Their daily archery practice was the highlight of their day, though. The Elvin Archery Creator had made a new bow and set of arrows for each of them. Blaze and Alaric were stunned at the beautifully crafted weapons gifted to them and showed their appreciation by practicing every day to be masters of the weapon and worthy of the gift. While they weren't as skilled at archery as the girls, they were improving more and more every day due to their diligent hours spent at the archery range.

While the teens were busy with their training, the adults were busy ensuring the Elven, Wolf, and Bear clans had the right defenses in place to protect their villages. Maia, Tati, and Kenna visited every village and performed protection spells on each home and building, reinforcing what had already been done by the villagers. The villagers had etched protection circles around each house and building, as well as one large circle around the entire village. This would keep the Darkness

/Hilda from crossing into the Villages, but if the unthinkable did happen, the reinforced houses would provide additional fallback points and added protection for all.

Maxim stayed on in Marqueria, supposedly to help in the search for his mother. He also began training sessions with Bram, learning how to tap into his magic. Having never known a human/elf hybrid before, Bram was interested in knowing Maxim's abilities and his limits. When Maxim wasn't training with Bram, he was with Tai and Kai, learning how to fight with short swords. He was quick to study and became proficient very quickly. After dinner, Maxim and Ulrika would find time to wander in the garden. Everyone knew there was definitely romance budding there, and she was the real reason Maxim stayed in Marqueria.

While everyone was enjoying their daily routines, there was an air of expectation and waiting. Waiting for something bad to happen. The adults tried to keep the young ones distanced from the worry of the Darkness/Hilda, but all four were very sensitive to the moods of those around them. In the evenings, Noelle, Ember, Blaze, and Alaric would gather in Kenna and Jamie's suite in the sitting room. They would game on their laptops, often against each other. They would also talk about what the adults were up to.

"I wish they'd share with us what they were planning. I feel completely in the dark about it. I don't like feeling this way; I'm so vulnerable and helpless. I want to know everything so I can protect myself," Noelle was saying to Blaze as they were playing Day of Dragons on their laptops. Blaze said, "They feel that they're keeping you safe by not burdening you with the details. They're parents; it's their job to protect you." "Yeah, but my magic is powerful, and so is Ember's. We could be helping, and it would make us feel useful. We've helped before," growled Noelle, who rolled her eyes, continuing to tap on her laptop. Blaze shrugged and smiled, his golden eyes twinkling, then said, "I think you'll get the chance to help when they have a solid plan. Then you can kick some ass." Noelle laughed and said, "You bet I'll kick some ass."

Ember, who was painting on a canvas in front of the fireplace, said, "I'd love to kick some ass, but on a dragon. Have you two ever ridden a dragon?" Raising an eyebrow at the boys, waiting for an answer. Alaric said, "No, we haven't. Dragons only bond with Elves, so Elves are the only ones who can ride them." Ember's face fell, and looking at Noelle, she saw that she, too, was very disappointed. Ember whispered, "Oh, I guess we will never get to ride a dragon, Noelle." Blaze, with confusion on his face, asked, "Why not? You're Elves!" Ember and Noelle both shook their heads, and Noelle said, "Only half. Our father is Bear." Alaric said, "Oh, yeah. I forgot. Well, maybe a dragon will bond with your elven side? You know there's never been an interspecies mating, so this is new territory. We should go down to the stables and see if a dragon chooses you." "What?!!" Ember shouted loudly. The boys were used to Ember's outburst, so they just waited for her to explain. "There's a stable full of dragons here?! Why didn't our grandparents tell us?" Ember asked, her expression a little worried as she looked at Noelle. Noelle said, "Maybe they didn't want us to be disappointed because we won't be able to bond with one."

The sisters were staring at each other quietly. The wolf brothers were also used to the sisters talking to each other in their minds, so they waited until it appeared they were done. Finally, Blaze said, "Ok, what are you two planning?" The girls gave the brothers huge smiles and waved them over to move closer. Noelle whispered, "Want to go with us down to the stables and help us find a dragon?" Blaze and Alaric exchanged a look, then looked back at the girls. "When were you planning to sneak down?" Alaric asked. "Now is as good a time as any," Ember said, grinning widely, and continued, "The adults are all busy in the War Room until dinnertime, so let's go now. The Bear brothers will be busy with that, so they won't be breathing down our necks."

Chapter Forty

The dragon stable was a sight to behold. It was as large as the main castle and just as round. Built with the same lovely white stones as the castle, its walls had the same twinkling jewels embedded into each stone. The structure itself was vast, with multiple spacious rooms designed to accommodate dragons of various sizes and breeds.

The interior was lit by the soft glowing light that lit the hallway to their tower of suites, plus softly flickering torches helped illuminate the interior. The air was thick with a mix of earthy scents and a hint of smoke from the torches and the dragons. The floor was covered with a thick layer of soft black sand, providing a comfortable resting place for the dragons' massive claws and bodies.

Each room within the stable was tailored to meet the specific needs of the dragons. Some rooms had high ceilings and open skylights, allowing the dragons to bask in the sunlight and feel the gentle breeze on their scales. Others were equipped with heated stones and mineral-rich pools full of warm water, providing a cozy and soothing environment for the dragons to relax and rejuvenate.

The dragons themselves were a breathtaking sight. They were many different colors, and their scales shimmered and glistened in an array of vibrant hues, reflecting the light in mesmerizing patterns.

Despite their formidable nature, the dragons within the stable exuded an air of tranquility. They coexisted peacefully, their presence creating an aura of awe and reverence. The sound of their deep, rumbling purrs echoed throughout the stable, creating a soothing melody.

As the four teenagers stood inside the massive dragon stables, looking around, they all wore looks of awe. "Where do we start?" Ember whispered. Alaric whispered back, "We don't know. This is the first time we've been in here. We've never been this close to dragons before." Looking a little exasperated, Noelle took the lead, waving to the others to follow her. She turned right down an exterior corridor, walking around the outer ring of the dragon stables. Ember caught up to her, grabbing the sleeve of her tunic and pulling her to a stop.

"Are you feeling the pull in this direction, or is it just me?" Ember whispered to her sister. Noelle nodded and said, "No, I feel it too. It's pulling me down this way." The wolf brothers exchanged glances, and Blaze shrugged and, with a smirk, said, "Lead the way, your Highnesses." Noelle glared at him and said, "Don't call us that. We have names, use them." This brought quiet laughter from the boys, who both bowed low to the girls. Rolling her eyes and growling low in her throat, Noelle turned and continued down the corridor. Ember just looked at the boys, shook her head, and said, "You have no idea what you're doing when you poke at her. She may seem mild and well-mannered, but she's tougher than I am, and her temper is worse." She then turned and followed her sister, leaving the boys to either follow or fall behind.

Catching up to Noelle, Ember reached for her hand, and together, they followed the call inside their head. The wolf brothers were right behind them, so quiet the sisters hadn't realized they had caught up to them. The group walked for a few more minutes before the girls suddenly stopped, both tilting their heads as if listening to something. "This way," whispered Noelle, tugging her sister towards a massive door to their left. The sisters each laid a hand on the door and waited. "What are you doing?" Blaze whispered to the girls. "Sshhh. We're listening," Noelle whispered back. Closing their eyes, the girls continued to hold one of their hands on the door.

"They're in here. Can you hear them, sis?" Ember whispered to Noelle. Opening her eyes and grinning, Noelle turned to Ember. "Yes, I can. Let's go in and meet them," Noelle said. Together, the girls put both hands on the huge door and pushed it open. Surprisingly, it opened smoothly and easily. The room behind the door was massive, with ceilings as tall as the stables themselves, and there were open skylights, allowing the cool night air to flow in. "Holy crap!" exclaimed Blaze when he caught sight of the two matching dragons inside.

Two dark green dragons were standing tall and alert, deep inside the room. Their bodies were sleek and muscular, covered in deep emerald green scales that glistened under the moonlight from the open windows above. Their wings were tucked neatly back against their bodies, but there were hints of intricate gold patterns on the sections of the wings that were visible. They had large, sharp claws that were a warm, dull gold, as were the two horns on their heads and the tips of the spines down their backs and tails. Their eyes were large and golden, very like the eyes of the Alpha Bear and Wolf families.

"Oh, you are both so beautiful," breathed Noelle. "Are you sisters?" asked Ember quietly. The emerald green dragons bowed their heads towards the girls, and then the one on the right said, "We are sisters, just as you are sisters." There came a gasp from behind the girls, and Alaric breathed, "I can hear them." This caused the dragons to chortle and chuff, and then the one on the left said, "Of course, you can hear us, silly wolf. We are speaking out loud." Alaric flushed a little and said, "Oh. I thought you were speaking into my mind." "No, little wolf. That is reserved for the rider we choose to bond with," the dragon responded.

Noelle asked, "Do you have names?" This again caused the dragons to chortle with amusement, and the dragon on the right said, "Well, of course, we have names, little elf bear." "Will you tell us your names?" asked Ember, standing with her hands on her hips. "Ah, you are the fiery one, aren't you, little elf bear?" the dragon on the right said, then continued, "But I feel your sister has a fire deep within her, which is slow to burn, but once it catches, it will match yours perfectly." "Yes, sister, I believe you are correct," said the dragon on the left.

"I am called Jade. My sister is Sage," the dragon on the right said. "It is nice to meet you, young ones of the Elf, Bear, and Wolf clans," said Sage. Jade said, "We have never encountered an Elf/Bear cub before. We are pleased to finally meet you, Noelle and Ember." "You know about us? You know our names?" Ember asked Jade and Sage. "We have been watching you since you first stepped foot into Marqueria. This is why we have not chosen our riders; we have been waiting for you to become aware of us. We have been waiting for you," Sage said, staring into Ember's eyes. Noelle took a step closer to Jade and asked, "We are the ones you wish to bond with?" Jade said, "You are. We have waited, and now you are ready." Jade stared deeply into Noelle's eyes.

There was total silence in the room as the dragons communicated with the sisters via their mind links. The wolf brothers knew to remain still and silent during this time. Witnessing a dragon bond with its chosen rider was a privilege, and the brothers were honored to be included.

For such a momentous event, the process took just a few minutes. When the bonding was complete, both girls had a dark green and gold tattoo on their left wrists. Looking at her wrist in wonder, Ember looked up at Sage and asked, "When can we begin our training with you?" The dragon sisters chuckled, and Jade said, "Patience, little cub. We will visit daily for the next several days and practice our mind links. The riding will begin as soon as we believe you are ready." Noelle and Ember both nodded their heads, and Noelle said, "Ok. We can meet with you after our Muay Thai and archery training sessions." "Yes, continue your warrior training. You will need it in the war to come," said Sage, nodding her large head.

"War? We are to fight a war?" asked Ember, eyebrow raised and head cocked to the side in an expression of disbelief. "Yes, little cub. You and your sister will be key elements for the victory of Light over Dark," said Jade. Noelle and Ember looked at each other, expressions showing a hint of worry. Turning to the Wolf brothers, Jade said, "As are you two. You both will play a large part in the coming war. You are to be the protectors of these two sisters. It has been foreseen." Blaze and Alaric stared at the dragon sisters in stunned silence. "Foreseen?" asked Blaze. "Yes, foreseen. Just ask the Alpha Bear grandmother of these two. She knows," replied Sage.

Noelle and Ember looked at the Wolf brothers in confusion. "They're to be our protectors? But we already have protectors. Tai and Kai are our protectors," Ember said to the dragons. Sage said, "Yes, the Bear brothers are your protectors. But these brothers here, they are your future. They are to be your mates." "What?! How can that be?!" cried Noelle. The dragon sisters both nodded their heads, and Jade said, "It has been foreseen. Ask your YaYa. Now, little cubs, it is late, and the castle is in an uproar over your absence. You need to return, and we will meet tomorrow."

"Oh crap," said Ember, turning towards the door. The four said their goodbyes to the dragons and left the room, making their way towards the main doors of the stables. When they reached the main doors, they were already open, and a group was preparing to search the stables. "Ummm, Hi," said Ember loudly, catching the attention of the Bear brothers, who looked murderous. Tai and Kai quickly came towards the four of them, golden eyes glowing, stopping in front of the Wolf brothers. "If you've laid one paw on the Princesses, I'm going to tear you apart," growled Kai to Blaze and Alaric, who didn't flinch or back down, returning stare for stare. Noelle and Ember stepped in front of Blaze and Alaric, their own eyes glowing and their hair starting to float. "Back off now," said Noelle softly.

Tai and Kai stepped back a pace; the looks on their faces were slightly hurt. "We have been sent to find you, Princess. It is our duty to protect you, even if it's from a friend," Tai said while his eyes roamed over the two girls, ensuring they were unharmed. "We are fine, boys. Blaze and Alaric would never harm us. They only came with us, so we weren't alone when we came to visit the dragons," Ember said, smiling softly at the Bear brothers. The brothers breathed sighs of relief, and Kai said, "You all need to come back to the castle with us. Your parents are waiting." Kai turned towards the castle, expecting the young ones to follow him, which they did, and Tai stepped in behind to be rear guard.

Chapter Forty-One

Kai led the four of them into the Library, where their grandparents and parents were all waiting in front of the fire. Jamie's face looked thunderous as the girls walked towards them. As they walked in, Ember reached out and grabbed Noelle's hand for comfort. The four teenagers walked to the fireplace and faced their families, soaking up the heat from behind and waiting. Blaze reached out and took Noelle's hand, and Alaric moved to stand by Ember, taking her hand in his. There they stood, holding hands and presenting a united front.

Kenna raised an eyebrow as she watched them and glanced at Luna, who was looking towards Kenna. They both gave each other a questioning look and then turned back to face their children. Jamie and Ulric moved towards their young ones, obviously upset over their disappearance. "Where have you been?" asked Jamie in a quiet, controlled voice. "Why did you leave the Castle?" asked Ulric in the same quiet, controlled voice. Ember whispered, "Oh shit. They're calm. This is worse than if they were yelling." Nodding her head, Noelle whispered back, "Yep. What's worse is the mothers are letting the fathers handle it. That means they're too angry to talk to us right now." "We're so dead," whispered Blaze.

From the group of four grandparents came the sound of muffled laughter. Ember looked over at her grandparents and gave them a wink. This was more than they could handle, and they burst out laughing, not even attempting to hold it in. "Seriously? This is not a laughing matter," said Kenna, staring daggers at her own and Jamie's parents. Bram, trying to compose himself, said, "We apologize, daughter. We mean no disrespect. This is just so entertaining and makes me feel alive. Which is something I've been missing these past thirty or so years." "Look at their united front and with such bravery," said Otso.

Jamie turned towards his father and said, "Enough, father. They need to understand how serious this is. They could have been taken by the Darkness." Jamie and Ulric both turned back to face their children, their faces even more stormy. This seemed to trigger Noelle and Ember, as their hair began to float and they began to glow. "We were just in the dragon stables. Blaze and Alaric have never been close to dragons, and we haven't either. So we went. You need to back down, please," Noelle said, eyes softly glowing. The fathers looked at each other, and Jamie shook his head in confusion and asked in a soft voice, "Do you think we are going to hurt you? We would never hurt you, Noelle. There is no need for you to use your magic against us." The girls slowly lowered their magic and took a deep breath. Blaze and Alaric looked at each other and then nodded. Together, they stepped out in front of the girls, and Blaze said, "It was our fault. We encouraged them to take us to the stables." Noelle let out a gasp and cried, "It was not! It was our idea; you tried to talk us out of it." Blaze turned around and said, "Hush!" This didn't sit well with Noelle as she began

244

to glow again and shoved a finger into Blaze's chest. "How dare you hush me! Nobody hushes me! Don't you ever tell me to be quiet again!" she growled.

Blaze took a step back and, in a raised voice, said, "I am trying to keep you from getting in trouble. If you weren't so stubborn, you'd understand that." Ember and Alaric took a few steps back from their siblings and watched in fascination. "I'm not the stubborn one! You are!" cried Noelle louder. She took a step closer to Blaze and again growled at him, "I had it all under control until you tried to play hero. I don't need a hero! I can be my own hero!" She poked him in the chest for emphasis. Blaze just stared at her in awe and then whispered, "Goddess, you are so beautiful and amazing, and you drive me crazy." Noelle stopped and took a step back, staring at Blaze in confusion.

Exchanging an amused glance with Luna, Kenna cleared her throat and said, "OK, let's all calm down. Why don't you four come sit down and explain what you were doing in the dragon stables?" Glancing at each other, the four walked to one of the sofas and sat down, Noelle and Ember in the middle, Blaze at the end next to Noelle, and Alaric at the end next to Ember. Noelle avoided looking at Blaze, but he kept sneaking looks at her. The sisters held hands and scooted back onto the deep sofa seat, leaning against the back with their legs crossed. The boys both scooted back as well but leaned forward with their forearms across their thighs. Across from them sat their parents, and on the sofa at the end sat the girls' grandparents, Bram and Maia, Otso and Tati. Luna said quietly, "Please explain." Ember sighed and said, "I might as well start since it was originally my idea. We decided that since you adults were busy planning on how to find the Darkness and not including us at all, I might add, well, we decided it would be ok to go down to the dragon stables and see the dragons up close." "Did you not think to let us know where you were going?" asked Kenna softly. Noelle bit her lip and said, "Yes, only for a moment, but then we figured you wouldn't let us, so we just went alone. Besides, Ember and I are very strong with our magic, and Blaze and Alaric are excellent fighters. We felt safe."

Their parents just stared at them for a few moments, saying nothing. Finally, Jamie said, "We're sorry we haven't been including you in the planning. We all agreed that you should be allowed to be young and carefree for a while. From now on, we will include you in the meetings about the Darkness." Kenna, Luna, and Ulric all nodded in agreement. "Now, is there anything else you need to tell your parents?" asked Tati. All four of them looked at Tati quickly, then away, flushing. "Hmmmm. Yes, it seems like there is something you need to tell us," said Ulric, watching his sons closely. Behind the girls, Tai and Kai gave low growls, making the boys turn around in their seats and stare at them. Blaze raised an eyebrow at the Bear brothers, and Kai said, "Try me, pup." This made Ember giggle and say, "Calm down, bear boys. Nothing like that happened. I don't know what that weirdness was between Noelle and Blaze a few minutes ago, but the Wolf boys were perfect gentlemen." This caused Noelle to elbow her sister and hiss, "Be quiet."

The adults all chuckled at this exchange before Tati said loudly, "Tell them what occurred in the dragon stables. Tell them everything." The girls stared at their YaYa in surprise. 'Tell them, sweethearts," she said again, giving them a soft smile.

Holding hands again, the girls looked at their parents. Noelle said, "Ember and I had been feeling a strong pull towards the dragon stables as if someone was calling to us. It's been happening for the past two weeks, and we just can't ignore it anymore. We didn't even know it was the dragon stables we were being pulled to. We were not aware you kept dragons, Papa." She gave her Papa a side-eyed glance, which was almost accusatory, and then continued, "We strongly encouraged Blaze and Alaric to accompany us there this evening." "Strongly encouraged, huh?" asked Jamie, raising an eyebrow at his daughters. "Well, we pretty much made them go with us," said Ember, grinning at Alaric, who rolled his eyes and nudged her with his elbow. This made Ember laugh.

"So what happened when you got to the dragon stables?" asked Kenna. "We followed the pull to the room where our dragons were," said Ember, smiling at her mother. "Wait, what? Your dragons? Since when do you two have dragons?" Kenna asked, her brow furred a little. The girls looked at each other, again speaking to one another via their minds. Ember sighed and said, "Fine." Blaze and Alaric both chuckled and shook their heads. They were used to their private conversations.

"Ember and I each have a dragon. They're sisters, too. They have been watching us since we came to Marqueria when we were toddlers. It was then they decided we would be the ones they bonded with," Noelle said, watching her parents. Jamie sat up straighter and asked loudly, "You're bonded to dragons?!" The girls both held up their left wrists and showed the dark green and gold tattoos around them. The tattoo was a dark green Trinity knot outlined in gold. Intertwined around it were green vines of Ivy with leaves outlined in gold. "In our minds, the dragons told us this tattoo represents our eternal bond and can never be broken," Noelle said, examining her own tattoo closely. Kenna stood up and walked over, kneeling in front of them, holding their wrists and examining them herself. She hadn't said a word since before the girls said they were bonded to dragons.

"What are their names?" Kenna quietly asked her daughters. "Mine is Sage, and Noelle's is Jade," Ember answered. Noelle said, "They are green and gold, like our tattoos. They want us to meet with them every day to strengthen our bond and mind connection before they will allow us to ride them." At the word 'ride,' Kenna looked up quickly, her expression worried. "Ride?" she whispered. She then stood up, walked back to the sofa, and sat next to Jamie, wrapping her arm around his and cuddling close to his side. Jamie disentangled his arm and wrapped it around Kenna, pulling her close and cuddling her into him. He knew Kenna needed comfort, and his scent helped her when she became anxious. Looking at where her parents were sitting, Kenna stared at them for a few moments, then said, "What is all of this about? You haven't told me anything about dragons and their riders. I want to know what this means for our daughters."

Ember spoke up, her voice raised enough to be heard, "Mama, there's more. Jade and Sage told us to ask our YaYa about our role in the war to come and about Blaze and Alaric's role in our lives. They said the boys are our intended mates!" Ember looked totally offended by this last part, much to the amusement of the grandparents present.

Chapter Forty-Two

Turning her eyes towards Tati, Noelle asked, "What did they mean, YaYa?" Everyone's eyes turned towards Tati. She nodded, then said, "I've had a vision. A prophecy was revealed to me by the Goddess. I needed to wait until you were ready to hear it. I believe now is the time."

In a realm of magic, where stories are woven,
A prophecy whispered of sisters unbroken.
With fiery red hair and eyes of green,
Their destiny entwined, a sight to be seen.
From the backs of dragons, they'll take to the sky,
With courage ablaze, they'll never be shy.
Beneath the moon's glow, the wolf brothers stand,
Protectors and guardians, Their love like a shield.
Their love for the sisters, fierce and unyielding,
In battles, they'll fight, their devotion revealing.
Through trials and tribulations, they'll face the unknown,
Together, they'll conquer, their strength clearly shown.
Their bond unbreakable, their hearts intertwined,
In unity, they'll triumph, their spirits aligned.
Two werewolf brothers, fierce and strong,
Shall rise as protectors, against all that is wrong.
With fur as dark as the midnight sky,
They'll guard the sisters with Golden eyes.

Red-haired and green-eyed, a radiant pair,
Their beauty and strength are beyond compare.
In the depths of the night, when danger lurks,
The brothers shall shield them from all that hurts.
With claws and fangs, they'll fight as one,
Defeating the Darkness until the battle is won.
Through moonlit woods, they'll roam and explore,
Guided by destiny, forevermore.
Their bond unbreakable, hearts intertwined,
Love and protection, eternally bind.
In times of sorrow, when tears may fall,
The brothers shall be there, standing tall.
Their presence a shield, their love a balm,
Embracing the sisters with warmth and calm.

Not a sound could be heard in the library but for the crackling of the fire. No one spoke. Jamie and Kenna stared at the four youths, eyes searching. Luna and Ulric looked at each other for a few seconds, then turned their eyes to their sons and the two girls. Noelle and Ember tightly held hands, and Blaze and Alaric had taken the girls' other hands in theirs while Tati was reciting the Prophecy. Their parents examined how they were sitting, seeing more than the four knew they were revealing. Turning to his mother, Jamie asked, "When did you have this Prophecy, Mother?" Looking into Jamie's eyes, her own apologizing for what she had to say. His mother said, "Two months ago." Kenna gasped and said, "But that was long before we all came to Marqueria and long before the girls met the boys." Tati nodded and said, "I had the prophecy about you two years before you were stolen away to the Mortal Realm. The Goddess foresees the future." Several minutes had passed, and still none of the teenagers had spoken.

Then Ember turned to Alaric and, grinning, said, "Well, looks like you're stuck with me. Hope you aren't in love with someone else." Noelle let out a snort and laughed before covering her mouth. Shaking her head, she said softly, "I love you, Ember." Ember laid her head on Noelle's shoulder and said, "I love you too, sis." Alaric said, "I have no interest in anyone else, Ember. I knew you would be mine the minute I laid eyes on you." Ember stood up and walked to the fire, then turned to face Alaric, saying, "But I will be just sixteen in a few weeks. I'm not interested in dating boys yet. I wanted to just hang out with you and ride dragons and shoot archery. Defeat the Darkness together. I'm not thinking about having a boyfriend, let alone a mate for life. How can you possibly know I'm that girl?" She was watching Alaric carefully.

Alaric stood up and walked over to Ember, taking both her hands into his. Even though he was just a few months older than Ember, he towered over her at six feet tall, indicating he wasn't done growing. Looking down into her eyes, he said, "Wolves mate for life. There is only one mate for us. We know the minute we meet our mate. Our mate knows as well, but with you being half Elf and half Bear and being raised in the Mortal Realm, where things are different, it may take some time for you to accept it. That is ok. I will wait, as we have time. I, too, am only sixteen, and I'm not looking to settle down either. We will continue as friends, learning to fight together, hanging out, and gaming. This changes nothing." Ember breathed a huge, exaggerated sigh of relief and said, "Oh, thank the Goddess, you're willing to wait, or I might have been married off at sixteen." Giving him the stink eye. Alaric flushed and said, "That is not how I meant it, and you know it." Taking his hand again, Ember said, "Yes, I know. When I feel threatened, I become even more of a smart-ass. It's my defense mechanism. I'm sorry."

Looking at their four parents, Ember said, "Don't start planning any weddings yet." Much to the amusement of all there. Noelle turned in her seat to face Blaze and asked, "Was it the same for you? Did you feel that way when you met me?" Blaze stared at Noelle for a moment, shook his head, and then said, "It felt like I was struck by a bolt of lightning the first time I saw you. I didn't want to scare you, so I've said nothing. Getting to know you and being friends is enough for now." Noelle blushed and looked down at their hands entwined. "I don't like my life decided for me. I don't care if the Goddess has deemed we are supposed to be together. If I don't fall in love with you, I am not becoming your mate." She looked up into his eyes, a soft smile on her face. He returned her smile and said, "I would expect nothing less from you, Noelle."

Jamie cleared his throat loudly and, needing to change the subject quickly, said, "Bram, would you please tell us exactly what it means for the girls to be bonded to the dragons?"

Chapter Forty-Three

"The dragon chooses who to bond with; it is a bond that will last the entire life of the Elf and the dragon, so it must be a good match. When they bond, their minds are linked, allowing them to communicate with each other, even when they are great distances apart. A bonded pair is also able to heal any wounds on each other, even from a distance," Bram said, standing in front of the fire, facing the group. "A few days ago, the girls asked if they could ride a dragon, and I said we'd talk about it another time," Bram said. Kenna nodded and said, "Yes, I remember. You were actually rather strange about the entire dragon thing. Why?" Bram ran a hand through his mussed-up hair and sighed, then answered, "It is because I wasn't sure they'd ever be able to ride a dragon. Only bonded Elves are able to ride a dragon, and only the dragon bonded to them."

"Ahhh. We are half Bear, and you didn't think a dragon would accept us, right?" Ember asked. Nodding his head, Bram said, "Yes, that is correct. Never in several thousands of years have dragons and elves been bonding, and has anyone other than an elf been chosen to bond with a dragon. Now, two have chosen to bond with you both. It is a week of firsts."

Kenna gave a sigh and said, "Yeah, no kidding." Then she asked her father, "So, the girls will ride on dragons. Exactly how is this accomplished?" Bram chuckled and said, "With practice, lots and lots of practice." Kenna said, "I'm not amused by this one little bit. I want you to assure me that my daughters will be safe." Her expression was fierce, as only a mother's could be in this situation. "Daughter, I would never put my granddaughters at risk. It is very safe. Spells are used to ensure the riders don't fall off, plus the dragon itself would never harm its bonded rider." Kenna sighed again and leaned into Jamie, breathing in his scent deeply.

"They will be fine, my love. I've never heard of a dragon rider falling off their dragon. Tomorrow, we will go to the stables and meet the sisters who bonded with our daughters," Jamie said, kissing the top of her head. "Ok, that works for me," Kenna said, yawning widely. Next to Kenna, Luna stood up and said, "I believe it is time for us to retire to our rooms. It is late, and it has been a stressful day." Pointedly looking at her sons, she raised an eyebrow. Blaze and Alaric said their goodnights to Noelle and Ember, then turned to the adults and bade them goodnight as well.

The Wolf family was the first to leave the library, quickly followed by Otso and Tati, then Bram and Maia. Kenna and Jamie sat on the sofa gazing over at their daughters, faces covered in concern, pride, and sadness. Tai and Kai came from behind the girls' sofa and sat on the sofa next to Noelle and Ember. Tai asked, "Are you two ok? Would you like some tea or hot cocoa?" Ember smiled softly at Tai and said, "No, thank you, Tai. I think I just need to go to bed. I'm exhausted. Something about bonding with Sage has wiped me out." "I know, right?! I feel as if I can barely keep my eyes open now," Noelle said, covering a huge yawn. The bear brothers stood up and walked to the doorway, waiting for the family to join them. Kenna and Jamie stood up, and each held a hand out to one of their daughters, pulling them up off the couch.

"Come, my sweethearts. We will tuck you in tonight; don't even argue with me on this," Kenna said, a sheen of tears in her eyes. They followed Tai out the door, down the long corridor, and to the elevator, Kai at the rear guarding them.

Chapter Forty-Four

In the Wolf suite of rooms that night, the Alphas were having a serious discussion with their sons. "Do you understand the responsibility involved in mating with these two girls?" Luna asked her sons. Blaze stood up and walked to the fire, staring at the flames. "Mother, I understand what it entails to take Noelle as my mate. Not only is she the Elven Princess, but she is the Bear Princess as well. Her magic is stronger than any seen in this realm, along with her sister's and mother's. I don't think it's going to be a quiet life we lead after we're married." Blaze chuckled quietly. Luna turned to Alaric and asked, "And do you understand what it will take to become Ember's mate? She is a free spirit and tends to get into mischief." Alaric grinned and said, "That is one of the things I love about her."

Luna sighed and said, "Don't misunderstand me. I adore those girls. I've been keeping an eye on them since they first started coming to Marqueria. I believe they are kind, brave, and loving. That being said, they carry the weight of the world on their tiny shoulders. They and their mother are Marqueria's only hope in defeating the Darkness for good. That is a heavy burden to bear." Alaric met his mother's eyes and said, "And I want to help ease that burden. I know I can help her." Blaze said, "I feel it is my duty to try and make this easier on them." Luna looked at Ulric and asked, "What do you think?"

Ulric studied his sons for a few moments before saying, "What will you both do if the girls never fall in love with you? You have both found your mates, but they were raised in the mortal world, and the idea of finding a mate is very foreign to them. Not to mention, they are half-bear and half-elf. While Bears and Elves find mates for life, these two girls are unique. They may not have the same instincts as the rest of us. Have you thought of that at all?"

Blaze and Alaric stared at each other for a bit, then shrugged. Blaze said, "She is my mate, and I am hers. I feel the Goddess has blessed our union. I'm not afraid that she'll reject me." Alaric nodded and said, "I feel the same. For all of Ember's wild mouth and attitude, she's a very loving and kind person. This feels right."

The two Wolf Alphas nodded their heads, and Luna said, "Then we will support you in any way we can. We wish for a happy union for you both, Goddess willing."

Kenna and Jamie were having a similar conversation with their two daughters back in their suite of rooms in the tower on the seventh floor. Kenna asked Noelle, "How do you feel about Blaze?" Noelle flushed a little and replied, "I like him. I'm comfortable with him. He's very handsome and kind, and we are becoming good friends. This prophecy has put us in a weird situation. He said he felt like he was struck by lightning when he saw me, but it wasn't like that for me. I thought he was cute, but my mind isn't on boys and dating; it never has been. That being said, I like being around him. I feel safe when he is with me." Jamie and Kenna gave each other a small smile, remembering how they felt when they first met and how Kenna was resistant to dating at first. She said she was never getting married; in fact, it was the second thing she said to him.

Jamie turned to Ember and asked, "And you? How do you feel about Alaric?" Ember smiled and said, "I like him. I really do. He's fun to hang out with; he makes me laugh. I feel safe with him, too. But I'm not even close to thinking about getting a mate and getting married. I want to live life before I settle down. I'm only fifteen! I have several years ahead of me before I think about taking a mate." Jamie and Kenna nodded at Ember with understanding. "Besides, they both said they would wait until we are ready," Ember said, shrugging. Noelle nodded and said, "Yes, and until that time comes, we can become good friends." Their parents stood up, and Jamie said, "Ok, munchkins, it's time to go to bed. Come on, get up, and let us tuck you in." As they walked into their bedroom, neither girl gave their parents guff about tucking them in. Instead, they gave each of them a kiss and a hug, which lasted just a little bit longer than normal. "Your birthday is in a few weeks. Start thinking about what you want to do on your day. Seventeen and Sixteen years old. It has gone by so quickly," Kenna said as she closed their door.

Chapter Forty-Five

The next morning at breakfast, one would expect there to be a certain degree of awkwardness, but there wasn't. It was as if last night had never happened, as if they had never heard the 'mating prophecy' as Ember had started calling it. The sisters sat with the wolf brothers, enjoying their breakfast and chatting about their plans for the day. Their parents, too, acted as if the prophecy had never been shared, but they kept an eye on their children all the same. At breakfast, they were joined by Maxim and Ulrika, who had been missing last night due to their evening walks in the garden. It was widely understood that they would be mated, as Ulrika had told her parents that Maxim was her mate. Maxim, much to his surprise, had discovered that his elf blood was strong here in Marqueria, and he was experiencing the urge to take Ulrika as his mate, too. This he shared with Bram, who, of course, shared it with everyone.

When breakfast was finished, everyone gathered in the Great Room to walk over to the dragon stables and meet Jade and Sage. Suddenly, Kenna ran down the stairs and asked in a panicked voice, "Has anyone seen Lucy? I can't find her. I can't even feel her around." The girls looked at each other, obviously communicating silently, and then Noelle and Ember quickly walked to their mother and joined hands. The three began to glow immediately. The others gave them space and continued to watch. After a few moments, the glowing stopped, and all three had tears streaming down their faces.

"What has happened?!" gasped Jamie, grabbing Kenna's hands in his. "We can't find her. It's as if she has ceased to exist," sobbed Kenna. The Wolf brothers went to stand by Noelle and Ember, wrapping an arm around their shoulders. "We will go search for her; I'll have everyone begin the search now. We will scour the Castle grounds," said Bram. The group headed out the front doors and into the courtyard to begin the search for Lucy. Kenna was whispering, "Oh, please let us find her, and please let her be okay. Please, Goddess, don't let Lucy be taken from us." Kenna, Jamie, and their daughters, along with the Wolf brothers, started walking left toward the gardens to search, and the rest of the group went in the opposite direction.

Lucy wasn't in the gardens, but they met the other group as they continued around the castle. "I'm leaving the Castle grounds to look for her," said Kenna, heading for the huge gate in the Wall. As they left the castle grounds, they were suddenly surrounded by two dozen Elves, Wolves, and Bears for protection. Noelle and Ember stayed close to their parents but held tightly to Blaze and Alaric's hands. Three hundred yards outside the Castle wall, they found Lucy.

There was a trail of blood behind her one hundred yards long, and she was still trying to crawl back to the Castle. "NO!" screamed the girls together and ran to Lucy, but Kenna got there ahead of them. The three knelt around Lucy, who had stopped crawling and was whining in pain. She had an arrow sticking out of her side, and blood was pouring from the wound. "When I tell you to, pull the arrow out. Not before

I tell you to," said Kenna quietly, her entire body glowing brightly as she laid her hands on Lucy. The girls grasped the shank of the arrow, ready to pull it out. "Now!" yelled Kenna, and the girls pulled it out in one quick jerk. Then they all three laid hands on Lucy, and Kenna said, "Picture the wound mending and healing; picture the bleeding stopping." The three began to chant while glowing brighter than ever before.

By the Power of Earth, Air, Fire, Water, and Spirit

I call upon the forces of Healing and Grace

To mend these wounds at a swift pace.

Oh, Goddess of Healing, we honor your name,

With trust and faith, we invoke your power,

To bring forth Healing this very hour.

After several minutes, Kenna and her daughters stopped glowing and opened their eyes. Lucy let out a whine and tried to stand up, but they wouldn't let her. "Let me check you out first, sweetheart," Kenna said, running her hands over Lucy's body, pausing in spots here and there. When she was done, she stood up, pulling her daughters up to stand next to her. Lucy stood up, and if it weren't for her blood-stained side, no one would know she'd been shot. Noelle and Ember leaned down and gave her a hug and kiss on the head. Kenna said, "She needs to be bathed and fed, but she will be okay. Hilda was here, and Lucy followed her. Hilda shot her. I saw it in Lucy's mind."

Gasps of surprise came from all around the group. "I think we will visit the Dragon Stables another day. For now, we need to return to the safety of the Castle Grounds and see to Lucy," said Maia firmly as she began to lead Lucy back towards the Castle. The rest of the group followed solemnly behind.

After Lucy had been tended to, her bed and food bowls were moved into the Library next to the fireplace so she could be more easily cared for. The group sat on the sofas around the fireplace, sipping on tea, hot cocoa, and coffee. "I don't know what I'd do without her," said Noelle in a quiet voice. She was sitting on a sofa next to Ember, with Blaze on her other side and Alaric on Ember's other side. Blaze put his arm around her back and pulled her into his side, then he kissed the top of her head and said, "You don't have to find out. She will live as long as you here in Marqueria." She quickly looked up and whispered, "Really? The truth?" Blaze said, "I'd never lie to you, Noelle." Noelle stared into his gold eyes for a few seconds, then looked quickly down at her cup of tea.

Across from the teenagers, their four parents were quietly watching their children and their body language. Kenna and Luna were sitting between their husbands, and Luna reached out and took Kenna's hand in hers. She leaned over and whispered, "They don't even realize, do they?" Kenna smiled softly and shook her head. She met Luna's gaze, and they both grinned. "What's so funny over there?" asked Ember loudly. "Mother stuff. You wouldn't understand," answered Kenna, smiling at her daughters.

"What are we going to do about Hilda? And the Darkness," asked Maxim, who was seated next to Ulrika on a small sofa at the end. Otso and Bram exchanged a look for a few moments, then they both nodded. Bram said, "We wait." This brought about a loud grumble from the teenagers and the Bear brothers. Otso said, "Enough! We wait until after we meet the Dragons of our granddaughters." "But why, Ukki? Why do you all need to meet Sage and Jade?" asked Ember. Tati spoke up, "Because I have been sent a vision by the Goddess. We need to continue our walk to the Dragon Stables today."

Lucy was left next to the fire, fast asleep, and the doors to the Library were spelled so she couldn't push them open. With Lucy secured, the group gathered in the courtyard to walk over to the Dragon Stables. Kai led the way, always on guard, with Tai taking rear guard. The walk to the stables was short, so they arrived quickly. Jade and Sage were outside, enjoying the sun despite the snow. The girls quickly ran to their dragons, laying their foreheads on the dragon's muzzle in greeting. Noelle stared into Jade's gold eyes, obviously communicating. Ember was doing the same with Sage. After a few minutes, the girls turned to the group. Noelle said, "I would like you all to meet Jade, my bonded dragon. Jade, this is everyone." Jade chuckled in a low rumble of a voice and said, "Little one, this is not everyone. Everyone would not fit in this courtyard. But it is ok; I know all who are assembled here." Ember stepped forward and said, "I would like to introduce you all to my bonded dragon, Sage." Sage inclined her giant horned head and said, "While it is lovely to meet the people in my little one's life, we want to say how sorry we were that Lucy received injuries today fighting the Darkness. We did not sense how close she was, but that will not happen again. Now, parents of my little one, if you would be so kind as to step closer, please."

Kenna and Jamie moved forward to stand next to their daughters. With shining eyes and a look of reverence, Kenna said, "I used to dream of dragons when I was growing up in the Mortal Realm, and in my dream, a very large black iridescent dragon would visit me every night. She helped me get through so many hard times; even though I know it was just a dream, I've never forgotten her." Jade gave a purring sound and nudged her head gently against Kenna, then said, "She was real Princess. She visited you in your dreams because that was the only way she could see you. But she is very real." Kenna stared at Jade in stunned silence. Then she said, "I don't understand. If she was real, where is she now?"

"She is waiting for you, Princess. In the Sacred Grove of the Dragons, she has been waiting for your return. She and her mate both have been waiting," Jade said, a soft chuffing sound at the end of her sentence. Sage said, "Jamie and Kenna, lay your foreheads on each of ours, and you will see what we are going on about." Jamie laid his forehead against Jade's forehead, and Kenna did the same with Sage. They stayed that way for a few more minutes, then Jamie let out a gasp and backed up. "Are you serious?" Jamie asked the dragon sisters. Jade chortled and chuffed, then said, "While we are not always serious, this is one time we are. They are waiting for you, and now you know the way." Kenna, with tears in her eyes, laid a kiss on each of the dragon's noses, then stepped back and took her husband's hand. Sage said, "She will help you in your defeat of the Darkness, as will her mate. Go now, your Highnesses."

Jade said, "Your daughters will be safe here while you are on your journey. They are our bonded Riders, and we will never let anything happen to them. Besides us, they have two Werewolves and two Werebears most devoted to their safety. Go and begin your journey." The dragons turned and walked further away and deeper into the forested courtyard. Noelle and Ember returned to their group surrounding their parents. "Father, Mother. I know you worry about us, but this is a very important quest you must go on alone. We can't go with you, nobody can. We promise to stay within the Castle grounds and never to wander off. We will be able to communicate with you, even so far away. You need to leave soon," Noelle said, smiling at the excitement she saw in her mother's eyes.

"They showed me the way and where I can transfer the two of us, but the last part of the journey has to be on foot," Kenna was telling Jamie. Suddenly, beside them, Tati stepped closer, carrying a large backpack made of super lightweight but very strong material. When Jamie took it from her, he was surprised at how light it was. "Is there anything in this pack?" he asked laughingly. Tati chuckled and said, "I wove it myself, and while I made it, I wove spells into the fabric. It can carry anything and everything you need, no matter how big and heavy, and the bag will never weigh more than half a stone." Jamie gave Tati a quick hug and said, "Thank you for your thoughtfulness and for watching over our daughters while we are away." Turning to Tai and Kai, Jamie opens his mouth and starts to ask them to watch over Noelle and Ember, but he never gets the chance. The Bear brothers held up a hand to stop him from speaking and together said, "We will guard them with our very lives if need be. They will be safe here. May your journey be quick and your burden be light." The Were Bears each clasped forearms with Jamie and said, "Safe journey."

Kenna gave each of the Bear brothers a hug and kiss on the cheek and said, "Thank you for protecting our treasure while we are away. I know they are in good hands with you." Tai and Kai bowed deeply to Kenna and stepped back to allow her parents and Jamie's parents to say their goodbyes. When Kenna and Jamie stood alone, the Wolf Alphas stepped forward with their sons. Luna gave Kenna a brief hug and a promise to watch over the girls as if they were her own cubs. Ulric gave the same promise to Jamie.

When Blaze and Alaric stepped forward, they bowed their heads briefly, then, with their right hands in tight fists, crossed their right arm over their chest, slamming their fist over their hearts. Together, they said, "We vow to be steadfast guardians, defending their rights and safety and well-being. We will stand by their sides, never wavering in our dedication. We will use our skills, knowledge, and resources to protect them from harm and ensure their security and happiness. Trust in our abilities. They can rely on us to be their shields and advocates."

Jamie stepped forward and grasped Blaze's and Alaric's forearms, saying each time, "I accept your pledge." The Wolf brothers stepped back to stand with their parents, but their eyes remained on Noelle and Ember, who were staring at them with a little bit of awe.

"Noelle, Ember. Come say your goodbyes," said Bram, with mostly repressed mirth. Flushing just a bit, the girls hurried to their parents, throwing their arms around them and creating their signature family hug. Kenna said, "I love you both more than anything; I hope you know that." Then, taking their faces in her palms, she gave each of them a kiss on the forehead. Jamie did the same and said, "You are more precious than air to me; please be safe while we are away." Then, with a final hug, Jamie and Kenna joined hands and disappeared.

Epilogue

Jamie and Kenna appeared at the base of a giant mountain covered in trees and boulders. It reminded Kenna of Mount Rainer, but much larger and with many different colored trees mixed in with the Evergreens. Staring up at the trail, Kenna groaned and said, "That's quite a hike, isn't it, husband?" Jamie grinned at his wife and said, "I have all the confidence in the world that you will be able to take on that mountain. Did the dragon sisters tell you how long this hike should take?" Kenna shook her head and said, "Nope. We're on our own out here, aren't we? Do you realize this is the first time we've been away from home alone since before the girls were born?" Kenna was staring at Jamie, the look on her face a little sad. Jamie said quietly, "They will be ok, sweetheart. They promised to stay in the Castle grounds and not to go off alone." Kenna smiled and said, "I know you're right; I just worry. They're my life," she gave a sigh and said, "Now, let's get climbing, husband."

"Papa, it's been several days, and they're still not back. I haven't been able to reach them through our mind connection; neither has Ember. I'm very worried," Noelle was saying to her Papa. Bram patted her shoulder and said, "Calm, granddaughter. I'm sure they're fine. Your mother is the most powerful magic wielder in Marqueria, and your father is the most powerful Bear, with the exception of Otso. They can take care of themselves, sweetheart." Noelle gave a great heaving sigh and left the room in search of Ember.

She found Ember in their suite in the sitting room, playing a game on her laptop, Alaric across from her. Looking around, Noelle spotted Blaze sitting on the other couch with a sketchbook on his lap, sketching something that held all his attention. When he realized Noelle was standing close by, he quickly closed the cover and stood up. "What did Bram say?" Blaze asked quietly. The look on Noelle's face told Blaze all he needed to know. He gave a quiet sigh, then asked her, "What do you want to do? What is your plan?" This caught the attention of Ember and Alaric, who closed their laptops and stood up too.

"Sage and Jade said they should have been back by now. They have been unable to make contact with our parents or their dragons. I think we need to take the dragon sisters and ride them to where our parents were going and start our search from there," Noelle said. Ember asked, "Can't we do the transfer thing like mom did? We're strong enough." Noelle bit her lip, considering it, and then she said, "Let me contact Jade and see what she thinks." Noelle closed her eyes and was very still for a few minutes. Then her eyes popped open, and she grinned. "The dragon sisters believe we are strong enough to transfer several people to the spot Mom and Dad were going. They said they would fly to the spot and meet us there. They've already left." Ember, eyes shining with excitement, said, "Pack your bags, boys. We're taking a trip."

"Not alone, you're not," growled a low voice from the back staircase door. They all turned towards the back of the sitting room. There stood the Bear Brothers, Tai and Kai. Already dressed for travel, each with a bag slung over a shoulder. Ember tilted her head to the side, raised an eyebrow, and asked, "You're not going to try and stop us?" Their faces fierce looking, they shook their heads. Tai said, "We know better than to try. You'd only sneak away. This way, we can go with you and be added protection." Turning to Blaze and Alaric, "Boys, go grab your short swords and bows, but don't let anyone see you doing it. Also, travel clothes and supplies. We will meet at the dragon stables in fifteen minutes." Blaze and Alaric quickly left for their suite of rooms.

"Go get changed, Princesses. Grab your bows and your short swords, too. Hurry! We, too, have a bad feeling."

Don't miss out!

Visit the website below and you can sign up to receive emails whenever Shana Ren publishes a new book. There's no charge and no obligation.

https://books2read.com/r/B-A-XRPCB-FGKTC

BOOKS 2 READ

Connecting independent readers to independent writers.

Did you love *Through the Tree*? Then you should read *Comes the Darkness*[1] by Shana Ren!

[2]

Return to the Land of Marqueria and join the family on another adventure through this magical realm. Jamie and Kenna have gone missing after setting out on a journey to find their Dragons. Their daughters, Noelle and Ember, embark on a rescue mission, only to discover that the Darkness is hunting for the sisters. Their quest will lead them to the enchanted lands of Marqueria and back to Montana, where they will encounter old friends and new

---

1. https://books2read.com/u/3kOrnK

2. https://books2read.com/u/3kOrnK

foes. Will Noelle and Ember be reunited with their parents? Will the Darkness find them? Discover the answers in the second book of The Land of Marqueria series.

Read more at https://www.shanaren.com.

Also by Shana Ren

The Land of Marqueria
Through the Tree
Comes the Darkness

Standalone
Comes The Darkness

Watch for more at https://www.shanaren.com.

About the Author

Shana is a retired RN, who when not writing, can be found romping through the mountains of Montana with her family, cooking new and exciting(?) meals, playing with her grandson and her crazy Mastiff, and caring for her two chronically ill teenage daughters. She's a wife, a mother to four daughters, a mother-in-law to a wonderful son and she is YaYa to her darling grandson.

Read more at https://www.shanaren.com.